THE FALLIBLE

STORIES

DAVID EWALD

ISBN-13: 979-8-9889795-0-0 (print)

ISBN-13: 979-8-9889795-1-7 (ebook)

This is a work of fiction. While, as in all fiction, the literary perceptions and insights are based on experience, all names, characters, places and incidents either are products of the author's imagination or are used fictitiously.

Grateful acknowledgement is made to the following magazines where these stories first appeared: *Spectrum*, "We Apologize for the Inconvenience"; *Metazen*, "Trupo's Hand"; *The Bend*, "Can't Keep the Spider"; *The Island Fox*, "Update"; *Denver Syntax*, "The Entomologist"; *BULL*, "500 Kilometers to Cairo"; *Eclectica*, "Ten Who Made America!"

The author would like to thank Jeff Bard, without whose critical eye this book would not exist.

An excerpt from *The Fall* by Albert Camus appears in "We Apologize for the Inconvenience," as does a brief excerpt from *A Portrait of the Artist as a Young Man* by James Joyce.

*for my mother
and
for my sister*

CONTENTS

We Apologize for the Inconvenience

My hope: you won't turn away when I tell you what happened in the spring of 1997, when I was eighteen and close to graduating high school, two years before Columbine. I'd like to think it's a funny story, a comedy. Still, Time has had its say.

First, a bit of background: every Monday, Tuesday and Thursday, Anomar High School (known better to its student population as Cow Pie High) would allow the senior class to go off campus for lunch.

It was a blessing, freedom—if you had a car or knew someone who had one. I had a 1986 Ford Tempo I called The Great White Hope, not because I was a racist but because it would have been a miracle if the ghost-colored death trap lasted past graduation.

On this particular Thursday, I was walking across the grassy lawn toward the student parking lot when I met up with one of my friends, Josiah, or J for short. In terms of size, he was David to my Goliath, which is why I should have better anticipated what came next.

He waved to me and said, "Kevin, where you headed?"

"Lunch."

"Uh, I'm starving. Mind if I come with?"

"Sure. I think Dominick is coming too. And maybe Luke and Brode."

"That sounds good. There is one problem..." Josiah raised an eyebrow—his right, always his right. "I kinda left my campus ID at home this morning."

"No way you're getting off campus then. You know they check everyone."

"Can I go in your trunk?"

I laughed.

"I'm serious, Kevin. They're not going to look there."

"How do you know?"

"I know, all right. C'mon, don't be a brode."

"Okay, okay. Let's go then," I said. "Time's a wasting."

THE TRUNK SPRANG OPEN. I looked around. J did the same. No one was watching us; AHS seniors were headed toward their cars with one thing on their minds. I turned to J and he was already sliding inside the Tempo's trunk. Two of him could have fit. I closed the lid. That was easy; getting off campus was another matter.

TRAFFIC in the student lot jammed up, grid-locked, and I was pissed because lunch had started at 12:40 and we had to be back at precisely 1:10 or else we'd be marked absent—not tardy, but absolutely absent, no questions asked. Mrs. Donna Feng taught my fifth period class. Her last name said it all—when she bit, she dug in deep. Although the school year would be over in just two months, and with it my high school "career," I had already racked up several tardies to fourth period on account of Jill and also served Saturday School for falsifying an attendance report. One more mark against me would send my mother over the edge and, in her words, "permanently destroy my acceptance to college." But I had to take the chance. I was a senior, I was hungry, and I was with friends.

These other three friends of mine had gotten into the car just as The Hope was inching up to security. Dominick, Luke, and Brode flashed their campus IDs in front of the big guys, who okayed them. I showed the enforcers my card and they waved me on. The Hope passed through the gates and sped out onto the road that led toward the main part of town. I looked at the car's clock as soon as we hit hallelujah: 12:50.

Dominick, my friend since elementary school, sat in the passenger seat and scolded me for the radio station I had on.

"Kevin, when are you going to stop listening to this crap?"

"It's Steely Dan."

"It's seventies."

"So?"

"So it's no good. I can't believe you listen to my mom's music."

"Yeah, Kevin, you listen to old people's music." This remark came from Brode in the backseat. He was ultra-religious—but not pushy about it. We called him Brode because that was the name we liked best; it originated from a couple of amateur movies we'd made the previous year (*The Incredible Brode, The Incredible Brode II: Brode in Danger*). It had stuck, and now he had it for life, probably, or at least for the rest of high school. He was big and pale, like an iceberg, and had bad acne on his chin, though his cheeks remained relatively unscathed. He had the blackest eyes of anyone I knew and was also hairless. He was not a swimmer.

Luke was a swimmer. He wasn't ultra-religious but was a devout athlete. He wore glasses and took them off whenever he was on the court, or the track, or in the pool, or trying to impress the girls at Cow Pie. He was cut, tanned, and lanky. Once I caught him crying in the band room in ninth grade for reasons that still aren't entirely clear to me.

Luke said nothing, which was his nature. The other two talked up a whirlwind.

"Kevin, why don't you listen to 91X, dude? 103.7 The Planet is crap."

"You're crazy, Mister." Brode often called me Mister. "You should be wearing some bell bottoms or somethin' with whatever this stuff is you're listening to."

It's a good thing I didn't know the meaning of the term 'Steely Dan' at the time. If I had known, I may have let the definition slip and offended Brode in an irreparable way.

Dominick turned the station and relaxed in his seat. The song was loud, I mean really loud. "Here we go. Now here's music, Kev. Alanis Morrisette is *good* music."

I didn't mind my friend of almost nine years dishing it out to me on my musical tastes because I knew that he wouldn't be in the car for long and, to be quite honest, we didn't hang out all that much anymore since we were both so busy with school and extracurriculars. He had musical theater and show choir; I had the academic bowl and the school paper. But it wasn't just that we were busy, it was that we had grown apart, and now that he was in the car I kept thinking of how I could talk to him like I used to. The radio station seemed of little importance at this point. My mind was on the desire to dish something back at Dominick—something that would catch him off guard—and, of course, the time constraints and the road. I forgot about everything else. It was that way with me in high school—turning on the radio and tuning out everything and everyone else.

Without thinking it through completely I said to Dominick, "You taking Meg to Prom, right?" I did my best to make it sound like an innocent, unloaded question, though the truth was we'd all seen how it had ended between Dominick and Meg at winter formal.

"Don't know yet," Dominick said with his usual cool. "What about you? Who are you taking?"

"Still thinking."

I'd been doing a lot of thinking since Christmas. I'd taken Elaine Sanderson to homecoming and had a good time, but since the start of second semester I'd gravitated toward her best friend, Jill Donnelly. They were both ultra-religious, members of the same church Brode attended.

"Just say it, Kev," Brode said from the back. "You're going to ask Jill."

"Would you be upset if I did?"

"No. What do I care. But you better not lead Elaine on."

"I won't. How about *you* ask Elaine?" I challenged.

"That would just be weird," Brode said.

"Why?"

"It just would."

"Stay away from that church, Kev," Dominick said. "Even Brode'll tell you that."

Brode nodded. Then he blurted out, "Oh my gosh!" He was looking at the long line of cars outside Burger King—most of them student-driven vehicles that crowded the parking lot and crammed the drive-thru lane.

"Rho. We're not getting food." Dominick put his head against the window.

I glanced in the rearview mirror at Luke. He looked grim.

The clock read 12:54.

"We're going in," I said.

SURPRISINGLY, I had made the right decision going into the fast-food joint rather than driving through. The place wasn't as packed as we'd expected it to be. We saw some of our classmates like Pighead and Numbnuts—names I'm just making up now because I don't remember their real names. We said hey and they said what's happening. Then we queued up in line to wait our turns—all of us except Luke, who took a seat at an available table and began to eat his sack lunch.

Dominick tapped me on the shoulder. I turned around.

"I didn't want to say this in front of Brode but...you really should go with someone else. Not Jill. Not Elaine again either."

"Where is this coming from?" I knew I was showing too much of my heart, again, but the thought of Dominick just now bothering to talk to me about girls irked me. After a summer and senior year of mostly silence, the gesture struck me as ill-timed.

"From true friendship," Dominick answered. "Care. Concern. Knowledge. Have you gotten anywhere with Jill?"

"Is that all that matters? Making out—and more?" I kept my eyes on the menu above. Could I tell Dominick about the afternoon Jill and I spent watching *Trainspotting*, the one R-rated movie she'd expressed interest in seeing, and that after I'd popped out the VHS tape we had gotten, well, closer—without doing anything? I'd been ready, and she'd rebuffed me. She'd laughed off the situation, a comedy to her. That reaction had caused me to double down and commit to Jill with a determination bordering on the obsessive. Hell, I'd even attended her church once.

I was thinking about Dominick, I was thinking about Jill, I was thinking about Steely Dan and getting back to class on time without involving The Hope and my friends in an acci-dent. I would not get into another one. These thoughts on top of an empty stomach.

At 1:06 all three of us had gotten our food to go and we left with Luke still eating from his brown bag. He seemed to have an endless supply of carrots and trail mix.

With time not on our side, I took to the wheel and we ate as we drove. We inhaled our Whoppers and fries, guzzled our sodas and listened to Piss-ant Schlock Rock as The Hope sped back down Main Street and hung a left on Anomar Street. Just as I was turning left on Spencer Lane, minutes still from campus, Luke, of all actions, opened his mouth. He said, "Hey guys. Guys! Turn down the music."

Dominick did so and said, "Yeah?"

"No, turn it all the way down." Then Luke looked at Brode. "Do you hear that?"

Brode seemed deep in thought. He unbuckled his seatbelt and twisted to one side, leaning his head against the backseat and listening intently. "Oh my gosh!" he shouted.

Luke said, "Kevin, someone's in your trunk."

"I think it's Josiah," Brode said, facing forward again. "It sounds like him anyway."

"What's J doing in the trunk?" Dominick wondered out loud.

"Oh shit!" I screamed. "He *is* in the trunk!" I had thought for those few moments when the realization of my mistake was dawning that perhaps he wasn't in the trunk and that Luke and Brode were just hearing things or messing around with me. Fat chance of that now.

"Is he alive?" Brode was practically hyperventilating. He looked whiter than usual. "He's okay, right?"

"Ask him," Dominick said.

"Josiah," Brode said into the backseat. "Are you okay?"

Silence. We all listened for a response, which finally came, garbled and unintelligible to all but Brode, who still had his ear to the backseat. When J was through garbling, Brode looked at me.

"Well, what did he say?"

"I can't say it," he said. "It's not very nice."

~

SINCE DISCOVERING that Josiah was in the trunk, Luke and Brode took turns talking to him through the backseat. They asked him questions like "How's your air supply?" and told him, "Don't worry, we're almost there. Kevin's driving really fast," which I was.

The Great White Hope screeched into the student parking lot of Anomar High School at 1:11 in the afternoon. We were late—no, we were absent—by one minute.

As soon as I braked in my parking space, I turned off the car, jumped out and ran to the trunk. J hadn't said anything in a while and part of me was convinced he'd suffocated and I would be earning my convict degree in the slammer. Dominick, Luke, and Brode got out too, each of them still munching. They came around to where I was just inserting the key into the lock. I popped the trunk, and all four of us leaned forward to stare inside at Josiah, who was curled up in the fetal position, his hands balled into fists, his eyes scrunched shut, his teeth clenched.

"The light," he said. "Not the light."

Dominick and Brode helped him out, and when J was standing and through dusting himself off, wringing his hands, rubbing his eyes, he said, "You are one fucked up sicko, Kevin."

"Hey. You asked to be put in the trunk."

"Not with *this*!" J reached into the trunk and pulled out a gun. A pistol. It was black, real. It wasn't a toy gun. It was a real gun I did not recognize.

All of the unarmed took at least one step back. A few years earlier I'd gone through a phase, inspired, no doubt, by all the James Bond movies I'd seen (and, I'll admit, the real gun I'd seen at a friend's house when I was younger), in which I convinced my parents to allow me to acquire a BB pistol. Black, heavy, the pistol could easily have been mistaken for a weapon of deadly force. I only ever used it in the backyard, taking shots at a life-size cardboard cutout of a smiling businessman. My father half-heartedly joked that I was imagining him when I fired. The pellets were kept separate from the gun, in a plastic ammo box my parents kept under their bed.

Josiah hadn't lifted the current, the real, gun high enough to be noticed—yet. All of us had backed away even farther at the sight of it.

"Jesus, J! Put that back in. Security's gonna see you."

"Or anyone," Dominick said. "That's not the BB gun, is it, Kevin."

"No. I got rid of that months ago."

"So, what's with the actual gun?"

"I have no idea," I said. "I have no fucking clue. I've never seen it before in my life. How the hell am I going to go to Feng's and sit through calc knowing I have that in the trunk?"

"Deal, Kev. It's yours," Josiah said. "Unless someone planted it on you. Your sister?"

"I hope not!" Brode sputtered.

"Sandra wouldn't do that, right?" Dominick's look pierced what little was left of my naivety. "Put it back, J. Before anyone else sees."

"I was tearing up the floor here thinking there was a lever or something to pop the trunk. Instead I lifted up most of the floor and there was the spare tire and on top of that this blanket, and under the blanket this box with the gun in it."

"No bullets?" Luke asked.

"I'm sure the bullets are in the gun," I said, unable to look at any of them. "It's not mine. You all know it's not mine."

"We believe you," Dominick said, and when our eyes met I knew he meant it.

"I gotta get to class," Brode said.

Luke nodded. Josiah was already walking. "Remind me to never ever forget my ID again!" he said without turning.

I felt numb, shell-shocked and empty, as if I'd learned the most terrible secret and lost everyone, all my friends, in the process. I placed the gun back where J had found it—in a transparent plastic box resting on the spare tire that was then hidden under a blanket and the floor of the trunk. I didn't recognize the blanket. Like the gun, it must have been a recent purchase. I closed the trunk and followed Dominick on to campus. We parted ways at the flagpole.

I couldn't concentrate on my last two classes of the day. I kept thinking about what was in the trunk and whether my unintentional secret would be discovered. I didn't really think it would; campus security in 1997, while good at making sure underclassmen and ID-less seniors didn't make it off campus during lunch, never searched student vehicles. Anything-sniffing dogs were unthinkable at that time, no police officers ever set foot on campus, and by sixth period I'd decided the worst the teachers at AHS pictured any of their students attempting was a pizza-ordering prank like Sean Penn's in *Fast Times at Ridgemont High*.

But a gun. It couldn't stay in my trunk even a day longer. Whose was it, why was it there, how would I get rid of it. I didn't want it. I hadn't touched any gun-like object in over a year—the last time was when I'd used my BB pistol as a prop in the *Brode* movies—and I'd since sold that item off.

I drove home fast, just careful enough to take the curves without spinning off Vincenzo Road. I arrived home in record time. In the driveway was a surprise: my father's car. In all my years living in that house, I had never seen my father home early, except once when I stayed home sick from elementary school and Dad begrudgingly agreed to come home and check in on me.

Not a good sign, I thought, and then my mind leapt at the

sight of the car to the truth. I knew to whom the gun belonged. Not my mother, who had not the temperament to complete such a purchase. Not my sister, who was too busy sneaking around with her boyfriend to buy a gun and hide it in the trunk of her brother's car.

I found the front door unlocked. I expected to find his body next, and when that expectation proved wrong I felt both relieved and silly. Of course I wouldn't find my father's body in the house. The gun was in my trunk.

Dad was lying on the couch, his hands resting on his stomach. His head was turned to face the TV, which was playing his favorite Western, *The Searchers*. Spread out on the coffee table: papers, files, reports from the office. A glass of Chardonnay hung on the table's edge; the near-empty bottle stood close by. I remembered my mother once telling my father not to drink so much, all that alcohol couldn't possibly mix well with the medications he was taking.

I stood watching him. He didn't seem to know I was there. I'm not sure my father would have acknowledged the presence of anyone that afternoon. He continued watching the movie while I waited for a commercial break, at which point I spoke.

"Dad," I said.

"Oh hey son…" His voice sounded different, as if he'd just woken up from a nap.

I asked if everything was okay.

"Sure…. Could be better. I decided to take home some of what I have to do. You know I wish the employees under me could do this, but…it's gotta be me."

"Is that problem at work solved yet?"

"What problem?" My father looked perplexed.

"The one with the woman who wants your job, or's complaining about you…?"

"Oh. That." My father shifted and sat up. He looked at all

the work before him as if he wanted to put a bullet through it. "That's still an issue," he said.

I was going to bring up the gun in what I prayed would be a tactful way, but at that moment the commercial break ended and *The Searchers* resumed. My father patted the spot next to him on the couch. "Come sit with me," he said.

I couldn't remember the last time my father had made such a gesture. Perhaps he never had. I complied. Together, we watched. At one point, Dad said, "This is my favorite Western."

"I know," I said.

An old man on the screen cried out, "*It's this country killed my boy!*"

Of my father's effects, I have framed just one: a piece of writing in his hand—but not in his own words. They are the words of one of his favorite authors, and they read as such:

I say 'my friends,' moreover, as a convention. I have no more friends; I have nothing but accomplices. To make up for this, their number has increased; they are the whole human race. And within the human race, you first of all. Whoever is at hand is always first. How do I know I have no friends? It's very easy: I discovered it the day I thought of killing myself to play a trick on them, to punish them, in a way. But punish whom? Some would be surprised, and no one would feel punished. I realized I had no friends. Besides, even if I had had, I shouldn't be any better off. If I had been able to commit suicide and then see their reaction, why, then the game would have been worth the candle. – Camus

John Wayne firing relentlessly at the buffalo just to pull the trigger, because he can.

I knew then what I would do. I would not mention the gun to my father. Doing so would destroy this moment we were sharing, this moment I wanted as an unblemished memory. I had so few memories of him like this, and so little time left. I would instead wait. I would wait for my father to pass out in an alcoholic stupor, as he invariably would, and then I would take the keys to his car and place the gun in his trunk, under the floor, on top of the spare tire and using the blanket he'd purchased. The gun he'd purchased, I was sure of it. Had to be his, because it wasn't mine.

That was my decision, my commitment, in the spring of 1997, before all that would befall us after. *Old father, old artificer, hold me now and ever in good stead.*

Trupo's Hand

A corrupt cop places a handgun under his chin and commits suicide, with the blood spurting up onto the underside of a patio umbrella.

— *screenit.com*

MOST UNSETTLING—AND greatest—sequence from *American Gangster* (2007, dir. Ridley Scott) occurs toward the end, just after Russell Crowe's good cop Richie Roberts sticks a thumb tack right through the photo-forehead of number one target Detective Trupo. Gotcha now, sucka.

Cut to the newspaper—or do the pants come first? Definitely the pants. Those swank dark brown polyester leisure pants. Trupo from the waist-down seated on the edge of his bed, facing east. A faint light in the room, late afternoon, muggy outside, August or September of 1976. Behind him, buoyed by the bouncy mattress and braced by his backside, a full cup of coffee, fresh.

Distress, uncertainty apparent in Trupo's torso. To get up or not. He gets up abruptly. The cup behind him turns over, spilling its contents across the bed. A stain spreads, steam rises. Trupo leaves without noticing.

Then the paper. Trupo sets it down and picks up the gun, his service pistol, from the surface of the patio table. He sits and aims, barrel pointed in the right place, the way he understood.

When the shot goes off his wife doesn't hear. She is busy vacuuming in the darkness of the living room, her long dress swaying, her head bowed in reverence to the carpet, her husband's backyard end seen through the sliding glass door in the distance.

He always saw himself as a character in a movie. Who would play him? Who would speak the words he was writing on the scrap of paper? I'm not one to go out guns blazing. I've done enough. Sorry honey. Best this way. Fight those bastards. Don't let them take the cars, the house, the vacuum I hear now. Will you hear? We've worked so hard for this, don't make them tell you any different. We did it together. What of the real man, the real name? What future actor, not yet born, would be his age, 39, when he took the role of him?

A bird on the patio umbrella above. He'd stopped thinking he'd die in the line of duty long ago. This was how, his back to the house, her. He was shaking. He'd forgotten his cup, the one with the fish on it, the one she'd bought him in the Cape. It was the bird he told her about that morning, remember? Do you remember the bird? I think it's the same bird.

He had a dream he was in Texas holding a big gun. But he'd never been to Texas so it could have been some other place, maybe Mexico.

Like any child, he'd grown up believing he could be President someday. The moment before the bullet cut through his brain he saw himself as the President of the United States, years into the future, throwing the first pitch in some stadium in Texas, then retreating to the safety of the White House to strategize the war. The war wasn't going well, and it had been a long one already, started many years ago, and his advisers were telling him it was unwinnable even as they were devising new ways to sell its legitimacy to the American people. President Trupo? He didn't think that was his name. His name was something else altogether, something burning with anger of a questionable legitimacy, an authority sold to the American people.

And who was he now? It was the fall of 1985 and he was wandering the streets of San Francisco. He'd always been fond of that movie. He'd just gotten out of a showing of the new James Bond, this one set in San Francisco and featuring the final battle on top of the Golden Gate Bridge. Poor Christopher Walken, he'd thought then. If only he, Trupo, could be an actor. If only he, Trupo, could escape from his life by playing someone else.

He was someone else, again. He'd been to Ireland recently and now that he was back his wife despised him. They weren't getting along, it wasn't working out. They slept in separate rooms. His son was nearly seven now. Born when Trupo murdered those two men, sorry, assassinated those two political figures in San Francisco's City Hall, Czolgosz, Guiteau, Booth, Oswald, and now the city didn't want him, the new mayor had made a public announcement pleading with him to stay away. But he had to try with his wife. He had to see if he could salvage himself.

One night when it had been particularly rough he dreamt he was a bad guy in a Western being shot to death by a fourteen-year-old girl, her revenge, his stupidity. It was the fall of 1985 in San Francisco and he shouldn't have been alive because he was supposed to be someone else, he felt it, like a burst blood vessel at the back of the brain.

The song playing on the car's radio was "So Far Away" by Dire Straits, and he felt that, so far away. He was thinking of Ireland now, and he put in the tape, waited for the new song. The hose was connected to the tail pipe. The hose was dangling through the back window, cracked just enough. All the windows were rolled up. The engine was on. The song was playing. It had to end somewhere, so why not here, in his own garage, in the dark? He saw all his lives now, the many roles he'd played, the people he'd killed, the ways he'd been killed as well, and was any of it true? What if the end to the origin story had never happened? Was he still alive, beyond the exhaust? Could he ever die? Was that a movie, too?

Can't Keep the Spider

Back then, movies took longer to be released for home viewing. We're talking the early 1990s here. For most movies we had to wait almost a year for the VHS tape. But the wait was worth it. One night we were watching *Arachnophobia*—just my parents, my sister and me—in our darkened living room when something happened strange enough to distract me from the screen. My father was sitting on the couch with us when the movie started, but after a few minutes, as soon as the credits where through rolling and the scientists were roaming the jungle searching for the death-spiders, and my father knew these spiders were going to emerge soon, he did something strange. Or some *things* strange, I should say. First, he drew his legs up so that his knees were against his chest. Then he ducked his head down between his knees several times. He looked like a little kid that had lost a coin in his crotch. I ended up watching him instead. He was sitting right next to me, I just had to smile at his antics. Halfway through the movie my father took to the carpet and lay there curled up. I saw him close his eyes at the part where the spiders drop from the ceiling of the house they're invading. And in the end, when the nastiest spider of them all shows itself, my father actually yelped.

When the movie was over and the credits were rolling, he got up from the carpet and stretched. "That was good," he said.

"You were scared," Mom said.

"Daddy, you closed your eyes," Sandra added.

He denied these accusations and promptly went to bed before they could say anything else that might embarrass him.

I thought he'd been scared too. I'd never seen him scared before. I was only twelve at the time and still had a ways to go.

Just to make certain of my father's fear, I said to Mom before going to bed that night, "Looks like Dad's scared of spiders."

"He sure is," she replied.

"What kind of spiders?"

"Oh, all kinds, I think."

"He can't be scared of daddy-longlegs."

"I'm sure he's scared of even those."

"Daddy-longlegs are some of the most lethal spiders in existence, but they don't have big enough mouths to bite us. I read that somewhere."

"What a memory you have." And then she kissed me on the forehead. Her answers had given me confidence.

So knowing that my father had this weakness—that he was scared of something— really fascinated me. And spiders. I could take advantage of the fact that he was scared of spiders. They weren't intangible the way ghosts were, or radiation from the microwave.

I went outside one day after school, around the side of the house, walking close to the wall, until I came to the air conditioning unit. Behind the unit was a thick electrical cord that snaked in through a hole in the wall of the house. This hole was the lair of a black widow spider I'd been observing for some time already.

The spider wasn't around this afternoon; nothing was in its web. I decided to change that. I walked across the gravel and through the small square patch of lawn in the center of our yard, past the water plant-covered ridge and into no-man's land. I called this area of the yard no-man's land because (a) I was interested in World War I (or any war for that matter) and (b) the place looked like a wasteland, dry and barren with rocks dust-caked and strewn everywhere. I saw cracks in the ground. Fissures, I thought. You could fall into them at the slightest tremor. Swallow you whole, down you go.

I found a stick nearby, picked it up and carried it over to the nearest anthill. Red ants moved about sluggishly. That would have to change. I stuck the stick deep into the ants' home and they went instantly wild, incensed. I let go of the stick, which was still stuck in the hole, and stepped back as the ants rushed my feet, seeking out the enemy who'd attacked from above. They were nearing my shoes; I had to act quickly. Already a couple of ants were on the stick. I grabbed the stick and ran out of no-man's land, down the ridge and across the lawn and gravel, back to the air conditioning unit on the side of the house. As I ran, I watched the ants to see how far they'd come down the stick. I watched how close they were to my hand. I was smart. When they came down the stick, almost to the bottom end where I held, I grabbed the top end with my other hand and flipped the stick and the ants over. I did this three or four times before I reached the air conditioning unit, so the ants never got to my hands.

I came up close to the spider's web and touched the stick to it. The ants ran down the stick and onto the web. They wriggled there but couldn't get free. Their motions would signal the black widow sooner or later. I just wanted it to be sooner instead of later. So I helped the spider out by moving its web around with the stick. The web shook but didn't break; it was much too strong to fall to pieces that easily. I didn't want to break the web anyway—I wanted that widow to come out and feast. But it didn't come out. I must have sat there by the side of the house, gravel digging into my knees, looking at that messy web for about half an hour before giving up and going inside. I figured the spider didn't eat until later and besides, I had better things to do.

Nintendo called. Eight-bit bliss helped pass the time—but only up to a point. I couldn't wait for the spider forever. I had to capture it, not just see it, or else the plan I was developing wouldn't work.

I headed back outside to see if the widow had come out of her lair yet, and sure enough, one of the ants was missing from the web. I felt good. That meant the spider had emerged and devoured one of them. I picked up the stick from off the top of the air conditioning unit. Then I tapped the web again with the stick, and this time the black widow showed itself. It moved so quickly that I had to take a step back, because I'd read stories from people who swore that black widow spiders are excellent jumpers. This one lady'd been rummaging around in her garage when she came across a widow in a shoebox. The widow just sat there, watching her, I suppose. She thought it was dead. But as she leaned in close, it suddenly leapt at her! She screamed and fell back, fearing for her life, but lucky for her the spider landed on her blouse so she was able to beat it off with a shoe before it could touch her skin.

That's what I read, anyway.

I didn't know if this particular black widow was in a jumping mood or not, but I wasn't going to find out. I knew that if a black widow did bite me, I probably wouldn't die. I'd get awfully sick, though. Widows are able to kill only old people, unhealthy people and babies—that's why I'd never let my grandmother into the garage if she wanted to go in there for something. I'd always do it myself. She'd look at me with this strangely scrunched up face, but I didn't mind that look. I only thought, *I'm saving your life, Grandma*, and tried to transmit that sentence to her through my powers of psychic communication, the same as the radiation rays from the microwave. I was the microwave then. Or trying to be, anyway.

Garages used to scare me because of the black widows, but by the time I was twelve I'd overcome my fear. My father, at the age of forty, still hadn't overcome his.

Surprisingly, the black widow was ignoring the second ant. Maybe it was full. That didn't matter, because the spider wasn't going to be out here much longer. I ran back inside the house and grabbed a Tupperware bowl from out of an overhanging cabinet. Then I went back to the web and waited. The widow just sat there in its web, not moving. Maybe it was getting ready to jump. I braced myself.

"Are you playing with the spider again?"

I groaned. My sister really annoyed me then.

"No duh," I said. "Here, help me catch it."

She stood by my side. "With what?"

"With your hands."

"You're weird."

"If I'm weird you're just as weird. We're related, you know."

"I'm going. And I'm playing the Nintendo."

"You're *what*?"

"I want to play the Nintendo."

"*You*...want to *play*...*Mega Man 3*?"

"Yeah. Why not? Or some other game. Come on. You're not playing it now."

"I am too playing it now. I'm just taking a break, that's all."

This was a new development, my sister wanting to play my video games—any video games, really. She had never asked to play Nintendo before. Had she suddenly gotten smart or something? I would have to watch this development closely.

"Maybe later," I said. "After I'm done with the next level, maybe. Or tonight."

"Okay. But you know you're gonna have to let me."

"Don't you want to help me show this black widow to Dad?"

"No way. He'll kill you."

Maybe he would kill me. I hadn't thought of that.

"Fine," I said. "Go watch the microwave."

"Dumbass." She punched my arm. It didn't hurt.

Sandra left. I stood there holding the Tupperware, thinking of all the ways my father could kill me. He could drown me in a toilet, or stick me in an overflowing bathtub and then throw in a plugged-in hair dryer. That happened in a James Bond movie I watched with him once.

There were all sorts of options available to him, but none of them seemed like interesting ways to die. I'd have to think harder. And I'd have to think later. Right now I needed to get the black widow into the bowl, without my sister's help since she was being such a wimp.

Then I really thought hard and decided I'd need two bowls for this job. So I went back inside and came out with a glass dish about the same size and diameter as the Tupperware bowl. I took these two objects and approached the web. The black widow was crawling for its lair. I'd have to act fast. I held the Tupperware bowl upside-down above the web. I held the dish just below the widow and its web. Then, with a quick slam, I put the two items together and there—there! The black widow was mine, caught in between the dish and the bowl. That pleased me.

Lucky for me, I could see through the dish up at the spider. It was struggling, bouncing around, having quite a tough time trying to break through the barriers. No use, of course. You can't bust out of Tupperware—not if you're a spider, anyway.

I ran back into the house, anxious to get things going. My father wouldn't be home until later that night. I looked at the time on the microwave. 4:42. I had about three hours to annihilate.

I got a little farther in *Mega Man 3*, just not enough to stick with it for longer that evening. So I turned on the TV and watched a good portion of the basketball game. That's how I spent most of those three hours. Before I really got comfortable out there in the living room I put the black widow container on top of the refrigerator; I didn't keep it with me in the living room because I thought the TV might have an adverse effect on the spider. Maybe the flashing images and glow would make it go wild, or sedate it. Either way, I couldn't have that with my father coming home. The top of the refrigerator was the safest place, far out of range of the microwave, which would give off its radiation rays and cause the spider to mutate into something monstrous. I couldn't wait.

Every fifteen minutes or so I'd check on my spider just to make sure it hadn't died, or knocked the Tupperware bowl over and gotten out. Whenever I checked, the widow quieted down and sat still. It was really a very good little pet. I wondered if it was watching me. I thought that would be cool, but I'd read that widows couldn't really see in daylight. That would make the night so much better.

Mom came home a little before seven. As usual she was tired and immediately started rummaging around in the cabinets, looking for something to eat. She would stick something in the microwave for dinner later, but for the moment she needed snack foods that were never there because my sister and I always ate them.

She came into the living room where I was just finishing up the basketball game.

"Where's the Triscuits?" she asked.

"I don't know," I said.

"You haven't seen them around, have you?"

"No."

"Does your sister have them?"

"I don't know."

"Where is she?"

"Her room." I pointed to the hallway that led to our rooms.

Instead of going to my sister's room, Mom returned to the kitchen. I heard her open the refrigerator. That's when I jumped up from the couch and ran to warn her.

"Mom!"

She was bent over, just picking out a few TV dinners to microwave. She turned to me. I pointed at the top of the refrigerator. She looked up but didn't seem all that surprised by what she saw. "Oh," she said, and set the dinners on the counter. "Did you find that in here?" I shook my head. "Out there?" I nodded.

She didn't seem concerned that there was a potentially lethal spider sitting trapped on top of the refrigerator. She didn't show concern that the only thing separating her from possible death was plastic. I was surprised by Mom's calm demeanor and, also, a little scared of how she wasn't reacting, like she'd been turned into a zombie-mom by the radiation rays from the microwave. Maybe she'd gone into shock from seeing the spider; that would be something to tell Dominick when I saw him at school.

"We can't have that in here," she said without looking at me.

Uh-oh, I thought. I wouldn't be showing my black widow to my father tonight. I waited for Mom to continue, but she didn't say another word and instead concentrated on fixing our dinners. She looked the boxes over as if she were inspecting something more important than food. That meant our conversation was over. She hadn't exactly given me an order, so I didn't know what I was supposed to do with the spider. Nintendo called. I went into the living room.

Mom took a few minutes before coming out and giving me the order for spider removal. "Get rid of it, Kevin."

"How?" I held back from pushing start on the controller. I didn't really want to play this game; I'd beaten it before.

"It's your responsibility. Black widow spiders are dangerous."

"I know, Mom. How?"

"Take it out front, I don't care. Just get it out of the house before your father sees it and has a coronary."

I turned off the console and went back to the kitchen, where I took the spider's cage down with both hands. "Oh...okay," I said, trying to make it seem as if she'd really hurt me by not letting me keep the black widow in the house. Mom didn't notice my attempts to gain her sympathy.

Not surprisingly, I'd lost focus by this point. Why had I brought the spider inside? To show my father, sure. But there was more to it than that. I wanted to scare him, just because I'd never scared him before and now, for the first time ever, I knew of something that truly frightened him.

I'd even thought briefly of putting this arachnid under his pillow. Maybe it would lay its eggs there. Maybe it would bite him. I'll never know because I took it outside to the rose bushes in front.

The porch light illuminated the way. Almost as soon as I stepped outside, I heard a low rumble, a car, and looked up to see my father pull into the driveway. The headlights lit me up. The spider must have freaked because I could feel skittish movement from within the cage, and for a moment I also felt fear. That left me, though, because I realized my position: here I was holding this Tupperware bowl and this plate together, and my father had just gotten out of his car. My chance, right here.

He approached me. "What d'ya got there, Kev?"

"A spider," I said in a low voice.

"What?" He leaned in closer.

"A spider," I repeated, and then, loudly: "A *black widow* spider." I held up the cage so that it was directly in front of his face. My father's eyes widened. He sucked in air quickly, sounding like a whistle.

Then my father ran inside the house. I stood there smiling, and less than a minute later the front door burst open and my father stepped outside, a can of insect spray in each hand. He came toward me, slowly. I didn't dare move.

"Set it down, son. And step away from it."

I obeyed. He rushed forward and kicked the Tupperware bowl off and away. We both stood there, close beside each other, looking down at this black widow spider that wasn't moving at all. "I killed it," I said.

"Let's make sure," he said, and shook both cans.

The spider moved. My father shrieked and started back toward the front door. "Don't go near it!" he warned.

My spider crawled away from the plate, toward the rose bushes. I let it go. I looked for my father, but he'd already gone inside.

DINNER WAS EVEN MORE tense than usual that night. After he'd finished eating, my father got up from the table and rummaged around underneath the kitchen sink. He brought out four cans of insect spray and walked over to where I was still eating my dinner. He tapped me on the shoulder and motioned for me to follow him. We headed for the door.

"Where we going, Dad?"

"Spider hunting," he answered.

We ventured out almost every night after that, until the novelty of the hunt wore off and we returned to the way things would always exist between us. But I will always remember those nights. On those nights he insisted I go with him all over—around the sides of our house, into the garage and then around the fence in the backyard. Searching. Black widows only come out at night, you see. That's what he said. I wasn't entirely sure about that. We did find widows some nights, and with my father it was always the spray. One time Mom tried talking him into using a different technique: "Why don't you use a shoe, or a broom, like I do?" But he'd just shake his cans and go about his business, a true professional.

Those nights usually lasted late. Once, it was nearing eleven and he still hadn't found a black widow to satisfy his urge. (They'd probably all moved to the hills by then.)

He was still as obsessed as ever when I entered high school, only then I refused when he asked me to go hunting with him. By that time, I had better things to do.

You Too Have Weapons

Killer walked down the street with a rat on his shoulder. Everything else about him remained the same: the way he walked, driving his legs into the asphalt and pumping his arms as if he were marching in the army; the way he dressed in his black jeans and striped button-up long-sleeved rayon shirt, his buzzed dirt-brown hair with actual dirt in it; how there was no separation between his caterpillar eyebrows. On this particular September afternoon I was shooting hoops in the front driveway. When I saw him approaching, I dropped the ball and ran inside the house, locking the door behind me. I thought about the gun.

On a dreary rain-logged day early in the previous year I had gone over to Killer's house with Dominick, my only true friend at the time. Killer opened the door and ushered us both inside where we had hot cocoa from the microwave and talked about games of strategy. We played Risk. This got us talking about military engagements and the conflict in Vietnam that had happened a couple decades earlier, as well as the current war in the Persian Gulf that was just wrapping up. Killer claimed that his father had fought in Vietnam and asked if either of our fathers had done the same. I answered no; my father had his number called when he was twenty-two or twenty-three, but by then they were already pulling troops out and there was no need for him to go. Dominick was pretty sure his stepfather had fought but he wasn't about to ask him.

Killer said his father had a gun and that he kept it in the house. This gun, he claimed, was in the chest in front of his parents' bed. He asked if we wanted him to get it. Dominick said sure and Killer went to get the gun. I didn't look at Dominick. I watched the walls instead. The rain continued outside.

Killer came back with the gun and showed it to us. He admitted it wasn't loaded but that he could load it.

I didn't care much about the gun. I thought it looked cool, and I thought it looked even cooler when Killer said it was the gun James Bond used in all of his films. A Walther PPK.

At first the gun was a good thing; I felt exhilarated holding it and pointing it at various places in the room. I liked watching Dominick pick it up and wave it around with satisfaction on his face. Killer seemed pleased, too. I actually thought, at that time and at no other after, that we might remain friends.

He took the gun from us and aimed at certain things in the room—the television, the couch, the kitchen counter, the overhanging cabinets, us. When he pointed the weapon at me I recoiled; Dominick did the same. We didn't like being targets, even if the gun was unloaded. But, I thought then, maybe Killer had loaded it. That's when the situation got uncomfortable. Things didn't feel right anymore. I remember I made up some excuse about having to be home at a certain time, and then I ran down the street in the downpour. Dominick stayed. I thought he was a dumbass. I thought Killer would shoot him.

I meant to keep the gun a secret, but one thing I'm definitely not is good at keeping secrets. As soon as I walked through the front door I told my mother. She flipped out when she learned that I'd come into direct contact with a loaded pistol. Even when I made it clear that the gun was unloaded she didn't listen and picked up the phone. My father agreed that I was not to go over to Killer's house unless his parents were home, and if Killer ever showed the gun again I should make up another excuse and leave the house as quickly as possible. Break a window and jump through that if I had to. They told me I had done the right thing. Their approval made me feel good, but I still wondered what had gone on between Dominick and Killer after I'd left.

And now here I was going around locking all the doors and closing all the windows in my house so that not even Killer's creepy rat could get inside. Having finished with the lock-up, I went to the dining room window and peeked between two blinds. He was on our lawn now. My anxiety spiked the way it always did when I had to fend off a Killer-coming-over. This time was different though because of the rat, which might have had rabies. Killer might have had rabies, too. I watched him stride across the lawn and over to our front porch. There was no stopping them. The rat, so big that I'd at first mistaken it for an opossum, scurried up and down its owner's back and neck, clinging to his shirt with sharp claws. I was sure Killer had seen me outside, and now there was no way to get rid of him nicely. What's worse than having an ex-friend that still thinks he's your friend? An ex-friend with a gun and a rat.

"Open up," he shouted into the door. "You're in there, I know and I'm coming in whatever it takes. I'm not leaving till you let me in. I'm not. You let me in. I mean it. If I have to stand around waiting I'll go to every window and bug you to death I will."

I waited, my ear pressed to the front door. Maybe he would give up and go away.

About a minute passed and I thought he'd left. Then he spoke, his voice nicer now, not so demanding. "Let me in, Kevin."

His real name was Andrew, but only his mother called him that.

"Let me in," he said again. "I got something to show you."

"I've already seen your rat," I answered through the door.

"But Sandra hasn't. Let me show it to her."

I groaned. Leave my sister out of this, I wanted to say.

"Sandra isn't here."

"Yes she is, Kev. I saw the two of you walking up the street and she hasn't left this house since you came home."

Great, I thought. He even spies on us from his house, waits for the bus to drop us off. I figured the only thing to do at this point would be to open the door and let him in. The sooner he came in the sooner I could ask him to leave.

So I opened the door to Killer. The rat had ripped a hole in his shirt with its claws.

"You can't stay too long," I said. "My parents'll be home soon and we're going out to eat."

"Okay, whatever," he said, and then he walked right in. As Killer pushed past, his rat reached out and tried to grab on to me with its long claws. I drew back against the wall and stayed there until both the rat and its owner were a good few feet from me.

"Sandra's in her room, right," he asked, gesturing toward the back of the house.

"Yeah..."

Killer turned from me to head back there. "But wait!" I said. He stopped and looked at me. The rat looked at me, too. "Just...Let me go and get her, you know. It just wouldn't be cool to bring this rat to her and maybe scare her. Just let me prepare her, don't surprise her like that."

"Okay," he said. "I don't like it but okay. It's your house."

Yeah right, I thought. More your house than mine now.

Then he said, "Are you ever going to let me be in a room with your sister?"

"What do you mean?" I had this bad feeling I sometimes get when I'm sick with the flu, or when one of our cats has died, or when Killer is suddenly asking why I won't let him be in a room with my sister.

"I mean just the two of us, alone. We have things to talk about." He thought his pronouncement over and then made a correction. "*I* have things I need to tell her. Important things that don't concern you, Kev."

"What are you saying?"

"One of these days, Kev. One of these days your sister, you know, Sandra. She's going to start liking me, and that's when we have to start talking about future plans. The future, Kevin. Just her and me."

I wanted to run, but that would have meant leaving my sister at the mercy of my best ex-friend and his rat. And I couldn't do that, as much as Sandra had been getting on my nerves lately, hogging up all the Nintendo-time and inviting her noisy friends over for slumber parties that lasted until four in the morning. I couldn't run out on her because she was my sister and her alone with Killer was just too horrible an image to have in my mind. I would stay and see this through.

"Just let me go get her," I said, sidestepping talk of any future plans. What future plans? Did Killer really like my sister, or was he trying to get to me in a way he knew would work—through my parents and sister, my family, those who mattered most to me.

"I'll wait," he said. "I'll wait in the kitchen with Opie."

"Who?"

"My rat."

"Oh."

I went to my sister's room. Her door was shut as usual. I knocked loudly so she could hear me through the music blaring out of her stereo. She opened the door and poked her head out. "What do you want," she asked.

"Killer's here and he wants to show you his rat," I said.

"His rat? Tell him no. I don't want to."

"Come on, Sandra. Just this one time."

"No, Kevin. I'm not seeing a rat."

"Come on, it'll be really quick. You don't have to talk to him for very long at all. I promise. He won't leave if you don't talk to him."

"Kevin, what's wrong with him?"

I almost said, "He likes you" but censored myself in time. Instead I said, "I don't know. He's Killer. He's just not gonna go away without seeing you. Please?"

"Fine." She huffed a little but I got her to follow me into the kitchen.

Killer sat at the table. His rat was running around leaving claw marks on the tablecloth. That's where we eat, I thought. This is our home. So get out of here. If only I could say those things to him. But I thought then, as I'd thought so many times before but never really admitted to myself, that I couldn't simply tell Killer off. As strong as I saw myself, I wasn't—not really. I couldn't tell him off. I couldn't tell anyone off—I was that terrified of making a bad impression on people. Stricken with the Please Disease. I was so damn eager to please. I was eager to please my parents, my friends, my ex-friends, my sister, my teachers, my coaches, everybody I came into contact with I had to please or else I'd feel guilty and think I was an awful person. I couldn't tell Killer off because he too was a person, no longer my friend true, a crazy with both a gun and a rat true, but a person nonetheless who had feelings. I did not want to hurt those feelings. It would be many years before I would begin to lose my misplaced and misguided empathy.

"Hi, Sandra." Killer stood up from the table and I thought he would bow. He reached out for the rat instead, picked it up with one hand. The thing struggled as Killer placed it on his shoulder, and as soon as it was situated it relaxed and began tearing up his shirt all over. He came up close to my sister and she backed away, anxious to take off for her room. I watched all three of them—Sandra, Killer, and Opie the Rat.

"It's my pet rat, Sandra," Killer said. He tore the rodent away from his shirt with both hands and held it out to her as a kind of peace offering. "I brought it over for you to see. Do you like it? You like it, right?"

"It's cool." My sister looked at me and I avoided her eyes. Just a minute or two longer, I wanted to tell her.

Killer did not believe Sandra thought his rat was cool. He looked disappointed. "Okay," he said. "Because you know I brought him over here for you to see. His name's Opie."

"Hmm."

"Sandra. Do you really like my rat?"

"Yes. Now I gotta go, all right. It's been really really fun seeing your rat, but I really need to go to my room. I mean the bathroom. I have to go to the bathroom." She looked at me with urgency in her eyes.

"Well, if she's gotta go to the bathroom..." I hoped I made it seem to Killer that I had no control over any of this when in fact I was the ringleader, the culprit who simply could not say no to an unwanted guest.

My sister said goodbye to Killer and disappeared.

"I think you better go now too." I tried to sound authoritative, but I just ended up sounding like a pushover. Killer knew this about me just as I knew it in myself.

"Your parents aren't coming home for a little longer, right?

Can't I stay for a little longer, Kevin? I came by to see you too, you know. Not just Sandra. I came by to see you."

Killer coming over to see me—when it was obvious we were no longer friends and hadn't been in a while—was funny. Unfortunately, he took my smile as a sign of friendship. He held out his hand—or his rat, rather—and said, "Okay, now how about we play some Nintendo like you like."

Super Nintendo, yeah. My plan was to play a few rounds with him, beat him soundly at whatever game we decided on, and then send him home with his rat. I agreed to play and Killer and I went into the living room. As soon as we'd sat down and started up the system, taken our controllers in hand, Opie jumped off Killer's shoulder and landed on the carpet. My anxiety was back.

"Is he going to crap on the carpet?"

"No." Killer sounded offended. "Opie's a good rat."

Killer and I played *Street Fighter II*, and Opie kept interfering. The rat would jump on my back or legs or chew on the Nintendo power cords. I started to think Killer had brought his rat over to help him finally beat me at a game.

"Hey," I said. "Tell your rat to lay off me."

"Opie," Killer warned.

The rat stopped after that. I concentrated on the game, and soon I had control and was giving Killer a severe trouncing. He grunted after every match I won. We played more than I'd planned. When I looked at the wall clock I saw that one of my parents might be home soon.

"Hey," I said to Killer. He grunted again. "You gotta go." When there was no response, I said, slowly and clearly, "You really have to go."

"First I have to find my rat."

I'd forgotten about Opie. The little critter had run off without either or us noticing. Or maybe Killer had noticed and he hadn't told me.

"I think he's back in your room," Killer said. "I'll go get him." He threw down the controller, got up from the carpet and ran out of the living room and down the hall.

I sat there, mulling over what my parents would do to me if the rodent had gone off and defecated somewhere in a corner of the house, and if it had done its business in my room, well, that would be even worse. What if Killer couldn't find the rat? What if he never found it? That old anxiety intensified in me then. I thought of some wild things—of Killer coming over to my house, year after year, searching for his rat, Opie. It would give him an excuse to come over, wouldn't it? What if the rat had gone after my sister? What if Killer had gone after my sister and was in her room right now, while I sat staring at the video game menu?

I heard a knock on the door—and it wasn't the front door. I knew it! I jumped up and heard Killer say, "Sandra, Sandra. Open up. Is Opie in there? I want to know if Opie's in there. Do you have Opie?" When I got to her door he was pounding, screaming for her to open up, open up, she had his rat and he wanted it back, damnit. He'd lost it. I saw the anger in his eyes and I wanted to step away from him, far away, down the dark hall and into a hole where he'd never bother us again.

I thought about the gun, and that scared me.

"Hey," I said. "Hey, leave her alone. She doesn't have your rat."

He didn't listen, only kept banging away on her door. I thought he'd break it down so I yelled in his ears, "Stop it, stop it. She doesn't have your rat!" I lost it in a different way than Killer. I showed my emotions. When I got angry or frustrated I often resorted to tears, and they were falling now. "Would you just leave?" I pleaded.

The door opened and Sandra stormed out. She pushed Killer and went into the hall bathroom, slammed the door behind. It was quiet. Killer looked in her room, looked at me, and then pushed past. "You're disgusting," he said.

Maybe I was. Fourteen years old and crying because I couldn't get my way. I so wanted Killer out of my house, I would have given anything to have run him out. I should have a gun, I thought. If I had a gun, he'd know not to barge in. He'd respect me. He'd fear me. I would have my way if I had a gun. I stopped my crying, wiped my tears, and followed him. I could hear Killer calling out for Opie as he walked around the living room and my parents' bedroom. "Try the kitchen," I said in an even voice.

Killer found Opie on the kitchen counter. He picked the rat up by its tail and headed for the front door. I took a deep breath, exhaled and followed him. It seemed like I had been following him forever. I refused to follow him again.

In the open doorway Killer said to me, "You know, Kevin, I wanted to think you were cool but now I don't know. I really don't know." He left. I closed the door behind him and spent the rest of my time in the living room, watching the clock, waiting for our parents to return.

UPDATE

I'm a father now and live in Denver. I left Anomar in the fall of 1997 for college, and nine years later I left California with my wife and young son. At the time I told myself I wouldn't go back, not to California, certainly not to Anomar, but that little town has a way of sticking with you. Case in point: Killer's ending.

His real name was Andrew Bloch. He was two years older than me, graduating from AHS in June of 1995. Rumors circulated his senior year that Andrew had compiled a hit-list of all those he intended to shoot. Cheerleaders. Jocks. ASB leaders. Popular kids. Kids not like me or my friends. The shootings never happened, and graduation 1995 passed without incident, as it did in 1996 and 1997 and 1998. They had always only been rumors. From a young age, Andrew was destined to be dogged with a negative perception from others. He was always on edge, but how much of that edginess was caused by those who judged and bullied him rather than himself was up for debate. We called him Andy to his face, Killer behind his back. The whole school did—those who would give him the time of day, at least. Yet when it came time to graduate, Andrew walked the stage and slipped away without so much as a mumble. His parents moved to the East Coast, and he went with them. As for our role in his story, we forgot about him—that is until I took my wife and son to California to see Dominick in Los Angeles, then drive up to UC Santa Barbara and walk around my alma mater.

In the hotel bar, only after Charlotte had gone up to our room with Jackson to tuck him in, my longest-lasting friend opened up.

He told me about what had happened in Virginia. A shoot-out with the cops. Some guy had gone crazy and put a bullet through the head of his two-year-old daughter while she was in his sports car, and then the guy went inside his mother-in-law's house and shot her to death. Set the house on fire when he saw the cops approaching. Fired at them through the busted windows. Nicked one cop in the neck; that officer went down but would survive. As the officers continued to encircle and draw closer, and the flames and the smoke amassed, the murderer put his gun to his head and pulled the trigger.

It had happened only a few months before my visit and was all over Anomar-related social media, our high school alumni pages. The killer, of course, was Killer, Andy, Andrew. He'd started out as an elementary school outcast enduring the taunt *Bloch-head*, graduated to *Killer* by middle- and high school, and as a thirty-five-year-old, Fate had finally run him through.

It's a year later now and I can still watch the brief footage of the officer getting shot in the neck and going down, the house consumed by flames. I don't watch all that often—and certainly never when Jackson is in the same room. He's nine now. When he was two I didn't own a gun, and I still don't own one. To think what Andy did to his little girl, his daughter. To think what he would have done to his wife if she hadn't decided to pull an extra shift at the last minute. Financial troubles, bickering, the threat of divorce. She succeeded in leaving him, but he made sure she was unable to take those she loved with her.

(And when they asked if I would like to have the gun, I told them No.)

Just yesterday I saw Jackson agonizing over some words he was preparing to post. You may be taken aback at the thought of a nine-year-old with his own social media account, but my wife and I gave it a lot of serious thought. We reasoned that Jackson was an only child who would stay an only child, and as such he could use social media—just one platform, one account—to stay connected with friends and our extended family. It's worked. Our conditions are that all new friend requests must be approved by us and that all of Jackson's posts must be vetted before they go live. That means Charlotte or I invariably need to be present when our son's online.

I came up behind Jackson and asked what he was writing. Although it was mid-day, the room felt dark. We were well into July then and the thought of going outside and throwing the ball with my son passed briefly through my mind.

"I'm telling everyone I'm okay," he said.

"Why would you not be okay?"

"Dad. The theater. Last night. The shooting."

"Oh."

I've come to the internet slowly. I have no social networking page, no social media account, no online presence anywhere, really. I check personal email something like two days a week. It's like exercise with me.

I leaned in and read the update to Jackson's profile:

hey everyone

just wanted to say im ok I wasnt in the theatr where it happend. saw it this mourning and it was totes awsum, right?

"You're talking about the movie, right?"

"Yeah, why?"

"I'm worried some of your friends might think you mean the footage and news reports and stuff, or maybe the shooting itself, and not the movie."

"They'll know," my son said with the confidence of a kid who's set to start fourth grade.

"I just think you should say what 'it' is. That's all."

I'd heard the news reports from my son the moment he got up and jumped on his computer that morning. He was shouting "Dad! Dad! Some guy shot up the midnight showing!" I told him we shouldn't go to the 9:45 morning screening like we'd planned, but since it's always been his choice I didn't have much of one. We went to a different movie stadium, one mashed city over from where the massacre had taken place. In the theater we were two of only ten. My son was the youngest. Despite the reports showing up on his phone, he insisted we sit in the very front, and for a time I kept turning my head around to make sure no one with a drawn gun was behind us, aiming at the backs of our heads.

Everyone in there was jumpy, but nothing happened and I was able to enjoy the movie after the initial sequence, the one involving the plane. During that action, I tried unsuccessfully to keep thoughts of the shooting at bay. I thought, Was this the moment in the movie when the shooter appeared? Was the audience able to hear the movie's first gunshots before hearing their own?

In that first sequence, the tension rose the way it should have. Something bad's going to happen, the movie wanted us to think, and I thought of all the people unaware of what was going to happen. They had lived the point of the movie without watching more than ten minutes of it.

Later, the movie said: "No guns. No killing."

The movie held Jackson's attention in a way I rarely did. When it was over he was quiet, and when I asked if he was thinking of the shooting that had happened fewer than twelve hours earlier, he answered that he was thinking of the movie. There were some things he didn't get, or didn't catch that I had to explain to him. He could have looked them up on his phone, he told me, but he wanted me to help him that morning.

"I think I'm going to post it now," my son said, his eyes on the computer screen.

"Go for it," I said. "You've heard my two cents. You don't need anything more out of me."

But as I spoke that last sentence I realized he did need more from me. It wasn't enough that I'd clarified some of the movie's plot points, or that I was his way of getting to the movie, getting him into the movie as well. He needed me not to be me right now. He needed someone else just then.

So I told him a story. I pulled up a chair next to him and started talking. I had his attention the way the movie had it less than an hour earlier. He was staring at me with those wide eyes, his mouth slightly ajar, waiting to counter. When I spoke, my voice at first sounded unsure, but then it got stronger as I remembered.

I didn't tell him about Killer, or my father. I told another story. It happened a couple years before he was born, when his mother and I were getting ready to graduate college. It was, I thought, the night of February 22nd or 23rd, a Sunday, I was pretty sure. I had just gotten back from Vegas with a buddy of mine and my roommate was on his computer, not looking at me when he said, "You missed it."

"Missed what?" I'd said, and he went on to tell me how the night before, these five people, these students and friends of students, were walking along a street in Isla Vista...

"You know, the college town I took you to last year."

"I know."

I couldn't decode the look on my son's face. At the

moment he seemed hesitant to listen anymore. I was not the screen. I felt instead like an octogenarian in a nursing home about to unveil a war story to my great-grandson.

"And these five people, they were walking along, and then this car plowed into them from behind. Pinned some of them to the cars parked on the side, just plain mowed others down."

I paused for a reaction. There was none. I pressed on.

"And this…the car must have been going at least sixty, maybe seventy miles an hour, and you remember how narrow those streets were there…. Those kids didn't have any chance of escape. Four out of the five died. The guy who did it was some nineteen-year-old son of a Hollywood director. He got off later. I mean he was declared insane, in the end, so they sent him to an institution instead of to jail or death row."

I felt fine bringing up the topic of death. Movies had made it possible. Now my son was looking at me strangely, and I sensed at any moment he would ask why I was telling him this, where was the punchline, or, at the very least, where was the gun?

"The point is," I said, "it was a different time then, before you were born. People didn't react the way they do now. When my roommate told me, I remember thinking I needed to call my parents, your grandparents, but they'd called already. I called your mom right away, and she was okay, she'd spent the night in, studying and relaxing, she wasn't out partying that night. And your grandfather actually said he was glad I'd been in Vegas, it'd kept me away from danger. So…the point is…"

I could tell he wanted to turn away. He wanted to look at the screen.

"…those were the only people I ever thought of telling. We didn't need to tell the world. We didn't need to spread our safety around like it's a gift. For strangers, for pseudo-friends, it's not a gift. It's a gift to you, but not to them."

What I was saying was no longer coming from me but from another me, the father I was supposed to be. I thought of the first real sustained conversation I'd had with my son, when he was five, about worms crawling along the sidewalk after a heavy rain. I remembered a time, followed by so many others, when I'd wanted to say no to him and instead said yes, just so I wouldn't have to see him cry, he cried so much and no matter what we did during the pregnancy—the songs we sang, the books we read, the music we played, the food she ate—nothing could stop that trait from developing. I remembered, that July day leaning over my son and staring at his screen, a moment his mother and I had shared at the end of the first trimester, when we weren't doing so well. I'd asked how she was doing and she'd said Read the books, I wasn't doing enough reading, how was I going to be prepared if I didn't know what to expect? I wanted her to tell me what I had to expect, but she was tired, and with the information already all there, why didn't I take advantage of it?

My son has never seen a gun in real life. His mother and I were just kids ourselves when we'd had him, not an accident, we told ourselves, just as we told ourselves that the world, the country we were raising him in was a better, more innovative and stable and resilient country than ever. I wanted to believe, I know she did, but our son was a daily reminder of that lie we'd been telling ourselves about the future.

"They want to know I'm safe," Jackson said. Behind him the screen confirmed that minutes had passed since either of us had spoken. I had been sitting there thinking, remembering, and he'd been watching, waiting for me to give him the okay.

"Do they all want to know?" I asked. "How many of them are really your friends? How many of them are just...connections?"

This was the wrong conversation to be having at his age.

Stop it, I thought. You're going to make him hate you before he's supposed to hate you. Stop it now.

But I couldn't.

"When the tragedy in Isla Vista happened," I said, "everyone in the world didn't feel the need to be a part of it. They weren't making yellow and blue ribbons with the silhouette of a gaucho on them and then spreading that image around the internet. People weren't 'liking' the artwork of the tragedy. There was no artwork of the tragedy. People didn't feel the need to jump in and express their feelings about it without really being a part of it. There were the parents, the families, some news stories, and a trial that ended wrong. That's all that was needed."

"Then they'll forget it," said my son. He turned to face the screen. He started clicking something.

"They won't forget it. I won't forget it. I'm telling it to you now so...."

The details. Where were the details in my story? What time of night was it when it happened, when I got in to learn that it had happened? What was I wearing? What were they wearing? What kind of car was the murderer driving? Just how fast was he going when he struck?

How long had Andrew and his wife known each other? How long had they loved, fought? Where was that wife now? Had she moved on, met someone knew?

"How will they remember?" my son said in a voice that was low yet fierce, a flame.

"They have a memorial," I answered. "In a park, in I.V." My jaw seized as I remembered searching for that park, with my son, the year before, without telling him what I was looking for, and I couldn't find it, the park and consequently the memorial. I had read that it was there, but how was I to know for sure?

"How will they remember?" my son repeated, and this time his voice was little more than a whisper.

I don't know, I wanted to say, but I didn't speak. Instead I placed my hand on his thin forearm and felt it move back and forth. I heard him click. My eyes were closed. I knew his eyes were on the screen.

THE ENTOMOLOGIST

Her first memory is of rain. Sheets of it bearing down on the roof of her house, smacking the windows and tocking like the tongue on the roof of her mother's mouth. Through the window she sees the cul-de-sac pelted and flooding, a car moving slowly through the water as if it's floating. Somewhere above, a plane descends in an attempt to land. The engines roar and the rest is darkness.

When she is six her mother asks her to feed the dog. It's summer and sunny out. She ventures onto the back porch. The dog is in a far corner of the yard, digging a hole through the great grassy lawn. She watches the dog for a few moments then turns to the large plastic container. It's so tall she has to get on her tiptoes. Having taken off the top she reaches in without looking inside. Her hands sift through the dry dog food in search of the elusive tin cup used for pouring. Her fingers touch dry pellet after dry pellet and then...a skittering, a squirming little thing. More skittering, squirming things. She whips her hand out of the container and looks at it, horrified to see three earwigs crawling down her wrist. With a cry she flings them off and then runs screaming inside the house.

Later that summer, the summer of her sixth year, she walks around the rose bush in the backyard on the great grassy lawn. She hears a tremendous buzz and looks up to see the largest bee yet—its black furry hide seems to sweat in the sun. The sight of this too sends her into the house.

Over a decade later she is a teenager graduating from Reno High School, on the other side of the airport from where she lives. Her sport is volleyball, and she graduates captain of the team. Volleyball has been a great outlet, a lifesaver really, the source of her friendships and the slayer of her fears. On the court, she doesn't have time to picture what terrifies her. She pictures only the next kill. The court is at all times clean, shiny. It should be: she helps clean it when she can. On senior night, her teammates and coach honor her, but although she smiles and hugs and high-fives, her mind is elsewhere. Her mind is already on the future.

She's convinced Reno—and by extension the entire state of Nevada—can take her only so far, so she attends college in southern California. When she arrives on campus, a freshman, she is ecstatic. That first year she goes to the beach often, decides to major in history. Volleyball is again a priority and she works her way quickly into the captain position. The key is to keep the competitive edge sharp. The key, also, is to avoid contact with the dirty, slimy, wriggly, squirming things of the world.

One night during her sophomore year she is brushing her teeth in her apartment's kitchen as she always does. She can't stand to watch people brush their teeth. This includes herself. It makes her nauseous. She rinses her mouth out in the sink and when she looks up she sees a millipede crawling along the wall beside the light switch. She watches it for a time. Her complete revulsion at the sight of this creature just about sends her into her bedroom—but she forces herself to stay and watch. This has to be it, she thinks. I have to get over it. I have to accept them. Pause for Poise, her high school coach would have said. That's what she's doing now: pausing for poise. In the end, she does nothing to the millipede. She lets it slip away and then goes to bed.

In one dream she is lying in bed, covered by a white sheet. The room is all white, too. She lifts up the sheet to find the bed covered with earwigs. Slimy black little earwigs, their pincers working wildly. She sees that they are on the ceiling, the walls, they will soon black out the room. That's only one dream.

The story of a hamlet in the south of England, August 19, 1776. At just after noon on that day the village is beset upon by a vast horde of earwigs. The tittering little bugs move like a rolling carpet across the plain and descend on the homes, shops and livestock. The village's inhabitants flee. It will be another two days before they're able to return.

She begins to look at insects closely. Study them, in a sense, as only an amateur can. She watches their movements, takes notes on their activity patterns both night and day, and checks out books from the college library. She comes to believe that insects will be the next great species to rule the world. It only makes sense. Life began with the fish, ocean dwellers, and then came the reptiles, dinosaurs, great hulking beasts of the earth. After the dinosaurs died out it was the mammals' turn. Still their turn. But when the mammals die out what will be left? Insects have patiently been waiting their turn for millions of years. They're up next. She imagines the future, a post-apocalyptic world where insects have mutated from nuclear fallout. Great deserts patrolled by roving bands of giant wasps, scorpions the size of semi-trucks basking in the bloody sun. Jungles and city ruins filled with spiders, centipedes, the scolopendromorphs and the mygalomorphs. And the people. She wonders if any people will be left alive in this future epoch. She wonders if it will ever rain. She considers changing her major.

"Okay, Gregor. I gotta go."

He is lying on his back, his arms folded, his legs crossed over one another. She has been dating him for too long now.

"Hey, I mean it. It's time."

She shakes him. His legs come uncrossed and splay. His arms remain folded, mummy-like, but his head falls to the side now, a bit of spittle issuing. She can no longer see his eyes behind his glasses. His nakedness, for the first time, shames her. As she's seen in movies, she presses two fingers against the side of his neck and waits. After a minute, she calls 9-1-1.

She decides against the study of insects and graduates with a degree in history followed, a year and a half later, by a teaching credential. To her surprise, when she does earn her credential and finishes the requisite hours of student teaching, the job offers are few. It's not that she's a bad teacher, she thinks, it's just that there's not a lot of need for history teachers at this time. She applies everywhere—everywhere in California, that is. Hoping to stay in a beach city, if possible. But after months of no bites all up and down the coast, she begins to think maybe she's being a bit too picky. She branches inland. A high school in San Diego's North County is looking for a history teacher. She applies and is hired. Disappointed at having to leave the beach but well aware that a forty-five-minute commute each way down twisting cliff-side roads five days a week would do her in, she reluctantly moves to her high school's small town. Her apartment is efficient and sad, but the job is good and she gets a cat. She'd like to get another but fears she might turn into a Cat Lady.

That is not to be, for she meets a man, another teacher, who's been at the high school for a few years now. He's a local and—to her immense happiness—a bit older, handsome and outgoing and very much interested in her. That he's the boys' basketball coach and a much-admired P.E. teacher is another plus. They date for just over a year before he proposes and she accepts. Since he owns horses and has convinced her, during this time, to accept these creatures as family, they move a little ways out of town to a place he's been eyeing for years.

She had never imagined herself living in the country but here she is now, standing in front of an old ranch house that sits on a sprawling six and a half acres. She'll learn to at least like it. He says it just needs some fixing up. He was raised in the country, so he knows.

That first night they sleep on the floor in one of the rooms, surrounded by boxes, awaiting the bed that is only a day away. In the initial dawn-glow she awakes to find him against one of the walls, looking up, a shoe in one hand. Cautious, she approaches him.

"What is it?"

"Shhh. I think I got it."

She too looks up and sees, just barely, a black widow spider in the corner, sitting still in its haphazardly constructed web.

She holds down his arm. "Don't kill it."

"*Don't* kill it? You crazy?"

"It'll be gone in the morning."

"Honey. No way I'm leaving this thing in peace."

But he can't free his arm. She continues to observe.

"They're really beautiful," she says.

"They're probably all over the house. I'll pick up some spray today. See if we can get by without calling an exterminator."

"You'll have to wait till the night."

"I don't know why we don't have a broom."

"Just leave it alone. Live with it."

"You're telling me you can live with that thing up there?"

"I've learned to live with them all," she admits. "It's

taken...forever. My whole life, but now I feel at peace when I see them."

"Black widow spiders?"

"Any insect. Really. There's something religious about them."

"Okay.... I better not find any in our bed when we finally get into it, got it?"

Three days later she is on a ladder set against the side of the house. Washing windows. It is early summer and she wears a hat, gloves, sunglasses, shorts and a plain t-shirt. She wishes she were taller.

He comes by, his body bent, his face strained.

"Any more widows?" she calls out cheerfully.

He grunts but stops to watch her.

"I'll quit asking," she says over her shoulder.

He stands there, watching.

"You know I wanted to study insects, when I was in undergrad."

"Spiders aren't insects, honey."

She considers saying, Why not? but, seeing his look, decides against it.

Finally he says, "I'm gonna run and get us some sandwiches. You want the usual?"

She nods and he leaves. She hears the truck pull away.

The renovations have been coming along nicely. Already the sideboards have been painted anew, the window frames touched up—all except for those on this side of the house. She draws the hand-squeegee down the left side, the last side, of the window. The way she's positioned the ladder, though, she can't quite get it all. That very top left corner.... She reaches, and as she reaches she feels the ladder wobble—just a bit, but enough for her to freeze. Pause for Poise. She looks down at an overgrowth of weeds and figures it's at most a six-foot fall. Nothing that would kill her, but still. She puts one foot on the next lowest rung and then pauses. That corner.... Determined, she stands back up and throws her arm out. It's enough to nab the spot. It's also enough to send the ladder toppling to the left. For an awful moment she feels nothing beneath her, it's as if she's weightless, and then she feels the blood rush to her head, feels—for a few seconds—the weeds—and then something else: wood. Old, brittle wood. She lands on this wood, hard, and breaks through. An ugly crack rings out and she's falling, continuing to fall, her arms outstretched. A cellar? she has time to think. Weeds give way to webs and then she feels them, all of them, on her at once as she lands on her back in what could be dirt. A sudden jolt, her eyes open and close. For them, she opens her mouth, and the rest is darkness, thousands of silent screams, faces never thought to smile, shiny, taut skin, a new look, the last beauty borne.

500 Kilometers to Cairo

My first night in Hurghada I wore the wrong shoes.

"What's that? What's that?" the boy beside me nettled, joined in chorus by another of the same height and look: beige robe, no shoes, a mess of black hair falling halfway to his eyes. Both of them pointing at my shoes. "What's that?" they said again. And again: "What's that?"

Jana glanced at me, her mouth a tripwire. I gripped her hand tighter and lengthened my steps. The kids stayed beside us. One of them held a wooden box for polishing shoes. The other tapped at the pockets of my slacks with every other *What's that?* He was feeling for something. He wanted to know where it was.

The main street of Hurghada was rigged with men fishing for tourists outside their shops, restaurants, and coffee houses. If Jana and I got too close the men would smile wide and say what became a mantra: "Hello, my friend. What is your name? Where are you from?" Some of them got creative: "My friend, hello. Where are you from? My name is Karim. What is yours?"

"What's that? What's that?" went the kids.

"Look—" I started, but was cut off by a hard shout in Arabic and the boy on my right, the one with the box, scampered away down the street. The other boy was grabbed by a broad-framed security guard in a black cap and uniform. Hauled off to Lord knows where. I thought I saw fear in the kid's eyes, but any pity I had was overwhelmed by relief that he wouldn't bother us anymore. I squeezed Jana's hand. Only later that night, as we undressed to turn in, did I notice the orange streak of paint running across the front of one of my black dress shoes.

When we were under the covers and close I said, "Come with me to America."

"I'll come to America when the koruna is stronger than the dollar."

"That'll never happen."

"You and your money," she said, and pinched the flabby bit of my waist. "Your little money-diaper under your pants. Are you not going to sleep with it?"

"I don't know," I said. "Can I trust you?"

Jana smiled and let this go. "Why don't you stay in Brno? They like you. You are a good teacher."

"I make no money teaching English."

"You make enough. You don't need more."

"It's not that. It's...."

"Say it. My country."

"I can't live in your country," I said. "Long-term."

She turned away, and it took some coaxing, a few minutes rubbing her neck and shoulders, to bring her back to my side.

"Why don't you like America?" I asked. "Your sister lives there. She's married. She has a family."

"My sister is the house, the yard, the land. When I go to see her I see these things, not her. The land is like a mouth there. Her house is a mouth."

Jana had always had her opinions about America, but I had never heard her talk this way. Her arguments against typical American excess, although pointed, had always been pat and imprecise. Now she was speaking in metaphors I did not care to understand. I suppose I should not have told her about my inheritance and explained to her the concept of a trust fund, which was ultimately what brought us here and provided, in great part, for her.

"Give it six months," I said. "I've been in Brno for six months. This English-teaching thing lasts a year, and then...."

"Then you leave me."

"No, then you come with me. Right?"

"Which one do you want more?" asked Jana. "Your country, or me?"

I sighed. "All I know is I can't stay in the Czech Republic. There's no..." I was about to do it again and couldn't stop now. "There's no infrastructure."

"What does that mean, infrastructure? What does that word mean?"

"Opportunities, I guess."

Jana pushed away from me and stared up at the ceiling. It was warm for February, and the mosquitoes had yet to strike.

"Six months," I said. "That's all I'm asking. We are married, aren't we?"

"If that were the truth. Only *here* we are married. To them we *must* be married."

She had been clear about this on the plane. "Because it's dangerous to say otherwise?" I tried to make my voice sound innocent.

"You don't believe me?"

"I believe you," I said. "I just think it may be dangerous either way."

～

JANA'S first trip to Egypt was with her parents and sister. All four of them were taking in the pyramids when they heard shouts and screams. In the shadow of the largest pyramid, an Egyptian man was being kicked and clubbed on the ground by the tourist police. Scattered in the bloody sand were an assortment of trinkets—alabaster pyramids, replicas of gods and the like. The beating continued. Tourists watched and a few took pictures. Eventually the hawker, who had reportedly tried to trick some money out of a tourist, was hauled off bleeding from the head and mouth.

I used to wonder what became of that man. Was he thrown in prison, or worse? What became of that boy who'd helped to paint my shoe?

WE'D HEARD we could hire a taxi to drive us the 500 kilometers to Cairo for no more than two hundred dollars total. It was either that or the tourist bus.

"Not possible," the first travel agent told us. "You must have the police with you at all times. Even in Cairo. Because of the bombing in Khan Khalili...."

I didn't buy it. Solo travel couldn't have been restricted that much. The trains still operated and besides, Cairo was a sprawling city with plenty of foreigners and ex-pats. Could the government watch every one of these people? Follow each one to the market, to the restroom? Was a tourist cop stationed on every street in every suburb of the capital?

"We should do the taxi," I told Jana once we were outside. "We can't let fear control our trip."

"Has fear controlled our trip?"

"I'm just saying. I think the terrorists aren't the only ones terrorizing here."

"So dramatic," Jana chided.

"No, seriously. They're trying to scare us into an organized tour, into forking over more money. I guarantee any other agent here will say the same thing. We can get a better deal on our own."

"You're worried now about your money?"

"I'm worried about being *constrained*. I want an adventure."

Jana bowed her head and smiled.

"What," I said.

"*To nic.*"

"No, what?"

"You look like a little boy."

"Do I?"

"I like it when you're a little boy."

His name was Nizam and he must have been in his sixties, maybe early seventies. His rusty, beat-up Corolla bore nothing indicating a taxi. In an alley off the main drag in Hurghada, underneath oil-wet awnings and beside a still-life of fruit stands, Jana made arrangements with the man in Arabic.

"Two hundred?" I asked when she came back.

"Two hundred," she said. "And he will take us anywhere we like in Cairo."

It didn't feel like our lives were in danger, even though our seatbelts didn't work and the back door on my side popped open at random times before I rigged it closed with Jana's bandana. The car rattled and bounced along, kicking up dust into the mid-day. At some point we fell asleep, and when we awoke it was night and Nizam still had not spoken a word. Looming in the distance was downtown Cairo lit up like a circus staked and settled. On either side of the dim freeway, people tended to cars broken down and immovable on the shoulder. Regular police were out in force negotiating the traffic jam just ahead; at a crawl on our right a boy on a donkey pulled a cart full of reeds and palm fronds. Pasted onto billboards were smiling people drinking soda and looming like ancient deities.

Nizam dropped us off outside the Nile Hilton, where I had made our reservation. Aware of Jana's eyes, I gave our driver an Egyptian fifty-pound note. The old man smiled and pointed at his chest. "Nizam," he said. "My name."

"Thank you, Mr. Nizam," Jana said.

We walked along the Nile. Arabic music blared from loudspeakers on almost every cruise vessel and felucca on the river. Egyptian couples leaned against the riverside railing, chatting or gazing at the Nile and the Cairo Tower and Opera House beyond. Others strolled arm-in-arm—even men with other men. Boys as young as twelve walked past us with arms linked. Jana leaned in beside me. "Don't worry," she said.

"What? Why am I worried?"

"*Jo*. Why are you?"

"I guess I wasn't expecting—"

"It's the custom," she said. "In Arabic countries, men show their affection with other men. It's normal."

"I guess."

"They kiss both cheeks."

"The men do?"

"And hug with force. Be used to it," she said.

When the music and rush of men asking our names got to be too much, we dodged across the street and headed for Midan Tahrir, the main square. We didn't yet have a suitable map of downtown, so instead of finding nightlife in the main commercial district, we ended up lost in a neighborhood just east of the American University. In Bab al-Luq we found not one welcoming coffee house, no bars, and every side street with young Egyptians on it turned out to be a dead end. At last I stopped Jana and brought my mouth to her ear.

"Do you feel like we're being followed?"

"*Ne*. You are—what is that word?"

"Paranoid. But I'm not. I really think there's someone...."

The street was narrow and black except for a thin wedge of light from an open doorway. Not even the moon touched this place.

"Let's go back and hail a cab," I said.

"You give up? Now? We'll find it. I'll ask someone new."

"I have this feeling. It's not good."

"Maybe it's the Revenge of Tutankhamen."

I started to laugh and that's when I was hit in the stomach. A fist, and as I doubled over another fist hit me in the ear and sent me into the street. Jana screamed and I tried to lift my head but couldn't see anything. Hands at my pockets and I felt my wallet taken. Then a shout, some words in Arabic, and Jana screamed again. I got up only to find the street empty save for Jana sitting on the asphalt, her head bowed and her knees drawn up to her chest. I knelt next to her.

"Did you see them? How many were there?"

"Two. I don't know. I think there were two."

"Did they touch you? They touched you, didn't they? I swear I—"

"They did nothing to me. I hit them. I put my finger in one's eye." She held up her index finger and the tip of it glistened with a thick fluid.

"Jesus, Jana. Good job. Way to go."

"You shouldn't smile."

"I'm just happy you fought back. They took my wallet but it only had a few dollars and pounds. That's all they got."

"That's all they will ever get."

"What does that mean?"

A shadow hid half of Jana's face, and though I tried to help her up from the curb she would not budge. "I need to wash this," she said.

I wiped her hand with the bandana I still had from the cab

and her finger came away clean. Still she would not look at me, and now her entire face was covered in darkness, like so many of the women in burkas we'd passed along the Nile.

"It's okay," I said, "I knew the money belt was a good idea. Come on. Let's go find a cab and get back to the Hilton."

Our next driver never gave his name. His cab was marked and official but as soon as I told him we were going to the Nile Hilton he just laughed and started on a ninety-minute odyssey through the Egyptian capital. Half an hour in I recognized the area enough to know he had no plans to take us straight to our hotel. I tried reasoning with him in English and finally turned to threats, but even then our driver appeared not to listen. "Can you talk to him?" I asked Jana, but she shook her head. Finally, I just sat back and held her limp hand and waited for whatever was coming to us—the unnamed couple who would go missing, unable to be accounted for because we'd never been part of the accountable to begin with.

Nearing a full hour in the cab, our driver pulled over to a man on a donkey cart and engaged in an animated discussion that involved a lot of throwing up of hands. I asked Jana what they were talking about. How much ransom to ask for? The best method for our torture?

"Football," she said. "They're talking about football."

AND SO IT came to this: Jana and I standing near our tour bus parked outside a perfumery. We were waiting to cross the street, our goal to spend a few minutes in the local bazaar, away from our guided tour and the unstated obligation to buy things in stores like the perfume parlor, or the alabaster shop we'd descended on the previous day, or the carpeteria we were scheduled to visit in two hours.

"Psst!" I heard. "Psst!" Just behind us, among the parked cars at the curb, a man in a black uniform sat between the open doors of a tourist police truck. The officer, with thick black mustache and glowering eyes, looked at me sternly and with menace.

"Jana, I don't think we're supposed to cross the street."

She asked why not—after all, three young Egyptian women were waiting close by as well. But we were tourists, I told her, and as such the police in charge of protecting us didn't want us wandering around. They wanted us in the perfume shop.

But Jana wasn't budging and, frankly, I didn't want to budge either—tourist cop or no. We had the right to break out of the schedule if we wanted.

"Psst!" the officer hissed again, even louder this time. He held up his hand, his index finger shooting straight up. The finger did not move at all.

"Pssst!"

"I better go talk to him," I said.

"Wait. Look at his wrist!"

The officer in the back of the truck had his other arm handcuffed to the iron bar on the side of his seat. He wasn't tourist police at all. What I had taken as an officer's black uniform was just a simple dark sweater and pants, a citizen's clothing. No badge, no officer's cap. Not even a baton at his side.

Images flashed in my mind—what might have happened if I'd actually approached this criminal thinking he's a cop. I get a little too close and lean my head in; he grabs me by the throat, either breaks my neck right then or holds me hostage while demanding his release. A standoff ensues. Both he and I end up perishing in a hail of gunfire. The headline back in America: He Should've Stayed On the Bus.

~

WE HAD TO SEE THEM. How could we not?

"What do you think?"

"They're kinda small," I said.

Jana looked from the pyramids to me, her hand shading her eyes. "Maybe you have to be young," she said.

Walking around the largest of the three, the Pyramid of Khufu, we heard shouts off to our left. Two tourist police officers stood just beyond the string-barrier that kept us back from the site, AK-47s slung over their shoulders. They were obviously bored and gesturing emphatically for us to come stand next to them. They pointed at the camera slung around Jana's neck, then gestured that she was to take a picture of me with them—presumably for a fee. I wondered, Will they shoot us if we don't?

"No thanks," I said and started to leave.

The officers continued to pester. The muzzles of their machine guns had shifted, rising closer to our level.

Jana said something in Arabic while I walked away, my body tense and rigid in anticipation of the bullets.

She caught up to me. "They weren't going to shoot you."

"People with guns use them sooner or later."

You will find them on the streets of Hurghada, at the roadside checkpoints on the way to Cairo, perched in medieval-style brick and mortar watchtowers overlooking the ruins, behind the bullet-proof glass and metal detectors at the entrance of every hotel. On tourist buses you will see at least one in plainclothes seated at the front, behind the driver, nine-millimeter tucked casually inside his sport coat. In every tourist-trap outdoor market, outside the door to every perfumery, carpeteria and alabaster mall, in the most expected places and at the most expected times you will encounter them. They are there to protect you, the money, the lifeblood of the country. And just how much do they resent you for that? Just a little, or just enough for them to act on it?

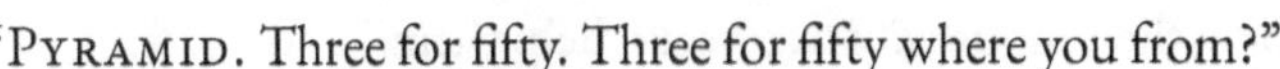

"Pyramid. Three for fifty. Three for fifty where you from?"

"Scarf for head. For when you go to desert."

"Cat statue! Cat statue!"

"Postcards of tombs. How much you want to pay?"

"Camel, camel. You want to buy camel?"

If it had been a real camel, and not the small, stuffed plush toy camel that this twenty-something hawker in ripped jeans and t-shirt was shoving in my face, maybe I would have played along. A real camel would have at least been authentic, something real, something *Egyptian*. But this toy camel was like everything else that had been pushed on me so far, and somewhat like this trip itself: overpriced, tacky, an undisguised rip-off, and I'd had enough of it.

"Why are you doing this?" I said to him.

Jana snapped my name and tugged my arm at the elbow. She said something in Arabic to the man, who laughed and said some words back. Then he grinned and again offered up the camel stuffie.

"You think I want your crap? I'll tell you something: I can go to New York, I can go to any damn Walmart, and get *the same thing*."

The hawker and Jana just looked at each other. The hawker's smile widened. I said to him, "You're a smart guy, right? Why don't you *do* something? Why don't you teach Arabic to tourists? Why don't you offer something *worthwhile*?"

Jana yanked me away and led me down the alley where our bus was parked in front of a papyrus shop. Robed women and poorly dressed children crouched at the tires, their palms cupped and reaching.

"What is wrong with you?" She had never been this angry with me before.

"What's wrong with me? I'm trying to help here!"

"But to tell it to them!" she said, and swung her arm to the beggars at the bus. "Why don't you throw all your money down their mouths? That would help them!"

"Okay," I said. "Hold on. Calm down. They're different. That guy could do something else. He *should* do something else. It's a matter of motivation."

"Oh, but it is very easy for you! It's always been easy for you. You don't know this country, its people. You don't know its leader Mubarak. But still you come and you judge."

"Sorry," I said, "I didn't think you were so...."

Jana stood apart from me, her arms crossed and her weight on one foot. The already dark circles under her eyes had only gotten darker and deeper over the course of this trip. She had not been sleeping well, and I wondered if we would ever sleep together again once we were back in Brno.

"I didn't think you were so..." Jana said, "...either."

That night we were exhausted and though I felt a real case of King Tut's Revenge setting in, Jana insisted we have sex regardless. As if she knew it would be the last time.

"A man is a man."

"Amen," I said.

When I woke up Jana was gone. Her side of the bedding had been thrown over me. There was a note on my nightstand.

I have been here before, and I have been with you before. To say you are all the same is not true, you are not all the same. But you share something I cannot understand, that is how you leave the good in you behind. Why is this? Why is it so important to be right? What is right? It is a word, an idea that has grown you up. I saw a little boy in you before, now I see a man. And what is a man? A man is right. A man is a word, an idea. You may search for this idea, after you read this, the only way you can.

But don't search for me. Don't bother. Money is your weapon. Go home. Use your weapon there.

Later I would say, to those who would listen: She just left. Just like that. But for that morning, perhaps the last morning, I understood.

JANA. The first time I saw her in the staff room at the language school. Her brown tangled hair and freckled face, angular nose and sharp cheekbones. The circles under her eyes, her little paunch. Surprising lower-body strength. The dark look she'd get when she was pensive. Didn't believe in writing any of her thoughts down; rarely told me anything personal. I remember biking with her and a few other teachers a hundred miles from Brno to Vienna. It took two days and Jana was in the lead the whole time. A long road darkened by thunderclouds stretching along soft hills. I remember watching her in the distance, the way her ass moved as she pedaled, pumping like chambers of a large heart I could never reach.

EVEN IN THE desert you can't escape the pull of the industry. On my final day of the trip I bought a head scarf and sunglasses from a vendor and rode—along with an army of tourists of varying ages and nationalities—ATVs through the desert. We were guided west of Hurghada toward the mountains and into a Bedouin village. Once there we drank tea from tiny cups and toured the facilities. An old Bedouin woman made herself some bread, stoking the fire with a stick clotted with camel dung. I took her picture. I took a picture of a goat, a well, a little Bedouin boy, the mountains at sunset, the Bedouins dancing and drumming and clapping to their song. When it was all over our guides had recorded the entire excursion for sale on DVD. I bought one. Then I was shepherded with every other tourist back to our ATVs lined up like so many fighter jets across the sand. The final leg of that journey we raced with ourselves across the evening desert, the landscape darkening except for what passed under our headlights. We were leaving, but I did not want to leave.

THE OPEN WINDOW

Not again, Jaz thought. *Seriously?*

The tapping was back, more insistent and prolonged than the night before. That night it had taken her several minutes to get out of bed and go to the window. Now she got up immediately. She left her phone. Her blackout curtains did nothing to dampen the sound. Click, click, click, click. The steady rhythm morphed into an attempt at a song that may have been "Summer of '69" but could well have been "Knockin' On Heaven's Door." She wasn't sure. She hadn't heard the entirety of either song in years. The night before it had been Collective Soul's "Shine," which lasted longer because the tapping was surprisingly accurate and Jaz wanted to see if the tapper could make it through to the end.

Patience was at a premium tonight. Jaz drew back the curtains and was not surprised, as she had been the night before, to see a woman in her mid-thirties dressed in dirty jeans and a nappy pullover. It was the same woman from the night before. Her unkempt hair looked unwashed. She was gaunt and fidgety. From her side of the glass she waved to Jaz, who shook her head slowly, her expression somber.

The woman lurched at the window and planted her palms against the pane. This action caused Jaz to take a step back, as she briefly thought the woman might break through. Instead, the woman stayed planted against the window, like one of those fish Jaz spied in the tank at her dentist's office. She watched as the woman, cast sickly in the moonglow, moved her fishlike mouth to form the words Open up.

Unlike the night before, Jaz hesitated. Tonight was different. The woman looked worse than before. Jaz hadn't thought that was possible, but the evidence was undeniable. With her mother, she was convinced now, it could always get worse.

Her mother frowned, then tapped again. She tried to make a funny face but ended up leering awkwardly. Her bloodshot eyes crissed and crossed and her tongue lolled. Against the goofing Jaz remained still, expressionless. Maybe her mother would go away. But she knew she wouldn't. For whatever reason, her mother needed her now.

Jaz sighed. She grabbed the window's handles and pulled inward. The cool night breeze entered. Her mother remained outside.

"I thought you weren't coming back so soon, Mom," Jaz said. She attempted a smile. Her mother smelled of pot and alcohol and some other drug, or drugs. The smell was far more pronounced than it had been the night before.

"Plan's changed...." Jaz's mother's words slurred somewhat; she was barely holding it together.

"Mom, what are you talking about?"

"I can't skip town after all. I mean I can, but I gotta wait. I gotta lay low. I was thinking...with you?"

"Papi's not going to like that."

"Shhh...." Jaz's mother put her finger to her lips. "He doesn't have to know."

"Mom. Seriously? He's going to find out."

"Oh. I'm sorry honey. I didn't even ask I'm so rude. Did I wake you up?"

"I was awake."

"I told you to put away that phone at night."

"Mom. I do need to get to sleep. So...I could ask Papi in the morning..."

"No, no. No need to ask him. It'll be our...secret."

"What will be?"

"Me staying with you."

"Where?"

Jaz's mother raised one bony index finger and pointed past her daughter.

"My room?"

"Sure."

"You can't live in my room!"

"Shhhh! You'll wake them up, honey."

"Mom, there's no room for you here. You can't even fit under my bed."

"There's the closet."

"Filled with my stuff. No."

"I can just take it out each day. Come on, honey. I mean, really, how many times does your grandfather ever go into your room?"

Her mother had her there. Still, Jaz would not relent. When she spoke, her voice was firm. "I can't, Mom. No."

"Honey. I need...."

Jaz watched in horror as her mother began to cry—albeit softly. She had never seen her mother cry before—though that wasn't saying much. For years, since the end of elementary school, she'd rarely seen her mother. She knew she existed, but the situation was a lot like knowing you had a great uncle who lived across the country. Jaz's father lived in Arizona, at the border. She hadn't seen him since first grade.

"What do you need, Mom?" Jaz tried to muster the degree

of compassion her question required, but the end result lacked any emotion. Her mother had been gone so long, too long, and, yes, she was her mother, she would always be her mother, and Jaz was supposed to love her unconditionally, as she had been taught in church. While all that was true, it was also true that her mother had loved her only conditionally, her father not at all. What was Jaz supposed to do with that? Just let her mother into her room and proceed with a secretive sleepover that could last months if not years? The idea would be ridiculous if it wasn't so sad. Like her mother, Jaz was on her own. She'd always been on her own.

Jaz waited for her mother to compose herself somewhat. "Mom, I can't," she repeated, proud of how emotionless she sounded.

Her mother's chest hitched. "Maybe you'll change your mind eventually...if I keep coming back."

"Every night?"

"Please, Jazmine. "

"Mom. Come on.... It's past two. I have to go to bed."

Her mother sucked up snot, an action that also seemed to suck up the rest of her misery. She now appeared as cold and collected as her daughter. "I understand," she said. "I understand." With that, she turned and retreated into the bushes.

Jaz stood at the window for only a moment. To linger much longer could invite a return. There would be no sign beyond this: Jaz shut and locked her window, drew the blackout curtains, returned to bed, and, before closing her eyes for the scant few hours of night that remained, turned off her phone entirely for the first time in years.

THE NEXT MORNING Jaz had to be woken up by her older sister, Ruby, who often drove her to school on her way to work. Ruby had graduated from Anomar High that June and was taking community college classes down the hill while managing the Pizza Hut on Main Street. She was eighteen and looking to move out by Christmas. Jaz was fifteen and a sophomore at AHS, with only the haziest of visions of one day leaving home. Most days it seemed as if she would stay living with Papi, her mother's father, her entire life. Jazmine and Ruby had the same mother but different fathers. Ruby's father was only slightly more in the picture than Jazmine's. At Ruby's quince, three years ago, he'd shown up with a stuffed animal and an envelope. Ruby told Jaz later that her father had won the stuffed animal in Vegas and the envelope contained two twenty dollar bills. "A lot for him," Ruby had said. He hadn't shown up since—not even to Ruby's graduation. It could be worse, Jaz was tempted to say to her sister. When she had her quince this year, Jaz's father didn't even bother to send a card.

"I thought you were going to try to get more sleep," Ruby said. She was behind the wheel, Jaz in the passenger seat with her head resting against the window. Their Papi lived in town, not far from the high school, so they always had to make their morning drive conversations quick. In truth, Jaz could have walked, but this short drive to campus served as one of the only alone times she had with her sister.

"I turned off my phone last night."

"That's a start. Big step."

"You don't have to say it like that."

"No, I mean it."

"Mom visited me last night."

Ruby was silent for a time. Jaz was just about to say Ruby's name when her big sister spoke. "What did you say to her?"

"Nothing much. I told her she couldn't live with me. In my room."

"She wanted to live in your room?"

"Isn't that why she went to your window a while back?"

Ruby was silent. Then she said, "I think she just wanted to see me, talk to me."

"To know you cared?"

Ruby nodded.

"Did you?"

"Mom's a fucking drug addict, Jaz. I'm surprised she's still alive, to be honest."

They had reached the high school. Ruby pulled up to the drop off zone at the front. Jaz gathered her backpack and opened the door. Before she could go, her sister said, "How did it end, last night?"

"Not good. She was crying when she took off. I turned her away…. Is it wrong I don't feel guilty? Am I a bad person for not feeling anything?"

"You shouldn't feel anything for her. I personally wouldn't respect you if you did. She cut us off when we needed her most, when we were young. Now…karma's a bitch."

"She said she'll be back."

"I'm sure she will be. She's so strung out it's going to take her forever to get the message. What you need to do is make the message loud and clear, like I did."

"How'd you do that?"

"Chewed her out. Said the most awful things a daughter could ever say to a mother. The most awful things a human being could say to another human being."

"I…don't think I can do that. I don't think I'm that kind of person."

"You're going to need to be that kind of person, Jaz."

"Okay."

"Look. I'm already late. You are too. We'll talk more, if you want."

Jaz gave a little wave, stepped out of the car, and got on her phone.

By FIFTH PERIOD that day Jaz was fading. She reasoned it wasn't entirely her fault. There had been her mother, and lunch, and it didn't help that fifth period was English, her least favorite class. She'd always hated English, always been bad at it. No teacher had ever been able to make the subject interesting to her; nearly every teacher told her to read, read, read on her own, and Jaz was a wreck when it came to reading on her own. Not even the audiobooks helped. Jaz would start off listening but within a few minutes her mind would trail off to food, her feeds, her friends. Like pretty much every student, the only way Jaz would read was if the reading was done in class, led by the teacher. And Mr. W was not about to kowtow to that wish.

Her English teacher's name might have been Mr. Werther, but he was undoubtedly the happiest teacher in all of Anomar High. Jaz understood the irony of her English teacher's last name because at the beginning of the school year he had explained Werther in the context of Goethe's *The Sorrows of Young Werther*. He didn't tell the class how the story ended. "For that," Mr. Werther said, "you'll have to read the novella yourself." Of course no one read the novella. One month into the school year and no one had read much of anything that was assigned. It had gotten so bad with the lack of reading, and class discussions were such train wrecks, that Mr. Werther had resorted to giving pop quizzes every other day. These quizzes, in turn, lowered everyone's course grade. As jovial as Mr. Werther was, he brought nothing but misery to his students.

Today was no different. As usual, he was all smiles. His reddish beard was as neatly trimmed and his eyes as bright as they had been every school day so far. If he'd been heavier and older, Mr. Werther might have passed for Santa Claus.

"I've decided," he announced, "to change it up a bit."

Silence from the class. There was as yet no indication as to whether this was a positive or negative development.

"We're going to begin a jigsaw reading!"

Several of the gathered sophomores groaned. They had not done a jigsaw reading in class yet this year, but they were familiar with the activity from freshman English. Jigsaw readings were the worst. They required you to talk to people you didn't want to talk to. Not only that, but you had to *look* at the people, too.

"Since it's now October, and October's a spooooky month, we're going to read some stories that have to do with ghosts, or the possibility of ghosts. Not all of these stories are scary, as you'll soon see..."

You had to hand it to Mr. Werther: unlike some teachers at AHS, he at least knew what he was doing. Before this sophomore class had taken their seats to start the period, he had numbered them off and assigned each numbered group a particular story. Jaz was in Group 5 and her story was by a man named Saki. The story was called "The Open Window." One of the kids in Jaz's group commented that at least the story was short. It *was* short—only two pages. A snap, Jaz thought. She avoided looking at her group members. She really didn't know any of them.

Before reading the story, Mr. W told each group to conduct research on their particular story's author. That was easy, as looking up facts on the school-issued laptops didn't involve conversation. Jaz went to Wikipedia and skimmed. Before long, Mr. W had arrived at her group's sloppy desk formation.

"So...what have you found out about this author?"

For a moment no one spoke. No one wanted to say anything because no one wanted to say the wrong thing and be exposed as stupid. At last, a female student said, "I found out Saki is a Japanese alcohol drink. Really strong."

The rest of the group laughed. Even Jaz smiled.

Mr. W widened his grin. "That's right," he said. "Saki is the author's name. Did you find out why he chose it?"

"Not yet," the same girl said.

"His real name was H.H. Munro," a male student said while reading from his screen.

"Yes! Good. And he was from the country of..."

Mr. W elicited more facts from the group. Through it all Jaz stayed quiet. She felt compelled to check her phone.

"Right," Mr. Werther said. "Written in 1911. Can you imagine? One hundred and five years ago. Life was different. Politics—even politics in England—were different. This was before World War I, which Saki would die in."

"Spoiler alert, Mr. W."

The male student looked up from his screen. "He got shot?"

"Yes. He was killed by a German sniper, in France."

"Sucks," the same boy said.

"My hope is that you don't feel that way about this story," Mr. Werther transitioned. "Now it's time to get to reading. I still have a few more groups to get to. It's up to you how you want to do the reading: out loud, silently...."

Of course they would read silently. That was the only way not to show your flaws in front of everyone else. Reading silently wouldn't expose you. No mispronunciations could be heard. No poor pacing. No lack of emotion. Dutifully, Jaz and her three group members picked up their pens or pencils and got ready to annotate. Jaz, however, had her phone out and underneath the table, resting on her left thigh. She kept her pencil in her right hand poised over the story. Her eyes flitted from the copy down to her phone over and over. She could be sent to the office for being on her phone, but she was certain that since she'd engaged in such subterfuge before in this class she could get away with it again. She did read a little of the story. She read the title and the opening, but the sentence *'My aunt will be down presently, Mr. Nuttel,'* said a very self-possessed young lady of fifteen; *'in the meantime you must try and put up with me'* did nothing to encourage her to read more. The language was so *British*, the writing so *old*. One hundred and five years. Couldn't they read something more recent?

Time passed. Jaz had intended to check her phone once and then put it away and go back to the story, but she never made it back. Before she knew it her group members had finished and were tentatively discussing what they thought of the story, and Mr. Werther was standing over Jaz with a slip of paper in his hand. The slip of paper was yellow. He dropped it on the desk in front of her. It had already been filled out. She knew what it was: a tech violation slip. She now had to take her phone to the attendance office and turn it in. She would be able to collect it at the end of the day.

Some students got indignant when caught on their phones. Some made excuses, got into arguments with their teachers, threw a pity party in front of the whole class. Not Jazmine. "Sorry," she mumbled. She got up with her phone and the slip of paper and headed for the door.

Several minutes later, she returned. The period was almost over and students were packing up. She handed the tech violation slip, which the office had countersigned to confirm she had indeed turned in her phone, to Mr. Werther, who smiled at her.

"Not the most exciting thing, Jazmine, I know."

Then why give it to us? she wanted to say.

Mr. W continued: "Please read the story. You're going to be speaking with students who haven't read this story, and there will be a quiz...."

"Ugh." Jaz took the copy of Saki's story and stuck it into her backpack. She moved her desk back into its initial position. As soon as the bell rang, she ducked out of Mr. Werther's classroom as quickly as she could.

JAZ COULD NEVER REMEMBER a time when reading was not a chore. When she was two, three, someone apparently read to her; she remembered her papi saying as much once. But that had been when her abuelita was alive. After Abuelita passed, Papi busied himself in his workshop even more. Jaz didn't see him much. When he wasn't in the garage he was at his job at the auto shop on Main Street, and whenever they did talk their conversations were always brief and rarely about school. Years and years had passed. Papi was looking old. Jaz wondered if it wouldn't be long before she and Ruby were living in the house off Elders Road on their own.

"It's just two pages," Jaz said aloud to herself. "I can read two pages."

She sat on the edge of her bed with the story in one hand and her pencil in the other. She had turned off her phone and positioned her abuelita's framed photo on the nightstand so that Abuelita could observe her granddaughter succeeding at something. The time was 11:46. Jaz was off to an early start tonight. She felt proud for staying on her phone only three hours this time. She glanced at her abuelita. Then she turned her attention to the first of two pages.

Click click click click click.

The timing was unreal, as if Jaz was living through a movie, or a story she was supposed to read. *No way*, she thought. *No freaking way.*

She approached the drawn curtains as if at any moment they might part to reveal her mother on the other side a vampire, a demon. Jaz's stomach churned. The clicking continued, now in the form of a song. Was it "Welcome to the Jungle" or "Livin' on a Prayer"? Jaz touched the edges of the curtains, ready to pull. Before she could, she stopped. Her hands fell to her sides. She leaned in, her ear against the fabric. From beyond the pane she could hear, in between bouts of tapping, her mother's sniffling. After about a minute, the tapping ceased. Jaz remained behind the curtains. She just listened.

"Honey. Honey I know you're in there. I know you're home. You're not over at somebody's house. You wouldn't be. Please open up. Please."

Jaz waited. She felt no emotion. On her bed she had left her phone and the story. She looked at both now.

"Honey. I'm sorry. I need you. I'm sorry for all I've done." Her mother was openly crying now. Jaz squeezed her eyes shut. She searched her memories for a true and good image of her mother as she wanted her to be, a loving, present mother, maybe at the beach, or walking along a street in Julian in the coolness of fall. No images presented themselves. When Jaz remembered now, she remembered the memes she'd spread, or the videos and posts she'd commented on and liked. Her mother did not belong there. She had no place in Jaz's present or her past.

"I can't leave you," she heard her mother say. "You mean too much to me. I won't leave. I'm going to keep trying every night until you open up."

Jaz placed one hand on her stomach and the other over her mouth. She felt close to puking. She might have if her mother hadn't left. Jaz sensed her go away. When she at last pulled back a curtain to peek out, she saw only the bushes, the cows in their fields, the horses in their corrals, and the houses beyond, all resting under a half moon. Jaz returned to her bed and stared at her phone and the story. She no longer had the motivation to read tonight. It was past midnight anyway. Jaz tossed the story onto the floor, picked up her phone, and slid under the covers.

JAZ DIDN'T OFTEN AVOID school, but she felt like skipping it the next morning. Ruby stood in the doorway, her arms crossed.

"You need to go, Jaz."

"Why?"

"Do I have to say it? Mom...."

Ruby had pulled the threat of Jaz ending up like her mother if she didn't attend school before, and each time it worked. It worked again this morning, though not without pushback from the younger sister. Jaz argued she could get just as much done, probably more, at home. The assignments were all posted, and it was a lot quieter in her room than in the classroom.

"I know you're just going to go on your phone, Jazmine. Get ready. We're going."

On the ride to campus Ruby asked if their mother had returned. Yes, Jaz admitted. "I wish she had somewhere to go."

"She does. She's still a part of the Summarien Fellowship."

"What's that?"

"I told you this. It's that wacko new age religion out there on 67."

"You probably did tell me."

"I did."

"Maybe they kicked her out."

"If they did she still has her druggie friends."

"Those aren't her friends," Jaz said.

"Yeah," Ruby said, quietly this time.

Jaz got out of her sister's car and, instead of looking down at her phone, looked up. She saw the campus. The gates, the security guard, the students milling about. Once she passed through those gates, they would be closed and locked and she would be trapped. She wanted to skip fifth period if anything. She hadn't read the story. She'd left it back in her room, still there on the floor. Two pages and she hadn't even brought it with her. Her reluctance had morphed into rebellion. She wouldn't read the stupid story. It might have been two pages, but it was single-spaced and the font was tiny. It would be more like reading four or five pages—too much. Could she ditch Mr. W's class? Where would she hide out if she did?

The warning bell for first period rang. Jaz didn't often feel confident, but in this she did: By lunchtime she would figure out how to ditch English class, and by the end of the school day she would come up with a plan to force her mother to change for good.

THAT NIGHT WAS A THURSDAY; Jaz would remember it well. She had shown up to fifth period English but left almost immediately after the bell rang to start the period. She complained to Mr. W of stomach cramps, girl problem. He wrote her a pass to the nurse. She took her time getting there, even after being stopped and questioned by campus security. In the nurse's office her vitals were checked and she was given ibuprofen and a tampon. She took her time in the office bathroom, was released to class, took refuge in another bathroom students claimed wasn't subject to search all that much. In this second bathroom, Jaz hit upon her scheme.

That Thursday night, nearing eleven, she prepared. She cleared a space at the back of her closet, then made a mess of her room. She yanked the comforter and blankets and sheets off her bed. She turned her lamp over onto her mattress. Her stuffed animals lay strewn across the floor. She cleared her shelves of the knickknacks, the snow globes and figurines and amulets. Finally, when she was satisfied her room looked ransacked, she turned over the story assigned by Mr. W and wrote a note on the blank back side. The note read

I can't live here any more. I have to leave. I'm going away with only what I need. You can try and find me, but it's not going to do any good.

Underneath the message she wrote her name out in big block letters, her signature. Then she went to the window, drew back the curtains, and opened the glass doors wide. The October breeze was blowing strong and hot tonight. Jaz took one of her tchotchkes and used it as a paperweight to hold down her note, which she placed on the windowsill. She left the window open and retreated to her closet. She sat in the back and covered herself with clothes. She was sure she would not be seen. Her phone was at her side, but she'd turned it off, only the third time. She would not allow this prank to fail.

As Jaz sat in the back of her open closet, she was certain her mother would get the message. Her mother would freak out, she would search for her. She would show she cared, if she truly did care. If her mother needed her, she would find her, and she wouldn't come back to her room. She wouldn't again go to her daughter's window. She would show up at the front door. She would beg forgiveness from Papi. They would hug, reunited in their determination to find Jazmine. And when Jaz was at last "found," not far from home, her mother would have changed. She would swear off her friends, go into rehab, get a job, start a new life with her daughter.

All that sounded wonderful to Jaz, who remained still and seated at the back of her closet. At times she would sneak a peek at the open window a distance away. The note could still be seen on the windowsill, the edges of the story fluttering in the wind.

Jaz could never be sure when she fell asleep, but it must have been early. Her phone was off and she couldn't remember much of the night, which meant she must have slept through most of it. Her body felt awful. Her back was twisted and she had a pronounced crick in her neck. She shuffled off the clothes she'd been sleeping under and slowly got to her feet. The window was still open, her note still untouched. Dawn was just beginning to break over the valley; Jaz heard a rooster crow.

Then she heard loud sobbing from inside the house. Was that Papi? Jaz went to her door and opened it. Ruby was just approaching from down the hall. She'd been crying.

"Jaz, you need to come with me," she said. She took her little sister's hand and led her into the living room. Two police officers sat in dining chairs across from Papi, who was on the couch sobbing into his palms.

Jaz looked at the scene and knew she wouldn't be going to school that day.

SHE WOULD NEVER READ the police report. It was enough to learn the story from the officers and, later, through her phone.

Shortly before eleven that Thursday night in October, Jaz's mother and a male companion were walking in a remote area off highway 67, in the vicinity of Mount Rocoso. The police suspected a drug deal was at hand. For reasons they had yet to identify, and possibly would never identify, the deal went bad. Shots were fired, likely from a vehicle. Both Jaz's mother and her male companion were pronounced dead at the scene.

Jaz did cry. She cried hard. Her mother had been many things, but *her mother* was one of them. Jaz cried at the funeral, and it was only that night, hours and hours later, that she looked at what she had done. She'd picked up some of her room; at least the bed was back to normal. Her closet was now closed. Jaz went to the window. She had not closed it since that night. She rested her palms on the windowsill. Her note, the story, was gone. She did care, but not about the things she was supposed to. Halloween was almost here. Mr. Werther had been right. Going forward, Jaz would pay attention. She would not only listen. She would speak.

Houses of the Guns

My title for this year is *Loss*. Last year's title is *Canceled*, and the year before that: *Forward and Backward*. I titled the 2017 – 2018 school year *Of Grubbing and Greatness*, 2016 – '17 *Trials and Tribulations*, '15 – '16 *Exultation*, '14 – '15 *The Year of Magical Teaching*, '13 – '14 *Survival*. Before *Canceled*, the years followed a typical teacher's trajectory: I struggled, made tenure, found my footing, encountered setbacks but hung in. It was during *Canceled* that my life, and the lives of my students, changed forever. The last day I saw my students in person that year was March 18th. We were just about to start *Into the Wild*. I remember looking out on my students and announcing that this would likely be the final day of their senior year, their high school career. Their faces were as blank as the whiteboard behind me. I wish I could say I liked that class, the Class of 2020, but I just didn't. I'd had so many as juniors and most refused to take me their senior year. I had only enough for one class. It was a good class, considering. One student stood out. She was new, transferred from another district beginning of second semester.

The morning I first saw Diana I made a comment about her shirt.

"Great show," I said.

Diana plucked at her shirt and gave me a nod.

That was all we could do at that point. It was the start of the period and I couldn't be making small talk about *Game of Thrones,* or drawing attention to my attention to a female student's shirt. Pauline had been dead six months at that point and I wasn't about to tank my career. I was lonely, true, but I would always remain a professional, and they would always remain my students, no matter how they looked or how they looked at me.

Diana was tall. I'd never had a female student who stood close to six feet. She was also the only female student with her long straight hair done up in a bun, a style which, I would later learn, served as a deterrent to her putting any stray strands in her mouth: a nervous habit. Her skin was pale, though her face grew quickly flushed whenever she was stricken with an unanticipated emotion. But what set Diana apart most from the other seniors in that third period class was the fact that she found her teacher more interesting than her phone. She had to have a phone—this was the start of 2020, after all. But I certainly didn't see that phone anywhere on or near her person. Not on her desk, not in her lap, not on the carpet next to her foot. The natural result: she paid attention. She did have a book out on her desk—a hardcover, no less— but she kept *Providence* by Caroline Kepnes respectfully closed. She seemed to absorb my lecture on Tudor England and the background to *Hamlet.* She even took notes. I was her screen. I mentioned Diana's focus when she met me at the end of class to receive the syllabus. She explained that her old school had a policy of no phones out in class, ever.

"How refreshing that would be here," I said. "Where's your old school?"

"Near San Francisco. But I was only there for a year and a half. I'm originally from the East Coast." As she spoke her eyes roamed the wall behind my desk. I saw her linger on the pictures of my wife and me, when Pauline was healthy. Diana stopped and caught her breath.

"You okay?"

"…Yeah, I'm fine. I gotta go. Thanks for this."

Stashing the syllabus in her backpack, she turned and hurried out of my classroom. The next period was my lunch, so I had time. My eyes went to everything Diana's eyes could possibly have taken in: the photos of my dead wife, messages and memorabilia left behind by past students, bric-a-brac left over from my college days. Was it the light green ribbon pinned to the wall? The photocopied yearbook page depicting a student decades before I returned to teach, who'd died tragically in a car accident? The "What's Your Plan?" sign I'd created from a piece of color printer paper? Whatever it was that had caused my new student to catch her breath, I didn't see it.

I did see something that made me catch my breath, though. I have a habit of looking up new students when they enter my class. Nothing insidious; I simply like to find out what other classes they're taking, who their teachers are, if any grades have been posted so far that might indicate if the student may be one who does work or chooses to slack off. I sat in the silence of my classroom, my door closed and therefore locked, and brought up Diana's student profile. At first nothing noticeable or alarming, no red flag for health concerns or parental conflicts. She was enrolled in A.P. U.S. Government and A.P. Statistics; smart kid. Then I looked at her contact information, which also listed her birthplace: Danbury, CT. Her parent, her mother, was listed as having a Bay Area number. No home phone was given. It was the physical address, the physical house, that caused my breath to catch. Diana's house was in my neighborhood, right around the corner from me, and what's more I *knew* the house. It was the Roberto Batiste house. The house where the tragedy had occurred.

TEACHING at one's former high school is at first a strange experience. It took me five years to accept the fact that I'd been clapped with the Golden Handcuffs and I didn't mind. I could've left, but my parents were in the vicinity and Pauline and I started talking kids, or at least a kid, and we thought we should just stay. Small town life in California's Central Valley wouldn't be that bad, we reasoned. We had some friends, we had my family, and hers were still in state, albeit down south. We could make it work. It *would* work.

And then it didn't. My wife of seven years got sick. It started gradually, as I suppose all cancers do, and she went in, and there were tests, and then a diagnosis, and then a plan of action which in the end proved futile. We're not there yet. We can develop several vaccines for COVID-19 but we can't develop one to stop the Big C. Does the type of cancer even matter? My wife is dead. I cried for a time, every day, used up a chunk of my sick leave that otherwise would have gone toward vacations, or caring for a newborn. Instead I found myself a widower at the age of 35 in the summer of 2019. I should have left. I had friends in San Francisco, a friend in L.A. and one in Austin. I didn't need to live in the house we'd purchased together. I could have left the walls, the windows, the doors, the *physicalness* of it all behind—and no one would have blamed me. Yet I stayed. I stayed because it was more painful not to stay, and I felt a duty to my alma mater, and to the students. I had been one of those students; I'd seen too many teachers move on after only two or three years to more promising districts, bigger, better cities. I would not be the person as an adult who had made me feel bad about where I lived and who I was as a teen. I would stay. I had to stay. My parents understood. They didn't need to give me their blessing. I had always had their blessing, just as, in the end, my wife had mine.

IT WASN'T until the end of the first week in early January that I again exchanged words with Diana outside of instruction. At that point she had made a friend, Zachary, who sat next to her in the front row of my horseshoe-shaped semicircle. I knew Zachary (never 'Zach') well; I'd had him as a junior the previous year. He was one I'd rather not have had again, and frankly I was surprised he was placed with me in his final year. As a junior he had told his parents about some of the books I was teaching—the graphic memoir *March: Book Three* by John Lewis, Luis Valdez's play *Zoot Suit*—and I was called in to speak with Zachary's parents and the assistant principal. Mind you, this was before hysteria over CRT really hit the nation hard, though I see now parents like Zachary's had been gearing up for a while. I defended the curriculum—and myself—admirably, and even received a "good job" email from the assistant principal later that day. But while the parents quieted down, Zachary's hard edge remained. In all likelihood he took me again just so he could argue with me and his peers.

Zachary's one eccentricity, though perhaps not so strange given the show's content, was that he fanboyed all over *Game of Thrones. GOT* was how he and Diana connected in class; one day they came in wearing nearly identical shirts. Hers read NOT TODAY and his, in a similar style but depicted as a joke, read TODAY. They had a laugh over that one. I took this as a good sign. Diana's presence seemed to take the edge off Zachary quite a bit. Until her entrance he had been the tallest student in third. Diana seemed relieved to find a student close to her height. For his part, Zachary now rarely uttered his usual verbal provocations regarding the literature at hand. It helped that we were getting into *Hamlet* then and I made my best effort to tie Shakespeare's play to the recently ended HBO series. Zachary occasionally still did his thing, reading too deeply into how I was modeling an interpretation, taking my teaching to be part of a larger "agenda," but for the most part he controlled himself better than he ever had before. He didn't want to show off for his buddies. Now he wanted to impress Diana.

For the first time that week I saw her smile—a flash of teeth that were quickly hidden once more. I felt good about that smile. Diana was fitting in. I thought I knew Zachary well enough. Even then, at that close proximity, after a year and a half of him as my student, I never knew who he was. Even the students who wrote me all the notes and letters I still have, did I truly know any of them, or were they all visions of a dream that will end only when I die?

I should have seen what was coming and separated them. I should have known Zachary better. I should have done my homework, moved him to the back, or at the very least to the side, still within range but far enough away from Diana for that connection not to have been made. But I didn't. I was only in my seventh year of teaching. It's true what they say: it takes ten years to get it right.

"Hey," I said when I saw Diana approach my desk at the end of class.

"Hi. I saw you walking yesterday."

"Did you?"

"Do you live in that neighborhood?"

"I do. For a while now."

"That's a nice dog you have. Is your wife still working at that time?"

"My wife passed away."

"Oh God. I'm sorry. I shouldn't have asked. I saw the ring and…"

"I can't take it off yet. Doesn't feel right."

"I'm just really sorry."

"It's okay. I'm pretty sure all my students know anyway, so might as well bring you up to speed too."

"So you live alone? With your dog?"

"Since this past summer."

"I'm so sorry. I should go then."

"Did you need to ask me something?"

Diana's eyes were no longer on me. I looked to where her gaze was fixed: not on a photo of my wife and me but rather on a small image, the smallest photo on any of my walls, cut out from a magazine. The image showed a little boy running across the grass, racing a school bus that's about to stop and pick him up. The boy is running toward the camera, the photographer, and on his face is a look of joy.

"Why do you have that picture," Diana said.

I took a moment before speaking. I remember the night in bed, Pauline beside me, when I read the brief review of the Sandy Hook documentary, *Newtown*, in *The Week*, and of how I began weeping uncontrollably at the sight of the very image I would later cut out and tape to the wall above my desk. Pauline had touched me as I cried; she didn't say much because she understood. She knew I feared bringing a child into the world. I felt for that photographer, that parent or family member, who had such love to embrace and captured that moment in the sun, so far from December I imagined, a moment that was both fleeting and permanent. I felt for that boy, Daniel, I wanted to feel his fear because I thought that if I could feel it I could make a little of it go away.

"I don't want to forget," I said.

"There's no way I can," Diana said. "I was there that day."

"Really?" The incredulity in my voice shamed me. Of course she had been there. Why would she lie about such a thing?

"Don't be one of those people that don't believe me," Diana said. "Please."

"I believe you. Wow. That's..."

The bell rang just as I uttered the word "terrible" and Diana, cursing quietly, turned to go. I asked her what she had next.

"Lunch."

"So do I."

"Oh. Then..."

"You don't have to rush out is all I'm saying. If you need to talk, I have time."

"Not today," Diana said. "Another time, next week." I followed her eyes to the picture of Daniel Barden. "I just wanted to ask," I heard Diana say, "do you believe in ghosts?"

Startled by the question, I disengaged from the picture and looked for Diana, but she was already out the door before I had a chance to respond.

I THOUGHT about Diana's question over the weekend. I certainly acted as if I believed in ghosts. When taking out the garbage at night, going around the side of the house in darkness, I would hurry. I sensed something at my back. The ghost of my wife? What did I have to fear from her spirit? I hadn't given Pauline cancer. Hadn't I been a good husband? If anything her presence would be a blessing, something to fill the nights that were always left empty by the screen. Her voice, if she could speak, would take the place of my music, those records that had brought me happiness when she was alive but now so often remind me of what I no longer have. I wanted to believe in *her* ghost. I didn't care about any others then. I only wanted her.

THE FOLLOWING Monday I asked to see Diana after class. She gave me a dubious look, yet when the bell rang she broke off from Zachary, who'd been standing with her by the door, and approached my desk.

"I do believe in ghosts," I said. "To answer your question from Friday."

Diana offered one of her slight smiles. She looked tired. She had looked tired at the start of the semester, and now she looked even more so. I told her as much. At that she turned and waved away the agitated Zachary, who took a moment to understand he was being dismissed. When he had finally cleared out, along with the rest of the students, Diana approached.

"I'm sure the last thing you want is to take up your lunch time with a teacher—"

"Sort of."

"—but I do get the feeling you want to talk. I'm just...I'm not a counselor. Do you want to talk to your counselor instead?"

Diana shook her head.

"You understand if it's something really bad, or even a little bad, I'm going to have to report it."

"They wouldn't believe you if you did report it," she said. "They wouldn't believe me either."

"What is it?"

"You know the house I live in now. You pass by it when you walk."

"I do know that house."

"Did something...bad happen there?"

I felt then as if the whole of my adolescence had rushed

back to strike me square in the face with a hard wet hand. Diana looked at me, expectant. My eyes settled on the image of Daniel.

"Yes," I admitted. "Something did happen there."

"You know about it."

"I was a student at this school when it happened."

"What was his name?"

"Roberto. Roberto Batiste. He was a grade below me. A freshman."

"He's not on your wall here."

I couldn't bring myself to put up a photocopy of Roberto's yearbook memorial page. When I first started teaching, I also took the role of yearbook adviser (*Survival*), and the past of my alma mater opened up to me. I experienced years I had never lived, bore witness to tragedies I had never known. So many memorial pages through the years, most years at least one but other years two or even three. When I turned to the back of the yearbook documenting my sophomore experience I knew what I would find, and there it was, yet I could not put the page up. Too close. His smile too haunting. Perhaps deep down I feared he would haunt me, a teen who had not been in the house at the time and who had lived so much longer.

"He's still in that house," I said, "isn't he."

"I've seen him every night. Since we moved in before Christmas."

"Every night?"

"Yes. Every single night."

Unrelenting was the word that came to mind. I said, "When you bought the house, they were supposed to tell you what happened there. By law, I'm pretty certain they're required to do that."

"Are they? If they did my mom didn't tell me. She may not have been paying attention anyway. She's...got a lot on her mind."

I chose not to press. The Bay Area number. The story of long-haul commuter parents was a familiar one at Grafton High School. Was the father in the picture? Why the move from the East Coast? The interior lives of my students I had no right knowing.

"By seeing 'him,' you mean his ghost."

Diana said, "If you know what happened there, I need you to tell me. Because Zachary doesn't know."

"You told Zachary?"

"I had to tell someone. Someone who'd believe me."

"And you told Zachary."

"You make it sound like he's as crazy as I am."

"You're not crazy, Diana. Zachary isn't either."

"But is something wrong with him I should know about?"

I held my tongue more than I should have. I did offer this: "Zachary has...very strong beliefs. That's not insanity. That's being opinionated. But...he's kind of open to a lot of things, and that may include the supernatural."

Education professional, I thought.

Out loud, after a moment, I continued: "I do believe you, by the way. I'm not surprised that house is haunted." I asked her what she saw every night. Was it the same?

Pretty much, Diana admitted. She would wake up each night around the same time—between one and two in the morning—and go out to the kitchen. She wasn't sleepwalking, nor was she dreaming. This was real, and she was compelled to go to the kitchen. There she would see the body in front of the oven, bloody, though she could not discern what had caused the fatal wound. A knife? A blunt object?

"No," I said. Then, matter-of-factly: "A gun."

Diana absorbed the truth without looking at me. At last she said, "I think I'm losing my mind. I think it has to do with Connecticut."

"Sandy Hook."

"I was ten that day."

"Dang. I've never known anyone who's actually been in a shooting. Any shooting."

"Not even Roberto Batiste?"

"I didn't know him. Not personally. He was just a kid a grade below me."

"Then you don't know."

"No. I don't."

"I could hear the shots...there was the intercom..."

"You don't have to relive this."

"I have to. I'm meant to relive it."

"Because of Roberto, you think."

"Not just him. It's like I'm being punished for what my dad did."

I opened my mouth to speak but held back. I waited, careful.

Diana gathered herself. "I'm not going to get into that now," she said. "Do you know what happened to him? Roberto, I mean."

I almost didn't tell her. I wish now I hadn't.

"There's a report, actually."

"A report?"

"A kind of...police report, or news report that reads like a police report. There's a whole bunch of them, actually, for things that happened to people in this town over the years. Not just Roberto."

I could see Diana anxious, expectant. I felt I couldn't let her down, I owed her this, for her past, what she must have heard through those halls that day as she huddled under her desk, only ten years old, and so I pressed forward.

"It's a website. It lists...well, everything. All these events. Deaths. All here. Roberto Batiste is one of them. That's where you can read about what they believe happened."

"Can you send me the link, please?"

"I'll send it to you by the end of lunch."

I didn't fear the district monitoring my communication. My superiors' surveillance wouldn't have made a difference in my decision to proceed anyway. My district is lax with so much; it would have to be something highly inappropriate, damaging, for anyone at the front office or the D.O. to call me in. What I planned to send to Diana was neither inappropriate nor damaging. It was simply the news: history.

So I sent it. Minutes after Diana had left, in the silence of my locked classroom, I switched to my personal email where I had stored the link in a message to myself from years earlier, when I'd stumbled upon the site in a fit of unrest. I copied the link, checked to make sure it still worked in my browser, then pasted that link in the body of an email sent from my school account. The addressee field auto-filled with Diana's full name and student ID number. For the subject heading I wrote "Research link" and hit send. I'm helping, I thought. I'm teaching. I'm what I'm meant to be.

Local Youth Killed in Gun Accident

Monday, December 6, 1999

The small town of Grafton was left reeling this past weekend when a fourteen-year-old, a freshman at the local high school, was killed in a tragic incident involving a discharge of a handgun. Authorities say the youth, Roberto Juan Batiste, was at the 429 Bering Lane residence of seventeen-year-old Timothy Olander when the fatal shot was fired. Officials say that on the night of Saturday, December 4, Batiste arrived at Olander's residence accompanied by another youth, sixteen-year-old Desiree Fernandez. The two male youths, acquainted with one another, proceeded to force entry into the locked liquor cabinet and consume some of the available spirits. Fernandez began to make food. Olander told Batiste and Fernandez his step-father had a gun in the bedroom and asked if they wanted to go outside in the nearby orchards and shoot with it. Olander had circumnavigated the locked door to his parents' bedroom and forced entry through the window using a knife. The ammunition was kept in the nightstand cabinet and the gun in an unlocked box under the bed. Olander told Batiste and Fernandez he had already used the gun a few times in the orchard. Batiste initially expressed disapproval with the idea, referring to the school massacre at Columbine High School that occurred in April, but Fernandez convinced him to see the gun when she expressed interest in the endeavor.

Olander left and returned shortly with a .9 mm Beretta. He demonstrated the proper insertion and removal of the clip and bullets and showed Batiste and Fernandez the safety feature. With the clip removed Olander then dry-fired the gun at the ceiling. He passed the weapon to Fernandez. The three youths took turns with the gun. Batiste said "Bang bang" when he dry-fired. The three watched TV for some minutes. During this time a verbal altercation arose in which Olander accused Fernandez of being unfaithful when the two had been dating earlier that school year. Batiste, though not romantically involved with Fernandez, was drawn into the accusation, and the conversation intensified. Batiste demanded Olander put the gun away. Olander complied by placing the weapon under a couch cushion. Fernandez then left the house with the intention of having Batiste accompany her; however, Batiste refused, as he lived in the neighborhood and could easily walk home. Upset by Batiste's behavior, Fernandez left the house abruptly, got into her vehicle, and drove to her house three miles away.

According to Olander, after Fernandez left, Batiste asked Olander to put the handgun back. Olander brought out the weapon and, while Batiste got the food ready to serve in the kitchen, removed the clip, not realizing that a round remained in the chamber. Olander approached Batiste in the kitchen. "Man, put that back," Batiste said. "Do you even know what this can do to a person?" Olander asked Batiste, intending to scare the younger teen as a way of joking around. "It's not just bang-bang, you know." According to Olander, Batiste asked, "Are you going to shoot me?" "Fake-shoot you, yeah," Olander responded. "There's no bullet in here now." "Liar," Batiste said. "I'm telling the truth," Olander said, and he raised the gun with the barrel pointed at Batiste. "I know what I'm doing." "You don't know shit," Batiste said. "Why do you even need to fire a gun?" "Because it just feels good," answered Olander. "Didn't it feel good when you did it?" "Does it feel good now?" Batiste asked. "Yeah," Olander said. "Then if it feels so good pull the trigger. I can't stop you." "You're right," Olander said. "You can't stop me." Knowing the clip had been removed and believing the safety to be on and no ammunition to be in the gun, Olander pointed the Beretta at Batiste's head and fired. Batiste was struck by the one bullet that remained in the chamber. The entry wound was at his temple. Olander returned the gun and clip to his stepfather's side of the bed. He then returned to Batiste's body and called 911. When officers arrived Olander told them what had occurred. Officers located the gun and ammunition. Batiste, who had been shot at point-blank range, was pronounced dead at the scene. Olander was taken in for further questioning and for a blood sample to be taken. Services for Roberto Batiste will take place this Friday, December 10 at 10 AM.

I ARRIVED LATE to the crab feed that Friday night of MLK Jr. weekend. Antonio stood outside the front entrance with his thick arms folded.

"Thought you might get cold feet," he said.

"Where's Wendy?"

"We thought me and you should do this one, just the guys."

Antonio and I had done "just the guys" before, when Pauline was alive, but now the phrase had taken on a new meaning. I was meant to find someone. Seven months—and seven years of marriage—had been long enough in the eyes of this friend couple.

"No ambush," Antonio said, in answer to my question. "This time let's play it by ear, loose."

Loose sounded all right to me. I headed in.

"Hold up."

I turned to see Antonio in front of a folding table on which two handguns were displayed. Antonio could tell you what kind; I had no idea. To me, they were guns, that's it. A gun is a gun is a gun is a gun is a gun. And that's it.

One of the guns looked like every other handgun: pitch black. The other had a royal purple handle and royal purple flourishes running along the barrel.

"Nice color." Antonio hefted the gun and brandished it at me. I've been with him long enough to know not to flinch. Antonio can handle any firearm. He wouldn't inadvertently kill me.

The old man seated behind the table said, "If you're going to shoot someone, take 'em out with a pretty piece like that. What d'ya say?"

"It'd be a beautiful way to go," Antonio said.

"Wendy would like it," I said. "It's her color."

Antonio set the gun down and forked over a twenty to enter into the gun raffle. As we went in he said, "You never know."

"No," I said. "You don't."

I'll spare you the atmospheric details of the Grafton annual crab feed, other than to say Antonio did try to hook me up with a couple of women—not at the same time, but when one encounter went south my friend of a few years kept up his cheery demeanor and moved on to the next target: Melanie, a colleague of mine at the high school, a science teacher several years my junior who'd recently broken up with her boyfriend. Our conversation, watched hawk-like by her trio of female friends and facilitated in large part by Antonio, lasted longer than my first half-hearted attempt, but I just ultimately wasn't into any of it. Someday, months or years from that night, I could be into Melanie, but not then. I had too much on my mind that pushed out any notion of a one-night stand. Ghosts, both familiar and unfamiliar, Antonio's children, whom I would soon be teaching, guns. The awkwardness of my ambulatory discourse was broken by the announcement that my friend had indeed secured the purple handgun. Antonio, his smile that of a newly minted Powerball winner, rose from our table and made his way to the front of the hall, where he collected his prize. Two of Melanie's friends cupped their hands around their mouths and shouted, "He won the gun! He won the gun!"

"Not bad for only twenty bucks," Antonio said as he reseated himself.

"How much is that worth, do you think?" Melanie asked.

"This? This would go for about $300, maybe $350, depending on the seller."

"Is it not a good gun?"

"No, it's a good gun. It's got stopping power. It'll kill someone if you need it to."

One of Melanie's friends said, "Your wife is *so* lucky."

"I think you have more guns than kids now," I said.

Antonio's grin didn't falter. "You know," he said. "I think

you're right." When asked how many kids he had, Antonio didn't shy away from the truth. "Six," he said.

"Wow. Busy guy."

"I started when I was still in the service, overseas."

The conversation then took the inevitable turn of focusing on my friend, my charismatic, physically imposing friend who, although only six years older than me, had six more children than me, a healthy wife, and an impressive record of foreign travel under his belt. I let myself fade from the scene. I, who had gone straight from undergrad into a teaching credential program, married my college sweetheart soon after, and settled in my hometown. I should go, I thought. I should go somewhere.

Later that night, after we'd loaded ourselves full of crab and bid the ladies goodnight, Antonio said, "You're down but not out."

"No. I'm out," I said. The door to my car was open. I knew not to offer Antonio a ride. He preferred to walk, even if a gun was half-hanging out of his shorts pocket.

"Next time," he offered.

I settled myself enough to smile. "You're right. Next time."

We hugged it out. Antonio's hugs might not have been on the level of Pauline's, but they meant something to me then.

"You be careful with that thing."

"She always is," he said.

On my way home, I called my mother.

"How's Dad?"

"Asleep."

"That's good.... How are you?"

"I'm okay. And you? How's your mental health?"

"Fair. Stable. I think I'm fine, Mom. Really. Just..."

"What?"

"They still don't know?"

"They won't know for a few more days. Be patient. He'll let you know. Or I will."

I couldn't say anything then. Mom spoke for me.

"I know you're thinking of Pauline. I'm sorry. But your father's different. Different body. It's not the same."

"I know. I hope."

"It's not the same. Try not to worry."

I could only worry at that time, before I took charge. The switch had been flipped for my father, just as it had been flipped for my wife. The sequence that precipitates the end. How naïve I was not to see that the switch had long ago been flipped for those I had sworn to protect.

WE WERE WELL into January of 2020 when an unfamiliar sense of foreboding came over me. Intense, undefined, unsettling, different from what I'd experienced in the early days of Pauline's diagnosis. In my wife's case we knew what was going on—and what was going to happen. We had the results, the numbers, the recommendations. But with this new wickedness, I had nothing. And so, January was rough. At first, I thought it was due to it being the start of an election year—since college, election years have always left me rattled—but it wasn't that. I'll admit it: I had trouble getting out of bed because for the first time since my first year of teaching I did not want to go to work. I had trouble making it to the shower, putting on appropriate clothing. I even had trouble feeding the dog. And it wasn't because of Pauline, I won't feel ashamed admitting that; it was because of Diana and what she was going through, and because of what I had given her, the knowledge provided by that website containing death after death, tragedy after tragedy, so many of which involved guns. She had read what had happened to Roberto Batiste, and she continued to be haunted. I could tell by how tired she looked when she rolled into third period every morning. Diana's perfect attendance made sense to me. If my house were haunted, I would do anything I could *not* to be in that house at any point of the night or the day.

The truth: I was scared. I was scared of showing up, scared of what I had discovered and what I had gotten myself into, the collective risk that is teaching. My parents are both retired public educators and when I was in high school, at the time of Columbine, I feared for their lives. They each taught elementary school in Grafton, and each morning as a teen I would go to school certain that if it wasn't my school that was the target it would be theirs. And quite possibly that's what I was experiencing in the first month of 2020, that old fear of going in to what could be anyone's last day. My parents have not set foot on a school campus in a while, but they go to the supermarket. They go to the movie theater. They go to restaurants, big box stores, the bank and the post office. Any place, any damn place could be the one. They go to their neighborhood not far from where I live. They go to their living room, their dining room, their kitchen, their bedroom. Any place. Any damn place.

And then it was the end of January and Kobe Bryant's helicopter had fallen from the sky, and a few days later the World Health Organization announced the emergence of a deadly strain of coronavirus—COVID-19. From there my fear mutated. It had a new target. I felt I could go to work without reservation.

For several days in January Diana's desk stood empty, so many days I began to worry. As a teacher I encourage engagement with the class by offering points for daily participation, and when a student blows off class and takes an unexcused absence, I'm forced to stick that student with a zero in the gradebook for that day's participation. Diana's course grade, off to a strong start in the beginning of the semester, had tanked by the end of January. She still turned in most writing assignments, but the absences were killing her chances of passing the class and walking the stage in May. I wanted to know where the hell she was and what the hell she was up to. I notified her counselor, who assured me she'd follow up. I doubted Diana's parents were aware. The dad: who knew his location, or if he was even alive. The mom: an obvious BAT. A Bay Area number meant a Bay Area job meant a Bay Area commute meant a Bay Area Transplant who left home early and returned home late. In the intervening hours the children have the rule of the roost. I could only imagine. The move of so many to our little town in search of cheap housing had signaled the end—when the transplanting began en masse in the late 1980s—of the glue that held Grafton's community together. Now I taught those children, the children of the BATs, and I could only imagine.

Friday, January 31st, the day after the W.H.O. made its declaration, I got up the nerve to say something about Diana to the student who knew her best.

Zachary had been in class far more often than Diana, but even he had uncharacteristically skipped some days, which happened to coincide with the days Diana had missed. I asked to speak with him after class ended. From the start he was resistant, but I managed to get out of him the situation I suspected.

"I've been with her a few times when she does it."

"Does what, Zachary?"

"...I don't think she'd want me to tell you."

"If it's embarrassing," I said, "we can bring your counselor in. Heck, even your parents if you want."

"I don't want that."

"Sure. But if this is dangerous, if she's in danger, I need to know about it now. Please."

Zachary bit his lip, something I'd never before seen him do. I was lucky he liked to talk so much. Even now he couldn't hold himself back.

"It's not embarrassing, and I don't think it's dangerous," he said. "But it is weird, and pretty creepy."

My mind went to the website I'd given Diana weeks earlier. "Are you hanging around the cemetery, Zachary?"

"Not the cemetery," he said. "Houses."

"Houses?"

"Yeah. Houses. It's weird. She'll pull up in front of a house early in the morning, then we'll just sit there while I listen to her read from these pages."

"She wrote something?" My question hung with hope. I knew the answer, though.

"I don't think she wrote it. It sounds like a news report, or something. It's all typed up, and the typing looks strange. I think she printed it out."

"Oh Christ."

"Do you know about this, Mr. H?"

For a moment I couldn't speak. I had to collect my thoughts and account for what I had done, for what I'd started.

"I gotta go." Zachary turned but looked back at me as he left. I must have appeared even more a freak in his eyes than usual, the way my mouth hung ajar and my eyes stared into the middle distance of nowhere.

When the room had cleared, I brought up my email. I no longer cared if the higher-ups knew what I had sent a student. If they pitched a fit, I could always admit the truth: I had sent that link because I thought it would help a survivor of Sandy Hook. I did not—nor could I be expected to—foresee just what that site I'd sent would cause the survivor to do.

I'm very concerned about your absences, I wrote to Diana, *and I wonder if it has anything to do with the material we discussed after class. I notified your counselor a while back; have you heard from her? I do care about what's going on. Believe me, I'm not just here for a paycheck!*

Anyway, let me know soon what's going on and if I can help in any way. I'm always willing to listen.

I left it at that, not expecting a response. So it was to my surprise when Diana reached out to me the next day, in person.

THAT FIRST DAY of February dawned brisk and overcast. I harnessed up Oblomov, grabbed Pauline's walking stick and a biodegradable poop bag, and headed out. It takes me fifteen minutes to walk the full neighborhood, the equivalent of one mile, unless Oblomov is feeling particularly nosy and slows me down to sniff and root. I had only just passed Diana's house, the Roberto Batiste house, when I heard a voice call out, "Mr. H!" I turned to see Diana standing in the front walkway. She wore jeans and a Yankees sweatshirt and sneakers—for a high school senior so early on a Saturday morning to be wearing all of that was a strange sight indeed.

I was so amazed and thrilled to see her—and to see her looking so well—that I waved my loaded poop bag in greeting. My grin must have been both shit-eating and goofy, but she made no mention of it as she approached me.

"Hi," she said.

"You're up early."

"I thought you'd be by. I know your route by now."

"Is that so."

She praised Oblomov, my corgi, and laughed a little when I explained the origin of his name.

"Your wife must have been a great reader, to read a book like that and remember it."

"She was a real fan of Russian literature."

"I'm sorry again."

At this I nodded and focused on the patchwork lawn.

"How are you?" I asked. "You look better."

"I am better."

"Because you're missing my class, is that it?"

"I'll be back on Monday, I swear!" She touched my arm as she spoke. I had to watch this. She had to watch this.

Diana withdrew, aware of how we looked.

"I'm glad to hear it," I said with some finality to my voice. Always the professional.

"I actually..." Diana began. "I actually was hoping I could walk with you, to explain what happened in January."

"That wouldn't be a good idea."

"And...knowing you'd say that I wrote this." She handed over a sealed envelope, unmarked.

"Is this like a confession?"

"It's admissible evidence, yes."

"I admire your wit, Diana. I haven't gotten a lot of that over the years. It's obvious..."

"Obvious what?"

I felt I had to finish. "...obvious you're from the East Coast."

For the first time that I'd seen, Diana laughed. She didn't seem to want to; she held back as she smiled.

"Have you ever been to the East Coast, Mr. H?"

"Once. When I was in college I flew out to see a friend in New York City."

"But you've never been to Connecticut?"

"Afraid not. Am I stereotyping you?"

Diana offered up her thin smile again. "See you Monday."

"I'm looking forward to it."

Fighting the urge to read the envelope's contents on the sidewalk, I finished the entirety of my walk. When I was back inside I let Oblomov loose and took a seat on the couch. The blinds were drawn. I left them that way now. Now mine was just another house with its blinds shut. What secrets were the other houses hiding? What secrets was my own house hiding even from me?

Inside the envelope I found two handwritten pages of stationery paper. Diana's handwriting was, as I expected, exquisitely rendered.

Dear Mr. H, Diana's letter read,

I first want to apologize for not being in class a lot of January. This is completely unlike me. In school I've always gotten perfect attendance. I've hardly ever gotten sick and when I do I just force myself to go. That's always been a thing with me, perfect attendance. I can't not go to school. I really like school, and I really like your class. You're obviously a great teacher, and yeah I do wonder why someone as good as you is in this town but I'm sure you have your reasons. I have my reasons too.

So why did I skip your class so many days in January when I could've skipped any other class? The truth is I couldn't have skipped any other class, it had to be yours. I wasn't angry with you or anything, but I felt you would be the one teacher who would understand what I was doing.

Zachary said he told you so you know what I was doing. But let me explain why and what happened. It helped me, first of all. It really did help me a lot to go from house to house, place to place, in Grafton and sometimes a town nearby. I had (I still have it) a printout of that site you tipped me off about. It's amazing how many of the reports list the actual physical address of where it happened. They don't do that anymore, do they? They make an effort not to reveal where it happened, no matter how it happened. I'm sure that's to keep freaky people like me (and you?) from doing what I did.

There have been so many tragedies in this town, this town of just over 20,000 people. And that's just one town. When I think of any place bigger, or the sheer number of towns across this country that probably have had these same kinds of incidents, probably the exact same kinds of deaths.

Most times I would only get two or three stops in before fourth period lunch was over. Even if it was a short report, a closed shut case, I would take my time sitting in my car, reading the report. Most times I'd read it out loud. It felt good, it's felt good to do this. Freeing in a way. It's like I'm paying tribute to the victims. You may think this is all creepy but I'm taking a chance because my bet is you won't think it's creepy at all, you'll understand. That picture of Daniel on your wall. I'm sure you'll understand.

Have you ever wanted to do what I've done? When you first saw the site, did you want to go to those addresses and see what the house looks like now, imagine what it might have been like in 1975, 1979, 1980, 1989, 1999, like mine in 1999? I wasn't even alive when what happened in my house happened. Some of the incidents go back to the early 1900s, like 1911, 1919, and the 1920s. Hunting accidents. Homicides. But there were accidental discharges even then. Young people didn't know how to handle guns. The grown-ups, the adults have a purpose, they know how they're going to use it most of the times, but there are those heart-breaking stories of the kids that just pick up the gun and then.

This town has so much history with the guns. These houses I park outside of, they contain so much. Are the guns still there, inside some of these places, buried? Still being used? If you're worried about me from what I'm writing don't be. I've found that with each house I've visited, each empty lot or mobile park my nights are way more manageable. I don't go to Roberto nearly as much now. I think that's because each visit brings me more into the collective history, or memory, or tragedy. I remember hearing the shots that day, and the screams. I'm not lessening what happened, it's as you said the greatest tragedy of the 2010s. But it's history too, it's our history, and with every gun, with every house or place of residence, or car or hill or private or public place, history is created, and I can't fight it, I can't stop it, I can only accept myself as part of it and try my best to feel what it must have been like that day, that evening, that morning or night. What music was playing, if any music was playing. How the silence hurt, or how the words sounded in their minds before they did what they felt they had to do.

I don't know if I'm making any sense, or if I ever made any sense to begin with. I'm not asking you to grade this, or give it extra credit because I know you wouldn't do that no matter what! If you give it to my counselor I'll understand and only be slightly disappointed. I believe I can trust you with this. I don't need to see a therapist. I'm not suicidal like so many people in those reports. The cars, the bedrooms, the bathrooms, the back-yards. I can't imagine doing it. I just can't. I did see a therapist after the massacre happened seven years ago and it didn't last very long because I didn't have much to say. I was scared, yeah, but they razed the school and built a new one and now maybe the ghosts are gone. I wish they hadn't done that. We need the place, which is home to the ghosts that are trying to tell us some-thing. We can't just be left with the guns. We need the places and their ghosts just as much. It's kind of like a battle. We have to keep the locations. Without them we lose the memories of what happened, and all we'll be left with then are the guns.

She had more to say but now is not the time for that. For the remainder of that morning I kept my music off, the house quiet. I thought of all that might have occurred in this house, my house, built in 1984, the year I was born, and of the previous occupants, cyphers in my mind. How many children, how much joy and how many tears. I kept quiet out of respect for them. I kept quiet out of respect for all of them.

WHAT IS TRAGEDY?

I ask my seniors that question every year as a way of

kicking off our unit on *Hamlet*. What is tragedy? I tell them not to look up the definition; I want their own personal interpretation of the concept. Despite my parameters and encouragement, most students come up with uninspired and uniform responses. Diana, of course, did not. I was not surprised when in early January, before she went on her daily morning house calls, Diana spoke up with this: "Tragedy is when something awful happens, like a shooting. It doesn't have to be a mass shooting. And it's sudden and shocking. It could be anything, but a true tragedy has to be sudden, and it has to shock, and has to cause a change to happen."

"What do you mean 'a change,' Diana?" I had to be careful here. "Change in a person?"

"It could be change in a person, yeah. Or...change in a lot of people."

"Change in a country?"

"Maybe."

I stopped short of claiming that in the case of Sandy Hook, no change could be just as terrible a tragedy. I could feel Zachary's eyes on me, and the eyes of his hunting buddies in the back. I had to say *something*. "September 11th changed our country." I felt silly saying it. But these teenagers, all of whom were born in the year after 9/11, needed to hear the obvious. To them it wasn't obvious. It was already so much ancient history. And 9/11 might have changed the country, the world, air travel, security, the lives of countless, but 12/14 didn't change the country, it didn't change the world. Diana knew this, and I wasn't about to call her out on it. Nor was I about to verbally tangle with a couple of my seniors who visibly displayed their NRA memberships. Zachary wasn't one of these, but he hunted alongside them, with a weapon of his own, and I had learned my lesson in the first semester, when discussions got overly heated. I thought about the day two years earlier when students organized a walkout to protest the

Parkland shootings. I remember offering my seniors in that particular period during the protest the chance to get up and leave class, just do it, they didn't need to be here, *Into the Wild* was ancient history. Only one student, a female, got up abruptly and left. It took her some time to do so. She was gawked at. Add that to the list of tragedies.

Diana wasn't in class when we talked about Kobe Bryant falling from the sky. She wasn't in class when I broke down, without breaking down myself, Hamlet's most famous soliloquy, which I performed, somewhat impromptu, for the class that last week of January.

"What does 'to be' mean?" I asked, only to be met with the white noise of the projector. I remember wishing that moment that Diana would return.

"If you 'are,' simply 'are,' what does that mean?"

"You exist," Zachary answered.

In October, at the start of our unit on Orwell's *1984*, I challenged the seniors by posing a question: Would it be a good idea to put a telescreen in every corner of every place where every human being in the world was living, if it meant we could stop all mass shooters from carrying out their plans? Would you sacrifice your privacy to prevent future massacres?

The class was divided. Many students expressed concern over loss of privacy—even as they fingered their phones.

"You can't prevent all massacres," I remember Zachary saying. "Someone's going to find a way."

And this from a responsible gun owner, I'd thought later that day.

Or not to exist. Although I delivered the soliloquy days before I read Diana's letter, I look back on that lesson now and see the connection. Or not exist. So many who used one on themselves. Many of them in Grafton were not a Roberto Batiste. No accident. Ernest Hemingway's father used a gun over sixty years old. And some of the online entries dating back to the 1910s, when Grafton was founded. An eternal solution. To no longer have to suffer, or force yourself to suffer, whether it's in your mind or body or both. To finally sleep when you've found you can't any longer. To stop tossing and turning, cease your crying, cease your wishing, your regrets. Why so many were young, so long ago. Not waiting to age, to stay that one age forever. To not even have the chance of feeling and of watching your body break down, be stricken, to not even have the chance of being hurt in love. In my third year teaching at Grafton High (*Exultation*), two seniors, not my own students, took their lives months apart. They knew each other as friends. Speculation persisted for some time that the second boy felt compelled to follow the first. Neither of them used a gun.

Perchance to dream of that undiscovered country.

I cried over the yearbook memorial page I had to create for them as the adviser that year. That was my last year as yearbook adviser. I never again wanted to create a page like that. Until 2020, those were the last two seniors Grafton High had lost.

DIANA RETURNED TO CLASS, and I continued with *Hamlet.* It's a difficult play to teach, and I don't even ask my seniors to do all that much with it. I doubt I'll ever teach it again, honestly. But in February of 2020 I was rolling with it. We completed Act III by mid-February, Act IV by the end of the month. For all of February, Diana came to class. She seemed alert, ready. The ghosts were gone. I watched the door, fingered the knife in my pocket resting against my wallet. It's a big knife; it could kill if I used it correctly. I'd figured earlier that The Hunters, Zachary included, didn't pose a real danger; they just loved their weapons. But with the door you never knew. Sometimes in the middle of third period I would glance at Diana and imagine myself the hero, when I couldn't have been that day in Newtown. I daydreamed about what I would do. I still do. To position myself to the side of the door, the knife out, gripped, ready. My students sobbing and gasping in the corner farthest from the door. As the gunman enters I grab at his weapon at the same time I strike at his throat. Sometimes he's wearing body armor, sometimes he's wearing a mask. Sometimes he's a teen, a student at GHS, sometimes he's an adult, my age. He's never a woman, and he's never me. In some dreams I slay him quickly, easily, and I am the hero drenched in the blood of righteous anger crying justice. In other dreams I die taking the gunman down with me, and I'm still the hero. Then there are the dreams in which I fail, I die, I don't save anyone, I'm incapable of saving even myself, and I'm just history at that point, possibly not even a name on someone's screen.

Those were my fantasies. I don't know if they're yours, but I know they were hers. I know that now.

In February I noticed Diana and Zachary had only intensified their interest in each other. I let it go. I wasn't sure what attracted Diana to Zachary, if it even truly was attraction; aside from a fondness for *Game of Thrones*, they seemed to have little in common. But during pair-share I observed that, once completed with the task, unlike other students who turned to their phones, Diana and Zachary kept talking. They smiled. They even laughed. In mid-February, Diana came up to me after class and asked if I would be chaperoning the winter formal.

"The last time I did that was my first year teaching. I don't really stay up that late anymore."

"Too bad."

I smiled. "You and Zachary are going together, I gather."

"As friends. We're not *together* or anything."

I nodded, knowing that in my day they would have been together—and also knowing this was not a conversation to let play out.

That February I continued to read the reports of the virus's spread. One case in Washington State, then a nursing home there, and I began to read articles that claimed an outbreak was inevitable. I had no idea at the time; none of us did. I made no announcement to my students; I did not pause the curriculum to talk about what was going on in the world. In my classroom we lived in the Renaissance, it was 1599, 1600, 1601. The Bard was alive while those on the outside, more and more, perished.

Then it was New York. The nursing homes. Bodies piled up in freezers. And still I didn't think it would arrive in little Grafton. Not really.

The day after the winter formal I found out what had happened. Diana wasn't in class. Zachary wasn't in class. The rest of The Hunters weren't either.

"There was a fight," one senior said, and no one would elaborate.

From Diana's counselor that late February day I learned the details: At the dance Zachary and his friends, Diana among them, mixed with other students, some of whom belonged to the Black Student Union. One of the BSU members got into it with one of Zachary's buddies about the president and his response to what was turning out to be a full-fledged pandemic. I imagine the argument was typical of teenagers who'd taken up strong political stances. This one, however, led to blows when Zachary interjected and started shoving the BSU member. Punches were thrown, someone hit the floor, and chaperones did what, as far as I can recall in the whole history of Grafton High School, chaperones have never had to do.

I should have been there. Instead I was at home, in bed, asleep, practicing for the end of my life.

All those involved—Zachary, his instigator buddy, the BSU member, the BSU member's girlfriend (who apparently threw punches as well)—were suspended for several days. Diana's suspension was lighter. She did not get physically involved but did fight with words. Her words, though, were directed at Zachary, and they were full of anger. I had suspected where she stood politically, and I wish I'd talked to her about Zachary's own political stance sooner.

I stared across the counselor's desk, aghast at what I'd heard.

"If you could not punish them academically for the work they miss in your class..." the counselor began gently.

"I won't."

"And it's a good idea to keep politics out of the classroom. These are...sensitive times."

"It's an election year."

"This is just the tip of it, I think."

"You think so?"

She indicated the door. "What's out there...we can't stop it, so...go easy on them."

"For the foreseeable future."

"For the future, yes."

I left the office that afternoon vowing to be different. I would take a different approach. I had been such a hard-ass at GHS for so many years I'd garnered an unflattering reputation, to the point where I suspected certain students thought it divine retribution my wife had died. Perhaps I was starting to believe that now, too.

I wasn't about to lose Diana, though. She returned from her suspension after two days, and at the beginning of class that first day back I asked to see her at the end of the period.

"Don't lecture me," she said. "I know it got out of hand. I

could've handled it differently. Like I could've found out about his political views sooner."

"*Hamlet* doesn't really bring out Zachary's views the way *1984* did last semester."

"It's sad, because we really do get along—at least we did until this crap. Now..."

"He hasn't threatened you at all, has he?"

"No.... Are you saying he will?"

"No. I don't think so. But just let someone know—your mom, your counselor, me, if he says or writes something bad to you. Okay? In the meantime I'm going to separate you."

"Something tells me he's not coming back to this class."

"He told you?"

"Just a feeling I have."

"I need you here, Diana. I'm always, always thinking of graduation. I want you there."

"I will be there."

"I need you in class so that I can make sure you get there."

"Do you want Zachary to get there too?"

"Yes. Even Zachary."

"He has a gun."

I took a moment before speaking. "What are you saying, Diana? Are you saying he's threatened you with it?"

"I'm not saying that. I'm just stating a fact."

"I know he has a gun. A hunting rifle he's very proud of. He's talked about it in this room for going on two years."

"Not the rifle. The other gun."

"Another one? I don't know about that one. What are you—"

"I'm not saying anything!" Diana shouted.

Her anger astonished me. It slipped from her like a sword. It struck me then that what was between them went beyond politics.

"This is a safe space, Diana."

"You think I'm safe here? *You're* going to keep me *safe*? Like every teacher I've ever had has kept me safe. You can't keep *any* of us safe."

They were the worst words any student had ever said to me. I had been called a lot of things, had a lot of things implied about me, over the years at Grafton High—some of it driven by honest misunderstanding, still more driven by the calculated need to increase a grade—but this was the worst because it had the weight of truth to it. Only in my mind was I a protector.

"Is he back? Roberto—is he back?"

Diana kept quiet. Her eyes were red-rimmed, watery. She looked tired again, like she did at the start of January.

"I don't know what'll make him go away," she said. "Maybe a gun will make him go away."

My entire body seemed to electrify at those words. "Diana —you're not. Are you—are you thinking..."

"No." She spoke with such force I was momentarily convinced.

"You need to see someone. You really do. I mean it."

"I am seeing someone." Diana managed a thin smile as she spoke. "I'm seeing you."

AND THEN IT was March and I found myself reading the *Times* more and making pronouncements in class concerning a virus I knew little about. "It lives on surfaces for up to two weeks," I said. I indicated Zachary's empty desk, as if the coronavirus thrived on its surface and had driven its occupant to swear off school forever. I made comparisons to the 1918 influenza pandemic and what experts were predicting about COVID-19. In short, I scared my students without realizing I was scaring them because I had lost my sense of them, who they were, who they might become. I knew the school would close, I just wasn't sure when. On March 16th my students submitted their essays on *Hamlet*; that Monday I began our unit on *Into the Wild* thinking I would have more time in the classroom. I had two more days. On Wednesday, March 18th, it was announced that all students and staff would be moving online for the next few weeks; the belief was that we would return to in-person instruction after spring break, the middle of April.

The first day of the shutdown, Thursday, March 19th, I woke up and began my online life. I had never spent much time on the computer; one of the perks of teaching, I felt, was the ability to get up and move around the classroom whenever I wanted. But I could no longer move for the rest of March. For a solid five-plus hours every weekday I was locked in on the screen, a servant to my seat. At first, I was optimistic. Students were encouraged to turn on their cameras, but if they didn't they were not to be penalized, and I did my best to understand. If they didn't want to show themselves, so be it. That wasn't going to stop my lessons. But within a couple of weeks my mood soured as the names never responded except through the chat feature, and students never turned on their cameras even when they were put into breakout sessions with those they assured me were their friends. Even Diana, though she regularly participated through chat, remained a faceless, voiceless name in a gray square. I made sure that any breakout session I put her in did not also include Zachary or The Hunters. They had returned, but they never responded to questions, never typed anything, and soon they quit submitting assignments. Most students dropped off in this way when the superintendent announced after spring break that we would have to continue online for the foreseeable future and that as such all assignments moving forward were to be used only to enhance a student's grade, never to lower it. At that point my most savvy juniors and seniors, or those who were awake anyway, Diana included, asked me, through email or chat, if this meant they didn't have to do any more work.

Yes, I responded. That's about right.

The policy proved to be a godsend for Diana, who had fallen behind badly in January and hadn't gained much ground in February and March. The policy saved her and so many others. It allowed them to graduate.

I do feel bad for the Class of 2020, just as I feel bad now for the Class of 2021. But 2021 hasn't lost any students; their understanding of tragedy is different.

By May I was letting my classes out earlier than ever. I would hit the required 20 minutes of live online instruction and then call it. Nothing I did mattered anymore. *Into the Wild* hadn't landed on them the way it had all previous senior classes. I had resorted to assigning social emotional learning-based quickwrites—worth just a couple points each—requiring students to express themselves on a random topic they could easily personalize. If you could take only three albums with you to a deserted island, which three would you choose? Explain what hobbies you have started, continued or would like to do now that your school is shut down and life is in lockdown. Occasionally, when assigning these prompts I would wonder what I was teaching, and I thought also of these students older, adults, and I as an old man dependent on their decisions and work ethics. Some students responded, most didn't. Some grades increased, most didn't, and in the end all my seniors passed, a happy outcome I had last experienced five years earlier.

On the Thursday after Memorial Day, the day graduation would have taken place had it not been corona-canceled, I was finishing up with my juniors in 7th period, the end of the virtual school day and the last class session of this strange school year, when Diana dropped in. She must have gotten the code to join the class from an underclassman. I heard her voice before I saw her gray-boxed name among the few junior names remaining.

"Mr. H."

"Diana? You...don't have to be here, you know."

"I know. But I need to talk."

I told her to wait: three names remained aside from hers. Diana responded by assuring me those students were asleep.

"Is that a fact?"

"They're all doing it."

"But not you?"

I knew she was right. Of course they were asleep. I was staring at the future.

I created a breakout session and sent Diana in. I joined moments later. To my surprise she had her camera on. That wasn't saying much, though. In her square: a whirring ceiling fan, a curtained window, shadows.

"I fear for the future, Diana."

"You should."

Her voice had an edge to it. Such an edge I'd never heard before that I was startled for a moment into silence. When I spoke it was to say I was just joking, sort of.

"Sorry," she said.

"Why? Because you're in the strangest situation of your life? The last time this happened was a hundred years ago, and I'm pretty sure if they held any classes back then they just took them outside."

Diana's laugh sounded tight, controlled. "Are you okay?" I asked.

She sighed. Her camera shifted. At last I had her face. It looked as if she was back to not sleeping.

"It's good to see you," I said. I meant that.

"I live right around the corner from you."

I waited. I was not, to my knowledge, being recorded.

"I'm sorry," Diana said at last, "for troubling you with all my problems."

My words were instantaneous and sharp. "Diana, you are not troubling me at all. Please don't say that. Don't think that. Please. You're one of my best students ever. Seriously."

"Thank you. It's nice to hear that. I just...I do feel that I've been troubling people for years now."

Eight years, I thought. And I knew then that I could not keep asking Diana if she had seen her counselor. It was too late for a high school counselor. Today Diana graduated. I had seen the montage of graduation pictures and videos seniors had submitted from home. Diana had not submitted anything. Nor had Zachary. I had to do what I should have done earlier—contact someone to intervene in what I now suspected could be a serious situation.

"Diana...I'm going to ask you something and I want you to please, please tell me the truth. I believe you'll be honest with me..."

She waited.

"Are you thinking of hurting yourself?"

Her *no* was such that I believed her. I had to believe her. And then she added, "I'm not planning to hurt myself."

"Good. Has Zachary...been in the picture at all?"

At this Diana looked away. She fell back into the shadows.

"What did he do to you, Diana?"

Silence stretched before she spoke. "It's more of what he could do. What anyone could do."

I looked at Diana in a new light now. I saw her for what she had become, and what she might always have been. I saw her without seeing her.

"In the beginning was the gun," she intoned.

"And the gun was good," I finished.

"What was the first gun death in this country?" Diana wondered aloud. "Was it a suicide? I doubt it."

"Homicide," I said.

"It's gotta be an English settler shooting one of the indige-nous people, right?"

"Or an English settler shooting another English settler. Who knows?"

"We'll never know," Diana said. "But it must have been in the northeast."

"What about Florida? The Spanish..."

"Let me show you something."

Diana got up and left the frame. I could hear her moving close to the computer, and I panicked.

"Diana do you...you don't have a gun, do you?"

Her face filled the frame. For a full half-minute we stared at one another, and in her eyes I knew the truth.

She said, "Don't you want to stop it from happening again?"

As an English Language Arts teacher I'm supposed to push students to identify the "it" in their sentences. That day I knew what the *it* is.

Placed before the camera now was a homemade poster—on it the enlarged face of the recently murdered George Floyd. I recognized Breonna Taylor as well. The acronym BLM, the words *justice* and *truth* and *cover-up* and #sayhername all found a place on Diana's poster. Something else, too: an image of a group of Black musicians. A couple weeks later, I would look at this part of the poster up close and find out the image was of the proto-punk band Death, which had been active from 1971 – 1977.

"That's all you have," I said, more to myself in relief. "You're doing the right thing."

"There's a protest here in Grafton."

"Here? Where in Grafton?"

"Don't sound so surprised. There's plenty of us. You should be with us, too. Teachers are going. Ms. Z. Mr. M. It would mean a lot to us."

I knew those teachers. They didn't care how they appeared in the community because they didn't live in the community. They lived in the large neighboring cities and commuted in. I had my parents to consider. I had my future.

Diana understood this without me having to say it. She knew me too well by now.

"Thought I'd try," she said.

"Where's your father, Diana? Is he—is he alive?"

"He's alive." Her words landed like jabs. "He moved to New Hampshire."

"Why not...with you and your mom?"

What Diana said next I couldn't imagine her revealing to many others, yet she spoke as if she'd told this story to everyone already. "My dad," she said, "and Adam Lanza's mom were together."

"Oh my God. They..."

"That's never been proven. My dad'll go to his grave denying anything like that happened. But they did go to the shooting range together. My dad and Mrs. Lanza and even Adam sometimes, toward the end."

"Jesus."

"I'm not sure if they did anything else, you know, together."

"I'm...I'm really sorry, Diana."

"I knew Adam. Sort of."

"You don't have to tell me this. Really. You don't."

"No, I do. He never babysat me or anything, his mom would never allow *that*, but he was in the background a lot, in rooms, just there. There but out of reach."

"Waiting."

"I guess. You know, it's obviously sad but...funny, too."

"What is?"

"This one time," Diana said, "when I was nine, only a year before the shooting, I was over at the Lanzas' house with my dad, he was just stopping by to give Mrs. Lanza something, and I asked to use the bathroom. So I went in the direction where Mrs. Lanza pointed. And I had to go through the kitchen. And there was Adam sitting at the table, eating something. I'm not sure what, and I'm not sure if something else caused this to happen besides just him, but he started choking."

"No shit."

"Yeah."

"You're serious."

"Yes! He was clawing at his throat, and his face was turning a dark shade, and it was awful."

"You must have been terrified."

"But I knew what to do. My parents had trained me. I yelled 'Help! Help! He's choking! Help him!' And Mrs. Lanza and my dad rushed in, and my dad did the Heimlich on Adam, and he saved his life."

"Holy crap."

"And I think...I just think..." Diana paused for a few moments before continuing. "I think what if I hadn't said anything? What if I'd just gone to the bathroom?"

"You can't blame yourself. It'll eat you alive."

"It already has."

"Diana?"

"You can come with me, if you want. We'd make a good team."

I shut my eyes. "I don't doubt that," I said. I was tired of talking, tired of connecting, or trying to connect. Maybe, I thought, teaching is now just a job, and a job is far easier to leave than a career or a calling. But to leave, after all the years I'd put in? To slip out of the Golden Handcuffs and risk what little I had left?

"Mr. H?"

"I support you, Diana, in whatever you do, whatever you

become."

"Thank you."

"I mean that."

"I know you do."

We ended shortly after those words. I never recorded any of my meetings. I wish I had recorded that one.

I FOUND out what happened through the teachers who had been at the protest firsthand. According to my eyewitness colleagues, the demonstrators began amassing at noon on Saturday, May 30th. I use the word 'amassing' because what was expected to be a small crowd quickly ballooned into a much larger force. Forces, rather. The numbers swelled in part because of the opposing side—those Grafton citizens, and some outsiders too, waving the black and white striped American flags with the single blue stripe prominently featured, some waving the flags with both the blue and red stripes, others waving 2020 election-themed flags in support of the sitting president. It was easy to tell one side from the other because of what they wore: the t-shirts, hats, jackets promoting the president, or making a dig at something the other side supported. And those gathering to protest the killing of George Floyd—the Black Lives Matter t-shirts, the unadulterated American flags that spoke for no group or individual—only a nation. The signs on either side—signs of hate and divisiveness, signs of anger and discomfort. It's come to this, I thought later when I saw the footage taken on one of my colleague's phones. I almost couldn't bring myself to watch it. But I had to. All that I had taught in the last several years—*The Great Gatsby, Hamlet, Into the Wild, March: Book Three, The Crucible, Zoot Suit, 1984*. What lived in the streets lived in those pages, and not everyone saw it. I watched as much of the footage as I could before I was warned. I see it even now. I hope it's been deleted; I fear it will never be, and even if it was, it will never truly be gone.

I see the two sides converging. At first the arguments appear in check—heated debate, similar to what I allowed in class. Then the voices rise to where it would be unacceptable in the classroom. Curse words, insults are hurled. Then the physicality—the finger-pointing, the wild gesticulating, the finger-jabbing. When the body gets involved.... Suddenly, swiftly, hands around a throat, an older person pushed to the ground, then fists launch and the two sides erupt at one another. Some—especially those with young children—flee. But I see teenagers swinging, shoving, stomping. A few of the teenagers are my own. I see The Hunters, I see members of Grafton High's BSU. I see Zachary for the first time in months. He's grown his hair out and he's wearing a shirt depicting the president as Rambo, the Terminator, brandishing a machine gun. But it's the person who emerges behind him, just outside the crowd, that holds the real gun: Diana, dressed in jeans and the first shirt I ever saw her wearing. It doesn't seem real. None of it seems real. This is California, I still think as I watch the footage again and again. How did this 18-year-old get this handgun? It's not hers.

It's his.

It is his. I've since found out that fact, that Diana stole the gun from Zachary and brought it to the protest.

There is where it should have ended for me, but day by day I found the courage, or rather the foolishness, the sickness, to watch the unraveling, to inch a little further toward the abyss. Diana sights her target. The police have yet to arrive. This, after all, is Grafton, which hasn't had its own police force in decades, instead relying on the county sheriff's department and the CHP. Diana's finger is on the trigger. Seeing her, the crowd convulses and scatters. Those aware enough to run find cover down side streets, behind trees or trash cans or buildings.

No one confronts the gunwoman. Diana moves forward. The thoughts and prayers I have as I watch don't matter. My thoughts and prayers don't matter. I can think only No don't no don't no don't.

I have never felt for Zachary. I feel for him now. He backs away as Diana stares him down with his own gun. He shouts, confused, not quite registering if what he's seeing is real or not, and he doesn't turn and he doesn't run. "My gun!" I hear him say. "That's my gun!"

As Diana, expressionless, remorseless, draws within a few feet, Zachary, whose fellow Hunters have deserted him, launches himself at his love.

It's unreal, not even a movie, to watch footage of a teen killing another teen. The gun goes off. The first bullet strikes Zachary in the chest, the second, in the throat. The third misses and hits no one.

Zachary's body lies on the ground. Screams and sirens. Now they arrive. Off-screen can be heard shouting, and officers enter the frame. They secure the area. A pair of officers run in the direction of Diana's escape route. Another officer kneels next to Zachary's body. Some distance away, shots can be heard.

"Oh my God.... Oh my God..." says my colleague taking the footage. He too is crying. He's a teacher at the time. He's not a teacher now.

What an empty vow I've made. What a coward I was not to go, to protect the people I am paid to protect every day, even outside of school. Instead I stayed home, taking refuge in a silent, empty house that has never had a gun in it.

Or has it. At the conclusion of her letter I read on February 1st, Diana closed with a dream, or a vision, she'd had since she was ten and there was talk of razing Sandy Hook. *I used to wonder*, Diana wrote, *where all the ghosts would go.* But she knew where the ghosts would go. They were in her dream-vision, the scene of that long wide street in suburbia Diana is now walking down, the street so many have walked down before. The houses on either side are not the cookie cutter houses of Madeline L'Engle's *A Wrinkle in Time*; they are distinct houses, each containing its own personality, its own souls. As Diana walks, she looks to either side and sees the people, the victims, gathered outside. Those who have walked before. Each one has found her or his or their home. Each one has found the house where it happened or it might have happened or it will happen. Each one is weaponless, downcast, yet welcoming. No one waves. Everyone gazes. Diana continues to walk, looking from side to side. The houses are full, occupied. There is no place for her. And then there is. She sees it on her right—a one-story ranch-style with nobody standing in front. Turning up the driveway, she proceeds along the walkway and toward the door, aware of the eyes, including my own, on her. The door is closed, but when she twists the knob it gives easily and she enters. The door closes behind her. And she's home.

TODAY, I think. *Today.*

THIS CLASSROOM, now that I'm back to teaching within its walls, is different without Diana and Zachary. I try to reason that the trigger would have been pulled eventually, if even decades from now. They did graduate, and they left me behind. They believed they no longer needed me. I had taught them what I could. In the end, that's what I have to tell myself, that's what helps me sleep at night: I did teach them, all of them, and they taught me. There is not much more a teacher can ask of this career. In the end, perhaps that's all we really can do.

The police investigation, and the subsequent district probe, ended soon after they began. I told them what I knew, and what I had done, but though I took blame they, in the end, assigned none to me. I wasn't there. I didn't know she had taken Zachary's gun that morning. I didn't know her motives, the substance of her sessions. I only knew so much, and what I knew amounted to thoughts and prayers.

Would I have gone with her, as she'd requested? Would I have stood next to her, unarmed, in support? Would I have fled with her to drive across this country, to visit all the houses we could before we were silenced?

I think about those questions now. Those questions are my ghosts.

It's now 2021, and the virus is receding somewhat, and the shots are going into arms, and we have a new president and those who were angry are even angrier and Diana was taken by her mother, whom I finally met, for burial back east. I expressed a desire to attend the funeral but due to COVID-19 restrictions it would be a small, private, family gathering. I understood.

I teach through a mask now. I still teach part of the day through a screen. In my free time, outside of my classroom, I try to make up for my errors. I do things I never would have done when my wife was alive. I go shopping in places I would never have thought of frequenting. I hold one piece after another. I feel the weight, the heft, the power. I take aim. And when it's time, when the school year is over and summer is underway, I'm going to load up and hit the road as she would have done. I'm going to visit all the houses I can. With the patience that has seen me through eight years of teaching, I will observe. I'll home in on the faces, the body language, the words and ideas. I'll look for the signs. I will be that telescreen. As long as the possibility of tragedy exists, so must I. Safety is the aim here. Safety is the child I can give this world.

EVEN MORE TROUBLE

I

Mrs. Melton's students feared her. They tried not to let on how much they were affected by what she said and did; still, it was hard not to show some type of emotion, no matter how much of it remained bottled up inside. Repression could've been what led a few of them to break her rules.

The other students—grades kindergarten through sixth—weren't scared; they didn't know what went on in the modular classroom where she taught. Melton liked that she was able to run things as she saw fit, without too much interference from the principal or the vice principal, both of whom only occasionally dropped in on her unexpectedly. Melton had received her credential from a university in the city, where she still lived even though it was a forty-five minute commute to the small town of Anomar and Gordon Lawrence Elementary School. She was married but didn't have children—that's about as much as the adults and kids in the community knew about her. When she was done with school for the day, Melton would lock up her classroom, stride out to the parking lot, get behind the wheel, key the ignition and peel away. She rarely stopped anywhere to do anything on her way out of town.

We could chalk up her bullying, cajoling, threatening, manipulating—anything to keep her students in line—to the fact that she was in only her second year. Looking back on those days, it's difficult to comprehend why she'd become a teacher in the first place. She certainly didn't seem to like teaching, so what was it? Did she like the power, the authority that came with commanding ten- and eleven-year-olds? Or was she just too scared of losing control? Regardless, her class obeyed, for the most part. Sometimes, though, students from the outside interfered. Once Daniel, a sixth grader, came in to deliver a message from the office. Mrs. Melton was kneeling down with her back to the class, head stuck in a cabinet. Daniel saw he was safe—he'd heard stories about her and he didn't want to talk with her—ever, if he could help it. There'd be mistakes he'd make in the conversation—mistakes his mom (another teacher) would find out about. He was not ready to face Melton.

So Daniel placed the note on Kevin's desk, right by the doorway. Kevin was about to say something but Daniel put his finger to his lips. Kevin shut up quick. The rest of the class also shushed. A few giggles, quiet enough for the teacher not to hear. Daniel smiled and left, shutting the door behind him. Kevin looked through the window and saw Daniel walking away, taking big strides toward the office.

Mrs. Melton came out of the cabinet and looked around the room. Most students smiled. She set her hands on her hips and said, "What happened, you all look different."

Kevin saw the note on his desk and picked it up. "Mrs...." he began, holding the note above his head. Melton took three steps to reach him.

"Thank you." She took the paper from him. "Who delivered this?"

He looked down, shrugged. Melton turned on the other students. "Who?" Her voice was much louder.

"The boy that's outside now," a student spoke up. "I think his name's, uh, Danny?"

The teacher mouthed this name silently. "Oh," she said and walked around Kevin, who still looked at his shoes. She opened the door, stuck her head out, and spotted Daniel, who had almost reached the grassy area near the main buildings. "Daniel!" she shouted. "Danny, get over here!"

Daniel froze. Then he started running.

"Danny!" she shouted again. "Don't you run from me! Get your butt over here!" Laughter from inside the classroom. Melton watched Daniel disappear behind a building. She gave up and went back inside.

The class was silent. She scanned the room. A snicker from the corner farthest from her. She grinned. "Wasn't that funny?" she asked, almost to herself. No one gave an answer; they knew she wasn't expecting one. "Everybody back to work."

SOME KIDS THOUGHT Norman had a glass eye. He would spend lunch period most every day telling any kid who cared to listen how terrible the operation had been, how the doctor had forced his eyelids open with two pairs of pliers while he was still awake, just so he could get the whole ordeal over with as quickly as possible. No anesthetic, no ocular Novocain. Nope, he didn't need any.

On the playground during lunch this one time Stan

approached Norman and started up something. "Hey," he said, "you ever take that eye out at night? I betcha do before you go to bed."

Norman tried to ignore him. He wasn't in the mood for this type of thing.

"Hey," Stan persisted. "Did the Eye Fairy give you that?"

"Nah," Norm said. Today he was awfully quiet, sitting by himself away from the rest of the kids with whom he usually hung out.

Stan wouldn't go away. "That thing's not real," he said.

"Yeah it is."

"No, cuz if it was you'd show me."

"How?"

"Take it out."

"I can't."

"Why not?"

"Not supposed to. Doctor says."

"Doctor schmez, man. You could do it, if it was real."

"It is."

"Then how about you show me another way."

"Yeah?" Norman looked wary. He had a right to be. Stan wasn't careful with anything he said to anybody. Sometimes he hurt people—one would hope—without meaning to.

"Take a hammer and smash your glass eye. That'll show everybody. Do it in front of everybody. Then they'll see."

"No.... You mean without taking it out?"

"Thought you said you couldn't take it out, no matter what."

"Uh...right."

"See, you're lying. I'm telling everybody that thing's not real."

Norman got up, pushed past Stan and walked away without looking back.

Norman could have beaten up Stan if he'd wanted to. He

was a big boy, one of the toughest in fifth grade. Still, his toughness wasn't enough to keep him from wearing glasses. He didn't want to wear them because he knew the other kids would tease him to death, but inaccurate vision wasn't appealing so he chose to stick with the glasses and somehow stay tough all year.

The other kids didn't see him as just a nerd then—they saw him as a tough nerd, a real rebel with attitude. When Melton told her students to cross their legs while they sat on the classroom floor ready to sing "Tomorrow" to piano accompaniment, everybody did except Norman. He kept his legs straight.

"Norman, cross your legs," Mrs. Melton ordered.

"No. I can't."

"Why not."

"The circulation in my legs—it's bad. My doctor says..."

"What's your doctor's name, Norman?"

"Um..."

"Fine, whatever." She flipped through her music book, ignoring him. "You're not worth the time or the effort."

That incident occurred in the beginning of the fifth grade year, and from then on Melton had it out for Norman. She wasn't one to have her orders refuted. Everything she said had to be obeyed, every student had to be on time to class, doing well on her assignments, their drawings perfect, their papers perfect. It could have been that she felt the need to compete with the other teachers and their students. If that was indeed the case, her own students never realized that it was this competition that drove Mrs. Melton to do things unheard of at Gordon Lawrence Elementary School.

KEVIN WAS out on the upper playing field, sitting against the chain-link fence, watching some of the kids a grade above play football. He was as old as they were. Older than a lot of them, actually. He should have been in their grade, sixth, and he didn't know why he wasn't. Something his parents once said about a decision they made. They were always making decisions on everything. It seemed to him that when you became an adult you had to make decisions and nothing else.

For now Kevin was happy just being a kid. He was happy watching the game and finishing his applesauce. Motts was the best. He kind of wished his mom would buy the cinnamon-flavored type. He would tell her this weekend, if he remembered to. Oh and today was Friday, which meant pizza and a movie at his house. Except he had to convince his dad to rent something cool, not "provocative"—the word his dad used to describe all the movies he picked out. It must have been because he was old.

Kevin finished the last of his applesauce and stuck the cup and spork back inside his brown bag. He looked around the field for his friend Dominick and that was when he saw Norman running through the game, breaking it up. "Hey!" some of the sixth graders yelled after him. "Watch it, snot-face!" One of them threw the Nerf ball at the back of Norman's head and pegged him. Norman didn't seem to care; he was at the far end of the field, over by the anthills.

Shouting came from below Kevin. He stood up and turned around to where he could see the modular classrooms on the lower field. He gripped the chain-link fence as he saw Mrs. Melton come down the ramp of her classroom. She wasn't just shouting—well, from what Kevin heard she was shouting at first and then it quickly turned to bellowing. He could barely make out what she was going on about. There was a name, though, unmistakable: "Norman!"

Kevin recoiled, as if it had been his name Melton called. He looked all around the upper field, shielding his eyes from the sun, but couldn't see Norman anywhere. Kevin turned back to the lower level and couldn't find Melton either. But there was that horrible bellowing still to be heard, farther away this time.

KEVIN FOUND out the cause of all this only after lunch had ended. Melton wanted to see Norman at lunch for some math tutoring. She was trying to help him out; she was just being nice, Kevin thought. When lunch rolled around Norman told her he was going to pick up the food his mom had left at the office, and then he split. He didn't come back to the classroom. By the time Melton realized he wasn't returning, lunch was almost over, and then her fury spiked. No one stood her up. Norman was a dead kid; Melton went after him, her deep-red lips parted back and her teeth gnashing. She might have been foaming at the mouth—that's what some of the kids said when they saw her storming across campus. They ran. Everyone ran from her, even other teachers and the yard duties. Melton's hair was blown in a puffed-out entanglement that made her look like she'd been struck by lightning. She only meant to chase after Norman, but she ended up chasing after almost the entire school. It was insane how she kept calling after him, like he was her son and he'd done something really terrible. Maybe he had.

For Melton the slightest thing wrong was taken as an attack against her. Kevin remembered one day she was furious with him over an assignment. The class was given the United States to color on the big wall map, and each student was given their own state. Kevin colored for a while before Melton came up and asked him what he was doing. She sounded like she was mad. Kevin took a moment to answer—he was unsure how to answer her. "I'm coloring."

"No you're not," she said. "Not the right way." Then she pointed at California. "You see this, Kevin. Didn't you hear what I said *before* we started this? Do you remember me saying color up and down only, or side to side only, but not *both*? Do you?"

Kevin didn't remember hearing this order before he began coloring. She probably gave the rules and he wasn't paying attention. He watched as she took a crayon and started coloring over his state. "You see how I'm doing this only one way? The way you have it looks all out of order, like a spider's web. Now fix it."

"But—"

"Fix It." She didn't shout this, but her voice was definitely louder.

He had done wrong; he was embarrassed because of his mistake. Several students were looking at him. Kevin had been in this position before and each time he'd done the same thing to protect himself—his face became flushed and tears came to his eyes. He faced the wall and wiped his tears with his shirt-sleeve. Whispers were all that were needed to make the situation worse for him. He felt a hard cry coming on, thought of getting out of the room but there was no time and besides, they'd talk even more afterwards when he was gone than they were talking now.

A hand touched his right arm. The hand wasn't Melton's. It was Norman's.

"Hey," he said.

"Hey," Kevin said back.

KEVIN REMEMBERED THAT MOMENT WELL. Nothing much came of it, but at least it was locked inside his memory as something important to hold on to. Lunch was over. He went back to class, hoping to hear from the other students what had happened between Melton and Norman. The door to the classroom was locked and a lot of kids were outside hanging around, joking and talking about what Melton had done and how Norman was going to get it big time from his parents. A couple of kids leaned over the ramp's railing and swung upside down. Kevin sat down on the ramp close to them and didn't talk to anyone.

"Hey you, Kev," Stan said from the other end of the ramp. "What d'ya think Norm's gonna get for running from Teach?"

"Don't know," said Kevin. He shrugged. "Trouble."

For some reason Stan laughed. Kevin thought this was weird because he didn't think he'd said anything funny.

"There he is!" Everyone looked to where Cassie was pointing. They saw Norman coming toward them. Melton walked behind him.

Norman's face was red from crying; Kevin could tell he'd been crying because of the way he squinted his eyes and tried not to look at anybody. Kevin knew what that was like. The strange thing about Norman was that he now walked with a limp; his left leg didn't seem to be working right, like it was dead weight and he was just dragging it along. His jeans were dusty at the bottoms, too.

Melton's head was held up while Norman's was lowered. Together they walked up the ramp—students on both sides— and stopped before the door. Melton didn't look at Norman or her other students. She took the classroom key out of her pocket, opened the door, and she and Norman went inside. The door closed behind them.

After about five minutes the door opened and Mrs. Melton came out. She appeared calm. "All right, everybody. Get inside and finish up your long division."

One by one, they filed through the doorway.

II

KEVIN HAD no idea what his dad did for work, but he knew it involved a briefcase. To Kevin, the briefcase looked cool. He imagined it might have a knife in it, the way James Bond's briefcase contains a hidden knife in *From Russia with Love*. Kevin doubted his dad was a secret agent. No secret agent would tell such awful jokes—in fact, no secret agent would tell any jokes at all. Still, it was fine to imagine, as Kevin was doing while touching the briefcase. His father had left it on the dining table overnight, and that's where Kevin was seated now. He was often up before everyone. The lights were still off throughout the house, but in the long glow cast by the open microwave, Kevin could see the edges of the briefcase. He was looking for the secret dagger compartment. Maybe you had to open up the briefcase first...

Kevin hadn't planned on opening the briefcase—except, well, yes, he had. He'd seen his dad open it a million times. He was half-expecting to see a knife—his dad, after all, slept with a nasty-looking blade on the headboard's shelf above his pillow. But instead of a knife there was only paper. Documents. The top document was nothing Kevin had seen before, it bore no official letterhead, the word MEMO in all caps. Instead, it had a title followed by short block paragraphs, each separated by a space or two.

Ten Who Made America!

1. John Henry:

America's original steel drivin' man. Took the nation by storm when he invented the steam engine. Fought racism to become the first black president of the Transcontinental Railroad. At the peak of his career, died of a heart attack while choking to death on a piece of steak. During Henry's funeral, the frosty Poet Laureate of the United States was quoted as saying, "So passes the finest man to ever drive a nail into his own coffin."

2. Paul Bunyan and his Babe:

A woodcutter from the backwoods of Maine, part-Canadian but with the blood of a Patriot, Bunyan was so big no house could contain him. Nor could it contain his wife, Babe, who was equally impressive in size. So they took to the road in an old jalopy, headed down Route 66, a banjo on their knees, to promote the benefits of eating flapjacks.

(five a day keep the doctor away)

They made it all the way to the golden state of California, but finding their message falling on deaf ears, they soon turned to picking grapes for a living. They started their own company, Grapes for Glory, and hired half the nation. Their hard work and determination single-handedly led us out of the Great Depression.

Kevin knew of these figures, these Americans. He'd watched *Pinwheel* on Nickelodeon and *Reading Rainbow*.

But this was different. There was more going on here with these little stories, and Kevin sensed he could learn—what exactly he wasn't sure, but he felt he had discovered something important, even precious.

He heard voices from his parents' bedroom. Time to close up and come back to "Ten Who Made America!" later.

IT WAS the day after Halloween, a day when no kid wanted to be at school. Kevin saw Stan walking his way, so he hurriedly started putting his lunch stuff back into his brown bag. Stan often tried to leech off of other kids.

"Hey," Stan said. "Kev, whatcha got in that bag?"

"Nothing."

"You got chips?"

"They're all gone."

Stan just nodded, like he was expecting Kevin to say that. "That's tough. What else ya got?"

"Uh...applesauce."

"Nah, that's no good, man."

"But it's Motts."

"Don't matter. Get some pudding. Pudding's good."

"Oh." Kevin felt a little embarrassed. Maybe he should've asked his mom to get pudding.

"Hey, Kev." Stan leaned in close.

Kevin thought about standing up and running, but no. It was easier just to sit. "What?"

"You ever see *The Exorcist*?"

"No."

"Well I did. Last night. Again."

"Again?"

"Yeah. I watched it every day in October. I know it by heart."

"Wow, that's rad."

"Yep, and now I'm possessed."

Kevin was puzzled. Could a movie possess someone like Stan? Stan was pretty smart, so it didn't make much sense. Still, it was *The Exorcist*. He'd heard it was scary. He wanted to see it too, but his parents had already decided he couldn't.

Stan twirled around. "I'm possessed...I'm possessed," he said.

The yard duty's whistle blew. Lunch was over. Kevin figured the whistle would stop Stan, but he kept twirling like he hadn't heard anything.

"I gotta go, Stan." Kevin stood, stretched, and headed to class.

As soon as all the students were seated on the classroom floor, Mrs. Melton sat herself down at the piano. "Music time, everybody. Now I'm going to start and you just listen to the song the first time. Then I expect you to sing with me the second time. Okay?"

Murmurs of assent. Melton smiled, turned to the music book, flipped a few pages and began to play. She sang in a gruff voice that reminded Kevin of his mother in the morning when she didn't have her coffee.

As Melton warbled the opening lyrics of "The Rainbow Connection," Kevin heard giggling at his back. He turned and saw Stan. Kevin was scared. He had to move quickly or else Melton might think he was the one who'd been laughing. Kevin wouldn't laugh at a song like that. Sure it was funny, but in a sad sort of way.

Melton had stopped. She turned to the class, her eyes narrowed. She pointed at Kevin, who shook his head vigorously.

"Kevin," she said.

"Not me."

The giggling started again. It turned into all-out laughter.

"Stan!" Melton shouted. "Stop this, Stan. I'm trying to sing 'The Rainbow Connection.' Now if you don't want to follow me then you—"

She stopped in mid-sentence. Her eyes widened.

Everyone watched Stan. He had straightened his legs while still in a sitting position.

Melton stood up from her piano bench. "Stan, cross your legs and sit Indian-style like the rest."

Stan managed to get out through giggles, "I can't, Teach. I'm...possessed."

"What?" Melton's face looked strangely scrunched up. Kevin had never seen her like this before. She looked confused.

Stan stood up.

"Stan, sit down Now!"

He waved his arms in circles and began to sing his own song: "There's a place in France where the ladies wear no pants...."

"Stanley Pangborn!" Melton strode over her students to get to the offender. She grabbed him roughly around his waist and lifted him up. She carried him back across the room, grunting, even though she was big and burly and Stan was only a scrawny kid. Stan didn't seem to know what was going on. He kept singing: "There's a hole in the wall where you can see them all!" Those were his last words before Melton dragged him to the door, opened it, and threw him out. Stan went spinning and would have fallen had he not grabbed the railing to steady himself. He turned to Melton and stuck his tongue out at her. She slammed the door on him.

Inside, the students looked at one another. No one dared to talk. Cassie looked at Kevin and mouthed something. Kevin didn't understand so he mouthed What? back.

"He's crazy," she whispered.

Kevin nodded, thinking of something else to say. Nothing

came to mind. He wanted to say something cool to Cassie, because he kind of liked her, although he wouldn't tell anybody that he did.

Melton was back at the piano now. She was just about to play when some students laughed. She looked to where they were pointing. Stan had plastered himself to the classroom window and was making funny faces. He pretended he was a puffer fish. His cheeks blew up then deflated.

"Ignore him," Melton ordered. "We're going to sing 'The Rainbow Connection.'"

Stan didn't do much more after the class started singing. He got bored and disappeared from the window. Eventually, Melton finished the song and went to open the door. She let Stan back in only after he'd promised to behave, and Melton, for her part, had assigned Stan two lunch detentions, one after school detention, and vowed to call home to his parents.

3. Johnny Appleseed:

He could not tell a lie. When his father asked him, "Was it you, my son, who chopped down this apple tree?" Johnny said, "It was I, Father." Young Johnny traversed the globe before settling down to the life of a soldier. He fought in the Revolutionary and Civil Wars, on the side of the settlers and the slaves. He killed many a poor man, and when the fighting had ended, he hung up his Smith & Wesson six-shooter and took a seat in the Senate, where he defended a woman's right to choose.

(and he never lost his love of apple pie)

STAN WAS CONVINCED Mrs. Melton was a Mormon.

"What's a Mormon?" Kevin asked. He was sitting with

some other kids at lunch over by the jungle gym fortress and the big iron fence. Beyond the fence was the wide open field and some new houses being built along the ridge. The bulldozer was on its lunch break too.

"It's someone who has a lot of kids," Lance said and then took a huge bite of his sandwich.

"Melton doesn't have any kids," Dominick said.

"Duh, dummy. She only got married last year. She was Ms. Tillitson before then."

"How do you know?"

"I know because my mom knows, duh. She'll have plenty of kids. That's what Mormons do."

"They go to church every day," Stan said. "I've seen their ads on TV. They come to your house to give you a book, and when you open the book a spinning light leaps out and brainwashes you into joining them."

Kevin wasn't so sure about that one. It was probably just another religion, like the Jehovah's Witnesses. That was a religion, right?

"I don't think Mrs. Melton can have kids," Kevin said.

"What," Lance said. "Can't her old man get it up for her?"

"No. I mean I don't think she *should* have kids."

They all pondered this for a moment.

"Teachers have kids too," Dominick said.

But Mrs. Melton? Kevin thought. His own mom was a teacher, and she was stressed out all the time. She didn't see him a whole lot because she had her own kids, her students, to worry about. They were more important than him, he felt. If his mom took her stress home with her after a long day of teaching, he couldn't imagine what Mrs. Melton would do.

4. The Unsinkable Molly Brown:

Starred in the longest-running sitcom, the cast of which

included several other survivors of the Led Zeppelin disaster. After toiling to save the dolphins and feed countless starving children, she started her own wildly popular daytime talk show and released a line of beauty products, Molly Made Me Up! She died having donated millions to public radio and fitness gurus worldwide.

(when she pointed her rifle, people listened)

THROWING STAN out of the classroom was hardly the worst of it, though. The worst of Melton's anger, directed toward Kevin, came on a test day. The rule to remember when taking a test was to never look at your neighbor's paper. Kevin wouldn't think to do that; instead, the trouble started with the three-sided boards.

They were tall and cumbersome for the kids, but because they were so big they ensured no eyes wandered. Every test the students took was enclosed on three sides. Later, they'd use similar boards for their science fair projects.

On this particular test day—the day before school let out for Christmas break—the students got in line so they could each get a board. Standard procedure, but this time Kevin must not have been thinking. When he picked up his board he moved to the right, too close to Melton's desk. He held his board flat in front of him and one of its corners knocked her bright plastic mug onto the carpet. The mug was full of water, but before landing on the floor it spilled all across her desk. Papers soaked, grade sheets and old tests ruined.

Melton hadn't seen; Kevin and a handful of other students stared at what he'd done, some of them looking around for her. There she was at the opposite end of the room, searching through a cupboard. Her back was to them. Had she heard the splash? How could she not have? There were whispers. Students shuffled back to their desks, sat down and set up their boards, hid behind them pretending not have seen.

Kevin was the last to return to his place, having taken so long to make a choice. He could tell her, or he wouldn't. It seemed simple, yet he was indecisive and of course scared. What would she say if he approached her? Better her come to him, seek him out. Maybe she'd be nicer that way.

Back at his desk, he heard Melton walk past him. He couldn't see her over the board. Cassie next to him giggled. He felt the urge to pee in his pants. A strange sound came from the direction of Melton's desk—a combination gasp-grunt. "Ah-ummm!"

Right away Kevin knew Melton didn't think the mess was an accident. It was his fault and now there'd be even more trouble.

"Who did this?" Her voice was calm. No one answered. Kevin could sense them watching him. They were waiting for him. Do something, they said. Get us out of this, you started this, Kev. Tell her.

Of course, *they* wouldn't tell on him. No student wanted to be a narc.

Her voice brayed again, loud and harsh. "I want to know who did this."

She was closer to Kevin now. He didn't breathe, held air in, scared of her but even more scared of what he was trying to do with covering up his mistake, making it worse that way. And worse for everybody.

"Norman, was it you?"

"No—not me," Norman said quickly. "It's—" He caught himself; Kevin heard him shift in his seat.

"All right, if I don't find out who did this in a minute, I'm keeping all of you after. And we'll keep going after until night, if that's what it takes. You want that, everybody?"

Silence.

Melton continued. "Someone's a coward...now who? Do I have to line you all up against the wall to find out who? You have a minute." She looked at the clock above.

This was not fair.

"Me," Kevin told Melton. "It was me."

"You, Kevin?"

"Yes."

"Get over here."

He stood up from his desk. He saw Melton's face for the first time since she'd brought the boards out of the closet. Furious, she pointed to her desk. "Do you see this," she snapped.

Kevin nodded. An odd detachment was about him now—he could feel it numbing him.

"So why didn't you tell me."

"I-I don't know. I didn't mean to knock it off."

"That's not the point, Kevin. Why didn't you tell me you did this?"

"I don't know," he repeated, weak. Why hadn't he just gone over to her? He was a criminal covering up.

"Don't hide things from me. You shouldn't have, Kevin."

Even though it was just the two of them really, he knew the rest of the class was watching. He didn't know how else to react, how to explain. Tears came swiftly, and suddenly he was sobbing, trying to muffle his cries. Melton cocked her head to one side then stooped to pick up her mug. When she came up she was a tower to Kevin and her eyes burned with red around their edges. "Sit, Kevin," she said. "Just sit. I'll clean your mess."

Kevin couldn't move at first, but he did when he saw Melton raise the mug high, ready to bring it down on his head forcefully. She may not have been brandishing the mug at him, but that's what Kevin saw, and there's no denying fear stifled the class.

Kevin returned to his seat. He didn't feel like himself anymore.

5. Hiawatha:

The little Indian girl that could. A tragic tale of love and redemption in America's Heart Land. Canoed the Colorado to the tune of Muddy Waters's "Wouldn't Take Nothing for My Premature Baby Now" before settling down in Zion and marrying Joseph Smith Jimmycrackcorn Josiah, a trial lawyer who later was called on by the Supreme Court to defend the Puritans at them Witch Trials of Super Salem Sunday. During the "These Charges are Bullshit You Must Acquit" phase of the trial, Joseph Smith Jimmycrackcorn Josiah grew ill and took to bedpan. When little Hiawatha learned of her husband's dying day, she turned into a seagull and flew to his side. Seeing his one true love in seagull form emboldened JSJJ with the blood of the Holy Spirit, and, using his newfound power, he turned into a grasshopper that Hiawatha carried, in her beak, to the sea, the sea, the great salty sea.

AFTER SCHOOL that day Kevin stood in line with the rest of the Latchkey kids. They were waiting to get their Icees. Cranberry today, cranberry every day. Kevin wanted something new—he'd even settle for pineapple if they had it.

"Kev, dude." Dominick punched his shoulder.

"What?"

"Whatcha getting for Christmas, you know yet?"

"No."

"I'm getting Tetris, I think."

"Wow."

"Yeah, you come over and we'll play it."

"Sure."

Dominick punched Kevin's shoulder again, in the same spot.

"Ouch."

"Here she comes," he said, pointing.

Kevin saw Mrs. Melton walking his way. She was coming straight for him. She looked like she did the day she chased Norman—only she smiled. The smile scared him because she'd never smiled at him before.

"Kevin," she said, standing in front of him. "How are you?"

"Good." He took a step away from her.

"I'm sorry I got angry with you today." She still smiled. "I get like that sometimes. We're still friends, right?"

"Yeah." Kevin felt dumb. He didn't know what she was getting at. Was it true? Could a teacher really be friends with her students? How many of his mom's students were her friends? Were any of them her best friend?

"Teaching...it's funny." Mrs. Melton laughed.

Kevin looked at Dominick, but Dominick wasn't paying attention to their conversation, or at least he was pretending not to pay attention.

"Kevin," Mrs. Melton said, "let me make it up to you." She reached for him with both arms outstretched. For a moment he saw his mother before him. He let out a gasp and then Melton's arms were around him, encircling his upper body, pinning his arms to his sides. She squeezed tight and Kevin closed his eyes. He felt like crying, and he didn't know why.

"You're such a good boy, Kevin," Mrs. Melton said, loud enough for the other kids to hear. "You're a really good student."

Kevin knew how embarrassed he looked to everybody. He'd be hearing about this from Dominick all vacation. It was bad enough that he cried in class. Now this. "Yeah," he said, "You sure?"

"Of course. You're one of my very best students. I, well, I just don't want to lose you, you know." She paused. "Have a good Christmas, okay."

"Okay, yeah."

She left soon after another quick squeeze. As soon as she was gone Dominick tapped Kevin on his arm. "She's crazy," he smirked.

Kevin stood silently. For the rest of the school year he'd probably be all right.

III

He would have been all right, except over Christmas, New Year's Eve to be exact, the bad thing happened. Kevin was in bed, must have been around midnight, when he woke up hearing his mother yelling. Not just yelling: screaming. She could only be screaming and yelling at his dad because the noise was coming from their bedroom.

Kevin got out of bed and went into the living room expecting to find himself in the opening of another nightmare. The lights were on already. He sat on the couch and listened. It wasn't long before his sister, Sandra, joined him. She said nothing. The door to their parents' bedroom was closed and behind it they could hear their mother still yelling. Kevin couldn't understand exactly what she was saying—or maybe it was that he didn't want to understand. His mom would yell for a little while and then she would stop and he could hear his dad's voice, very low behind the door. Then his mother would start yelling all over again. It happened like this a few times, and the whole time it did Kevin felt the insides of his stomach drop lower and lower, like they were going to push right out of his body.

Neither he nor Sandra thought to turn on the TV while

the yelling and low voice clashed. Then, suddenly, they heard a bang like a gun going off in a movie. They shot up. Now Kevin was sure something even worse had happened. A gun. But his parents didn't have a gun, at least not any that he knew about. No knife could have made that sound.

Kevin and Sandra stayed seated on the couch. After some more yelling—this time from Mom and Dad—the door opened and his mom stormed out. Once when he was younger he'd had a dream where she was at the other end of the house and he could hear her breathing heavily and snorting, like an animal. In the dream Kevin couldn't leave his bed; instead he stayed under the covers with his head peeking out. He couldn't even hide his face underneath the blankets—he could only wait. The snorting and breathing and stomping had grown louder, and he knew it was Mom—except it wasn't completely. When she appeared in his room she was wearing her bright red bathrobe and her eyes were blazing. She also had little red bull horns poking out of her head and smoke coming out of her nose. But that was just a dream, and Kevin had woken up before she could do anything.

The memory of that dream was in his mind when he saw his mom come out of the bedroom—only now a lot of things were different. Of course his mom wasn't wearing the red bathrobe—she'd actually gotten rid of it a couple years before —and she definitely did not have horns poking out of her head and smoke coming out of her nose. Her eyes weren't blazing either; instead, they showed she'd been crying a lot, and Kevin was surprised to sense more hurt than anger from her. It was a feeling he hadn't picked up much from his mom, this hurt, and it scared him almost as much as if she'd been angry.

At first she didn't seem to want to look at him, and that scared Kevin too. Then she came over, sat down next to him and put her hand on his forehead like he had a fever.

"I'm sorry, Kevin," she said, and she tried to smile even though the tears were sliding down her cheeks. "I'm sorry, Sandra."

Kevin didn't know what his mom had to feel sorry for. It couldn't be her fault because she'd been yelling so much. Was it his fault? His mom couldn't really smile then. Her soft mouth quivered like an arrow in a tree, and her green eyes were blacker, like a cat's, and reminded Kevin of the obsidian pieces in the backyard because of how shiny they were from the tears. Her hair was messed up, normally curly but now it was all over the place, a lot like Mrs. Melton's that day she'd chased Norman across campus. His mom reminded Kevin a lot of Melton right now; they both were commanding, both had the same job, and they both scared him with their feelings.

Kevin joined his little sister in crying. His mom hugged them both, and when he looked over her shoulder he saw his dad standing in the bedroom doorway. Dad was really tall, so it was weird for Kevin to see that he'd been crying too. He wasn't as bad off as the kids and their mom, but his eyes were definitely wet, and watching him Kevin could not ever remember him like this.

Mom let go and said, "Go back to bed, Sandra. You too, Kevin."

Kevin thought he'd get a chance to say something, even just an "okay," but his mom said her words as she was getting up off the couch, and by the time she'd finished her sentence she already had her back turned to him and was heading to the bedroom.

Kevin had always obeyed both his parents, but now he hesitated. If he went back to bed he wouldn't be able to sleep; he'd only cry. His parents seemed to know this, which is why Mom didn't repeat her command. Instead she looked at Kevin sadly—and so did his dad. What was going on? Why were they like this? What had happened? The door to the bedroom shut and Kevin was left without the answers he needed.

He must have stayed on the living room couch for another hour before the door opened again. By that time he wasn't even aware of what show he was watching—some comedy he was pretty sure he and his dad used to watch together. Kevin looked up from the commercial to see his mom coming toward him. She looked calm now, even though her eyes were still red. She sat down next to Kevin for the second time and held his hand. Kevin tried to find his father, but he couldn't see Dad through the open doorway.

Mom talked as if at any moment she was going to say the wrong thing. It didn't matter how careful she was; everything she said was wrong to Kevin. His father was going to live somewhere else for a while—not forever, but right now it was better for him not to be in the house. He wasn't going to be far, and Kevin would get to see him a lot. Kevin could even see him today—New Year's Day. As he listened Kevin thought of his father not living in the house anymore, what that would be like. Dad didn't live a lot in the house anyway—he was at work a lot or on business trips—but still it was sad, and Kevin started to cry all over again. His mom cried too, and then Dad was there and both his parents hugged him at the same time, and in their hugs Kevin felt they were fighting to see who could force the most love into him. He felt a lot like a doll, or a dog, and this made him cry even harder because if it wasn't his fault whose fault was it?

Finally he did go back to bed because he didn't want to feel that fighting over him anymore. In bed he tossed around with the lights off. He'd thought he wouldn't be able to sleep, but when he next was aware of anything the sun was just coming through the blinds, and he could hear his dad moving around the house. He stayed in bed and waited. After a while Dad came into his room. He looked tired and much older.

"I'm going now, Kev," he said—only as he spoke he seemed to be talking to the carpet. "I'll see you later today."

Kevin had never really hung out with his father in a place other than a movie theater or the beach of the mall. Dad would sometimes take him to see R-rated movies that Mom didn't want him seeing, and that was certainly a cool way to hang out. At home they would also watch movies or sometimes play chess, but what Kevin really wanted to do was never done. Now, though, later in the day, New Year's Day, Kevin set up his Nintendo with pride. His dad had taken the small TV and its stand from Mom and Dad's bedroom and rolled it into a corner of the Anomar Street apartment's wide living room. Kevin hooked up the console and plugged in the controllers. It took a little while to find the right channel, but once they had and Kevin saw the intro screen for Tetris he knew they would have a good time together. His dad only had to *try* Tetris and he'd see that Nintendo was worth playing. He would stop using the phrase "zoning out" to describe what Kevin did. Tetris wasn't like the typical games Kevin owned; it was a thinking man's game, and it was provocative.

"Provocative?" Kevin's dad sounded like there might be a fire somewhere.

"Yeah. Really provocative."

His dad seemed like he wanted to say something, but then he thought hard and kept quiet. Kevin offered him the main controller, but his dad said Kevin should take the lead here. Kevin went first, and while he played his father talked to him.

At first Dad talked to him about the game and about Nintendo in general. He asked Kevin how many hours he was playing a day, a question he'd asked before and Kevin always lied about. Kevin couldn't be blamed, though; they were the ones who'd let him play nine hours straight on his ninth birthday, the day he got his Nintendo system. They should've known letting him play that many hours would get him hooked.

Kevin definitely didn't feel bad now; his dad had told him to bring over the Nintendo, and his mom said it was fine. He and his dad had all afternoon and even dinnertime to beat Tetris—or at least get as close to beating it as they could.

Kevin didn't notice that the conversation had switched until he'd already answered his father's questions. At first he figured they were about school, but then he realized they were about home. He tried to remember the questions he'd just heard and the answers he'd just given, but all he could think of was the screen showing the falling blocks that needed to be moved around before they landed in the wrong places. He handed his father the controller, but Dad said he'd rather not play, he'd just watch, if that's okay. "I think I need more patience for this kind of thing," Dad said.

Kevin watched his dad, and when it didn't look like his dad was going to say anything more, Kevin stared at the screen too. He thought about continuing his game, but all of a sudden it didn't seem so worth it with Dad staring straight ahead without moving.

"Pretty loud last night," Dad said.

"Yeah," said Kevin. His finger was on the pause button, but he couldn't press it.

"I'm sorry we were so loud last night. We didn't mean to wake you and your sister up but..."

"That's okay," Kevin said quickly.

"Guess the door didn't help much. We thought you couldn't hear us." Kevin's dad paused, and for one of the only times that afternoon, looked right at Kevin, who turned away. "Could you hear us?"

"Not really," Kevin said to the controller. "I was on the couch."

"I saw that. But you didn't come up to the door, put your ear to the door, not once?"

Kevin shook his head. He wanted to start playing again and not listen to any more questions, and he was kind of annoyed with his dad for asking so many, but he knew if he did unpause his dad would get angry, and he sure didn't want that.

Then Dad said, "Your mom was upset because I didn't tell her something I should have.... I had to stay late at work and your mom didn't like that. We were supposed to go out to eat."

"Last night?" Last night was New Year's Eve, and Kevin's father shouldn't have had to work at all—even though he had been gone for part of the day.

"No, not last night. A different night. Right after Christmas, when Grandma was still here. She could've taken care of you but...I dropped the ball."

Kevin nodded again. "You stay at work late a lot, Dad."

"I know. I'm going to be better about that, from now on." In his dad's voice Kevin thought he heard the start of crying—but when his dad talked again his voice was normal: "This is only for a little while. It's temporary, Kevin. Did your mom say anything about last night?"

"Not really. She said I needed to come here."

"Did you—did you want to come here? To see me?"

"Yeah." Kevin was going to add that they were having fun—but he wasn't so sure they were having fun.

"So your mom didn't say anything about me, huh." When it was obvious Kevin wasn't going to speak, his father went on: "It must've been scary for you, huh?"

"Kind of."

"She was angry at me, Kev. Not at you. You understand that, right?"

Kevin's "yeah" sounded small. All his words sounded that way now.

"This doesn't have anything to do with you. It has do with us and what we haven't said to each other. We're just...we're having communication difficulties. Do you know what those are?"

"I think so."

"When two people can't talk to each other the way they should. Your mom and I haven't been talking so well lately. That's all. But we're going to work it out. We're going to see somebody who'll help us talk better." Kevin's dad stopped speaking and Kevin, used to hearing his father, looked up at him, alarmed. His father spoke right to him: "If you feel depressed about this in any way, son...you can talk to me, you know, and I can help you. And if I can't help you then we can find someone who will help you. It's no problem."

"Okay," said Kevin. When would this be over? Maybe it would never be over and he and his father would sit in this bare apartment in between all these unopened boxes, talking for eternity. Kevin had not felt such a strong need to go back to school until now. He would take Mrs. Melton's yelling over this kind of talk any day.

"You know I love your mother very much. And you know I love you and your sister very much."

Kevin said he knew. His finger actually pressed the unpause button right then, and the block started falling. Embarrassed and fearful, gasping a little, Kevin hit the pause button again. He almost looked at his father.

"I'm not a bad guy, Kevin." Kevin's dad looked so serious it was like his skin had turned the color of smoke. "I'm certainly nothing like Dominick's father."

Kevin nodded. This was true. Dominick's stepdad—*not* his real father, his stepdad—was a big biker dude named The

Badger, or sometimes just The Badge. Kevin's dad was not like him at all.

"Maybe you could write Mom a story."

"What?"'

"Maybe you could tell her a story—but on paper—and that would help."

Kevin's dad stared as if he had no idea what to do with the boy's suggestion. Maybe Dad hadn't written "Ten Who Made America!" But he had to have written it—it was in his briefcase!

"That's a thought," his dad said.

This time when Kevin unpaused the game he kept it unpaused. He turned from his father and continued to play.

IV

IN EARLY MARCH Kevin's dad moved back into the house. He brought back all the boxes, set them down in the kitchen and living room, and started opening them right then and there. In about two hours the boxes were all gone and it was like he'd never left. *Almost* like he'd never left. It was obvious to Kevin that now his parents behaved differently around each other; they had hardly ever shown affection, but now they kissed every day. Most of the time it was just a quick peck on the mouth or cheek, and after a while of seeing it so much Kevin grew suspicious. He began to think that maybe his parents were kissing just for his benefit, to prove to him that they loved each other. They'd been told to do this by whoever it was they'd been seeing, and if Kevin weren't there they wouldn't kiss but instead fight. Kevin was convinced of this because of the lack of hugging. To Kevin hugging was just as important—probably more important—than kissing. Kissing was all right, but with hugging you could feel all of someone's love. Kevin wished he could get more hugs. He still remembered how Mrs. Melton had hugged him after school the day before Christmas break began, and although it had felt weird and embarrassing then, he still felt that hug, which was more than he felt from his parents. His parents kissed him and sometimes hugged him—now more than before New Year's

Eve—but none of it seemed real. Kevin couldn't get past the idea that they'd been told, and that he and his sister and their parents were part of an experiment that some guy in a lab was conducting with beakers and Bunsen burners.

Mrs. Melton hadn't been nearly as friendly in January and February as she had been the day school let out for Christmas break. January and February had been filled with tests, science fair project instructions, long division and difficult subtraction problems, memorization of important dates in United States history, and rain—lots and lots of rain, rain pretty much every day. Those two months Kevin would hurry home to avoid getting soaked, get right to work on the homework he hadn't finished in class that day, and then play video games until it was time for dinner. In a way it was good that Melton was giving so much work because it took Kevin's mind off the fact that his dad wasn't there to have dinner with him and his mom and his sister. Those weeknights Kevin and Sandra and their mom would eat in front of the TV, and when they were finished his mom would retreat to the kitchen dining table to grade all the papers that had piled up, and Kevin would either keep watching TV or go back to playing video games or, if he was feeling nervous about a test, study until it was time to turn out the lights. On weekends he and Sandra would visit Dad or Dad would pick them up and take them out, down the hill to the city and to the movies. Kevin's dad never talked about Kevin's mom—and vice versa—in those two months. But Kevin knew they were seeing each other; they had to because they were getting professional help to work on their communication difficulties.

The professional help must have worked because when Kevin's dad came in through the front door that March day carrying the first of many moving boxes, his skin was no longer the color of smoke. He still looked too thin, but now he flashed a smile that Kevin felt was real. The kisses and hugs might not have been entirely real, but at least Kevin's dad was happy to be home.

One workday in March, not long after he'd settled back in, Kevin's dad arrived home early. He wore his suit and tie and glasses. He poured himself something to drink and asked Kevin for the mail. Kevin handed over everything to his dad except for the March/April issue of *Nintendo Power*, the one with *Super Mario Bros. 3* on the cover. This he set on the dining room table. Still standing, he flipped the pages, his eyes widening at the secrets revealed.

"What's that?" he heard his father say.

"My magazine."

"Must be pretty important."

"Yeah...I'm gonna get this game."

Although Kevin's dad didn't say anything, his look said plenty. It was a look Kevin hadn't seen often, but when he did he always wanted to curl up in his room with the door closed. It was the same look his father had given him when he came home the day before and found Kevin doing his homework in front of cartoons. The look then had said Kevin was too old for cartoons, just like the look now said Kevin was too smart for video games.

6. Davy Crockett:

King of the Wild Blue Yonder. Suited up and shipped out as leader of an exploratory mission to the Red Man's planet far far away, across the mighty black Las Vegas-lit ocean that no ship had yet crossed. The Nana, the Santa Barbara, and the Tonto were the names of the three flying saucers under Captain Crockett's command. Braving rough winds, cabin fever and mutiny, the convoy reached the mysterious Red Man's planet in October of 2149. Having landed, Crockett was the first to place his foot in the Red sand, and, driving a stake into the Utterly foreign soil, he proclaimed this new planet property of his majesty the Emperor of America. The next century was spent converting the illegal aliens to Christianity, and a hard, hard rain did fall during that trying time. A commemorative statue of Captain "Rocketman" Crockett now stands where the sun don't shine.

"Hey, Kevin, you got it yet?"

Kevin looked up to find Norman staring down at him with sweat and dust streaked across his exclamation mark face. It looked like Melton had been chasing him again, which would make sense since the day before during afternoon music lesson Norman refused to cross his legs. He'd also snickered—but then a lot of the class had snickered when Mrs. Melton sang the "mountain mama" part of "Take Me Home, Country Roads."

"What?" Kevin said.

"You know..."

Kevin looked down at the cover of his March/April issue. The claymation Super Mario with his raccoon tail smiled at him with one fist raised.

"Oh, yeah. Nah, not yet. My parents are giving it to me for Easter."

"Easter? Why Easter?"

"They give me gifts at Easter."

"Wow, lucky you," Norman said—and he meant it. "My parents don't give me squat for Easter. We just go to church and eat a lot."

"We do too," said Kevin. "Normally. They're in Mexico right now."

"Mexico? Why?"

Kevin hesitated. He was sure his parents had been told to go by the professional helper.

"They..." Again Kevin hesitated, only to seconds later blurt out: "They won a contest."

"No way. You're kidding."

"I'm not kidding. They really did. An all-expenses paid trip to Acapulco."

"So...how come they left you here."

"I have school," Kevin said, as if this was obvious. "Plus my grandma's taking care of me and my sister for a week."

Norman seemed to accept this. He said, "Well, I just got *Super Mario Bros. 3*. I'm playing it over at my house after school today, so..."

Kevin waited. Norman stopped altogether. He also waited. Here the two of them were, waiting for the other to speak when Mrs. M was about to appear and the bell was about to ring.

"So..." Kevin said. He didn't get it. What was Norman trying to say? "I'm playing it over at Dominick's place today."

"Oh, cool. That's cool." Norman's exclamation mark face turned into a period. It also turned bright red. He concentrated on the metal ramp. The bell rang and the other students on the ramp stood up and started forming a single line. Instead of cutting in behind Kevin, Norman turned and walked to the back. Kevin watched him go, wondering what that had been about.

7. Molly Pitcher:

As legend has it, the count was bases loaded with two out and Casey at Bat. No one could stop Casey. He was one mean sumbitch. All others Jell-O-ed in his presence. But not Molly. She came down from the stands at Ebbets Field that fine May Day and strode bravely across the green toward the mound. Bob Hope tossed her the ball. Molly cocked her head and tilted her cap and gritted her eyes. Across the way Casey popped his big league chaw. The crowd hushed. You could drop a needle and never find it. Molly's eyes shimmied to the right, to the left, behind to look out the back of her head, but it was just her and Casey now. So this housewife and part-time mall volunteer wound up her arm tight as an ass in a New England January, and with the collective history of native peoples on her side she let 'er rip! It was the pitch heard 'round the world. After witnessing the Mighty Casey swing air for the third and final time, folks everywhere took hammers and boots and fists to their televisions, and the revolution, at last, was underway.

DOMINICK HAD to have been the only fifth grader in all of Gordon Lawrence Elementary who still had all his toy action figures from when he was really young. We're talking the G.I. Joes, Thundercats, He-Man, Transformers, Star Wars. Kevin missed his Star Wars figures. He especially missed the four-legged AT-AT walker he'd gotten for his eighth birthday. Whenever he was over at Dominick's house and he saw Dominick's open trunk spilling out toy action figures, and his open closet showing the toy vehicles and fortresses, Kevin felt bad about having sold his own stuff at a swap meet two years ago. It was like as soon as the Nintendo entered his life, he had no more room for any of the little kid stuff. It was the kid stuff that made him feel most like a kid.

He and Dominick used to play action figures in Dom's room—not all that much, but sometimes. They stopped on the day Badger walked by the open doorway and stopped to stare at them with his iced over eyes and his big shirtless belly hanging heavy over his jeans. The Badge liked to stroke his long scraggly beard, but he was too angry to stroke it at the sight of Dominick and Kevin talking in their toy figure voices and battling each other.

Kevin couldn't remember much of what The Badger had said that day—definitely something about "sissies," "pansies playing wussy games" and other mean things. The Badge had never actually stepped inside Dominick's room, but from then on Dominick made sure the door was closed at all times, and even then they never again touched the action figures.

Even The Badger had been a kid, right? He must have had toys. Kevin's dad must have had toys, too.

Dominick was quiet as he guided Super Mario through the current realm. Kevin watched, mouth slightly open in awe of his best friend's ability to beat any game.

Still punching the controller's buttons and with his eyes always on the screen, Dominick said, "I hear this is gonna be Melton's last year."

"What?" Kevin's mouth hung wide. He looked at Dominick, and Dominick looked right back at him.

"Don't freak out, Kev. She's just a teacher, remember. It's not like she's your mom or anything."

"How did you, uh...how did you find out? Are you sure?"

"I'm sure. Mrs. Melton told Danny's mom, Danny's mom must've told Danny, Danny told Lance and Lance told me."

"She's just going to leave? Is she going to tell us?"

"I bet she will. She's mean—but she's not *that* mean. Dude, Kev, you sound, like, really scared."

"I just don't understand why she's leaving." Kevin felt like he was going to cry. Dominick was watching him like he expected Kevin to do just that. Dominick's look was a lot like Kevin's dad's look when he saw Kevin reading his *Nintendo Power* magazine or watching *Chip 'n Dale's Rescue Rangers* and doing homework at the same time. It was even, Kevin thought then, a lot like how The Badger had looked at them the day they swore off playing action figures forever.

Dominick was cool as he talked. "Lance said Danny said Melton's moving to Utah."

"Man. Utah," Kevin said.

Dominick said, "Don't you remember how she made you cry all those times?"

"It wasn't that many times."

"Kev. Come on, dude. That's not what everybody told me."

"Who's—who's everybody?"

"Everybody. Everybody in your class who matters. You know, Lance and Tom and Stan...and even some of the girls, like Cassie."

"Cassie?"

"Sure. They know she's made you cry—and they don't think it's fair either. I'm not the only one who thinks something's gotta be done with Melton."

"What are you....Are you talking about killing her?"

"No! No way! I wouldn't kill her!" Dominick laughed, but as he did Kevin twisted to look at the sheathed samurai sword hanging above his best friend's bed.

"Okay," Kevin said, and he turned back around. "So, what then?"

"I don't know. But something. We need to give her a send-off she'll never forget."

"We can't hurt her."

"We won't hurt her," Dominick said. "But we gotta do *something*. I'll think about it. You think about it too."

Kevin nodded without looking at his friend. He hit the start button and moved his thumbs.

8. Daniel Boone:

A brave American if there ever was one. Threw off the

shackles of Civilization to live among the Blessed Beasts and the children of this earth. Trained in the ways of the rifle by a marmot and the spirit of a squirrel. After killing him a b'ar when he was only three, Boone, with nothing left to learn and nothing left to lose, took off for Frontierland. In a final fit of fury, he fought valiantly but died inevitably alongside Uncle Sam I Am and Mickey the Moolah Mouse at the Battle of Bulgy the Bus.

V

June now, and the end of fifth grade was only a few days away. A week earlier Mrs. Melton had told the class she was leaving, but she didn't say she was going to Utah or why.

"She has to live there," Lance said right after the big announcement. "All Mormons have to live there."

"No they don't," said Tom.

"Yeah. Why not?"

"How come Eli's family's still living here?"

"Eli's Mormon?" Dominick said.

"They just haven't gotten the call yet," Stan said.

Kevin wanted to know the truth, so instead of going to morning recess he stayed behind in the classroom. Mrs. Melton asked him what was wrong. She looked like she was about to leave.

"I just want to talk," said Kevin.

"Let me...go to the bathroom, Kevin. I'll be right back."

Melton made him wait outside the locked classroom until she returned. When she did they went back inside and Mrs. Melton sat behind her desk. She shuffled papers and opened a drawer, and Kevin felt she was too busy for him and that he shouldn't be doing this.

"What do you want to talk about, Kevin?"

The shuffling and the opening and closing of desk drawers continued.

"Nuh-nothing." Kevin turned to leave and that's when Melton looked right at him.

"Kevin, it has to be something. What is it? I'm listening."

She'd stopped shuffling and searching, and now it was like she couldn't take her eyes off him.

"Okay. It's just...why are you leaving?"

Mrs. Melton folded her hands in front of her, like she was in church. Her words were as careful as his mom's had been the night the bad thing happened.

"It was a difficult decision, Kevin, but my husband, Mr. Melton, we agreed that San Diego is not the place we want to start a family."

Start a family? Mrs. Melton?

"Oh," Kevin said. "But you're going to Utah?"

Mrs. Melton smiled; at that moment she actually seemed kind. "Yes, we're moving to Utah."

"Will you be teaching there too?"

Mrs. Melton gathered herself by folding her hands in front of her and adjusting her position. "I've decided to rethink teaching. It's a lot of work, and it's not a job you can easily turn off when you go home. Your mom knows all about that, I bet."

Kevin nodded. It seemed like the conversation was over —Melton smiled and nodded at him, and he smiled back and turned to leave. But then the question that came into his mind felt important, it felt like he had to ask it, so he did.

"Is it, uh, hard to start a family?"

The question seemed to tickle Mrs. Melton. "You're an interesting boy, Kevin," she said. "I don't know if I'll ever have another student as sensitive as you."

Kevin waited, and when Melton saw that he really did

want an answer she said, "I don't know yet, we haven't started. But my parents did a pretty good job with me and my sisters."

"You have sisters?"

Mrs. Melton smiled. "And parents. Can you believe that?"

Kevin couldn't—well, the parents, yeah. He wasn't so dumb not to know that *everyone* had parents. But sisters? He'd always thought Mrs. Melton was an only child.

"How old do you think I am, Kevin?"

"Uh...." Kevin's dad had just turned forty and his mom was a year younger than that, so Melton had to be a little younger than them, right? "Um...thirty-five."

Mrs. Melton laughed. It was a more relaxed-sounding laugh than the one she'd given in December. It was also one of only five times she'd laughed all school year.

"I'm twenty-five," she said.

"Oh." Twenty-five was still old, but it was a lot younger than thirty-five.

"How is your family, Kevin?"

"Fine," he said. Then he added: "We're okay."

"That's good to hear."

Kevin knew better than to tell Mrs. Melton about the bad thing, or about how his father had changed after he moved back home. His father was trying to take a more active role in his son's life, he said. He was trying to parent more and to be a better dad all around. That's why he came home from work early now, and why he continued to take Kevin and Sandra places on weekends when Mom was sick or had too much school work to do. One time at the Horton Plaza mall Kevin saw his dad turn to watch a woman walk by, and Kevin felt strange. He thought of Mom. He never said anything to his dad about that moment, but he was tempted to tell it to Melton now.

The bell rang to signal fifteen minutes were up. Already some students were gathering outside, wanting to be let in.

"Why don't you take your seat, Kevin?"

Kevin said okay and did as he was told.

WATCHING Dominick work the controller now, in Dom's room, Kevin knew that his best, really his only, friend, would have handled that situation at the mall differently. Dominick would have asked his father why he'd turned and stared at that woman like he knew her or wanted to know her. Dominick was that kind of guy. He was tough. He didn't take any guff—not even from The Badge really. If Dominick had his real father living with him, and his father had done that at the mall, Dominick would have called him on it, and he would have called him on it with the same coolness and strength he summoned to play Nintendo and practice karate. Dominick was studying the arts of the ninja so that he could one day get rid of The Badger forever.

"Lance said you guys played Twister in your class today," Dominick said as he beeped and bopped, his eyes always on the screen.

It was true; they had played Twister in the afternoon. Mrs. Melton had taken it out of the cupboard in which she was so often searching.

"Lance said Melton looked pretty funny showing you all how to play."

Kevin agreed. But as he spoke he didn't feel like he meant what he said; a week ago he would have meant his words, but not now. Now he just felt like he had to agree.

"Lance said it was you and Cassie and Norman on the mat in the beginning."

"In the beginning," said Kevin. "Norman dropped out because of his circulation."

"That's probably why she made him go first."

"Maybe."

Dominick's low, quiet laughter, the Nintendo beeping and bopping in the foreground.

"She's crazy," said Dominick.

"Plum loco," Kevin said, feeling bad as he said it.

"Plump loco is more like it."

Kevin's laughter was quieter than Dominick's.

"Is she really plump, though?"

"Hell yeah she is."

"I don't know if she's really that...fat."

"Seriously? Kev, dude. You said so yourself at the beginning of the school year."

"I think she lost weight since then. Maybe she exercises."

"I doubt it."

Dominick handed the controller to Kevin. Then he said, "But you got all over Cassie when you were on the mat, right?"

"What? No. We didn't even touch."

Dominick arched an eyebrow. "In Twister?"

"Well..."

"You touched her, Kev. Cough it up, man."

"Okay, we were touching—a little. That's all. It's no big deal."

"It's a big deal when you like her."

"I don't like her."

"Jeez, Kev. Get real. The whole school knows you're in love with her. Why are you lying?"

"I'm not lying!" Kevin paused the game and stared at Dominick, who looked surprised. "I really don't like her anymore."

"Anymore. So you did..."

"Yeah, I did, okay? But I don't now."

"Why not?"

"I just...don't think I should."

Dominick shook his head and said, "It's no big deal, dude. She's just a girl."

"Sure. Just a girl."

Dominick sighed and shrugged off this last comment. He asked if Kevin was going to play. Kevin unpaused the game and punched the buttons hard. He sensed Dominick looking at him, but he didn't care what his friend thought right now. He didn't care what anyone—even himself—thought right now.

After some seconds Dominick said, "We're still going to get her, you know."

"Cassie?"

"No, Melton, man. Melton. Remember what we talked about?"

"You still want to do that? That was, like, three months ago."

"I've been planning it this entire time."

"I don't know…"

"Kevin. I thought you were cool," Dominick snapped.

Kevin felt like he'd been stabbed. He was cool. Did Dominick really think he wasn't? Neither of them could look at each other just then. Was Dominick really even his friend?

The next person to say something was Dominick, and this time he sounded nice. "She's not gonna get hurt, I swear. It'll just be a lot of fun."

"Okay."

"Besides. What do we got to lose? She's not coming back and neither are we. Next year's the middle school all the way."

Dominick was right. Gordon Lawrence Elementary had decided to move next year's sixth graders to the junior high school—part of a pilot program, Mrs. Melton had said. And because Dominick was his friend, the only person Kevin could talk to, he decided Dominick was right about Melton, too.

"What do you want to do to her," said Kevin.

9. Betsy Ross:

Born to parents who never made it past elementary school, Ross spent her formative years in an Indonesian sweatshop, where she labored 13 hours a day, 7 days a week sewing women's undergarments for US consumption. Though her life was a Living Hell, the Dream of America was always with her. In Amerikay, people told her, the streets are paved with gold! And so, at the tender age of nineteen, she emigrated to Old New York, gateway to the new world. The first thing she did was pay a visit to the CEO of the faceless corporation that sold those women's undergarments. The CEO, smitten by her skin-magazine beauty, offered her his hand in marriage and half the money in his coffers. Together they formed a more perfect union that worked to abolish the ACLU, the NGLTA, the NRA, the CIA, the WYSIWYG, the NIMBY, the KAFKA, and the TOLKIEN, all while promoting a more Prostate America. Betsy even sewed together a youth soccer league team banner that read, "This Bomb's for You." Tragically, she and her husband died in a plane crash over the Bermuda Triangle.

THE LAST DAY OF SCHOOL. At a little after nine in the morning all the fifth graders started forming their class lines in preparation to get on the twinkie-mobiles that would take them to the park and their graduation picnic. Kevin waited patiently in the line that had just formed for his class. Up ahead Melton stood at the front, her raised hand clenching and unclenching like a beating heart. This was her signal, and her students knew to look for it. Mrs. Melton wore khaki shorts, a button-up pale blue blouse and sunglasses. Sitting on top of her head like a lazy bird was a wide-brim Panama-style wicker hat, the kind Kevin's dad had gotten in Tijuana one time. Kevin watched the fist clench and unclench, imagined his own heart in Melton's hand.

The park was a little over a mile from school. Already it was teeming with fifth graders by the time Kevin stepped off the bus and onto soft grass. He surveyed the wide flat field and beyond that the barbecue area shaded by thick oak trees. He saw his fellow classmates playing football and soccer. Then he plucked the students, one by one, from the scene, removed them like he was using a magic eraser. Now he saw a park without anyone from Gordon Lawrence in it; instead he saw a great battle between the American revolutionaries and the British red coats. Cowpens. Saratoga. Bunker Hill. He tried to get the battle right, just as he'd seen it mapped out and dramatized in the books he'd checked out from the school library.

Betsy Ross. Molly Pitcher. Johnny Appleseed. His father really had taught him everything he knew.

He saw Dominick over by the barbecue pits. Dominick was sitting on one of the tables and talking to a kid Kevin didn't know. Kevin went over anyway. He had to talk to Dominick about their plan.

"Dom," he said. "So we gonna do it now?"

"Kev," Dominick said. "Chill. My mom's not here yet. We'll do it at the end."

Kevin recognized the tone and immediately backed down. He again wondered if he and Dominick were really best friends, and if they would stay friends in the future. Maybe this was a dream, an idea like the kind his father had about going off and being someone else for a change. It wasn't right, but it wasn't wrong either. He'd just have to do a better job of hiding himself.

Kevin drifted from Dominick and the other kid who were deeply engaged in conversation. He weaved through tables, grabbing a chip here, snagging a soda there, and stopped to watch his classmates around him. Most of the boys were in the field playing sports, but Kevin wasn't interested in any of those games. He'd played soccer for the last three seasons and he'd decided this year would be different. But he didn't have a new sport yet and he wasn't sure which one he should go for. He would ask his dad, only his dad and him weren't speaking so much lately. His dad had started staying at work late again.

A lot of the girls were down in the ravine that ran just beyond the shaded barbecue area. A wood-plank and iron-rail bridge spanned the ravine and led to the other side of the park where the volleyball courts were. The summer sun beat down on the sand that filled these courts, and beyond them, up a short ridge, was the road and all the houses in the hills. Home. Kevin stood at the edge of the ravine and watched some of the girls walking around down there, gossiping about whatever it was they gossiped about. Gossiping about him, maybe. What a crybaby he was in class.

He stared at the empty volleyball courts and thought of Dad. His father used to play volleyball in these pits with some of the local firefighters. Kevin would watch, and whenever a ball went down into the ravine Kevin would go shag it for the guys. His father expected that of him. One time his father made a joke about his son being a dog that was playing fetch. One of the firefighters had laughed, but no one else really. Kevin's dad had stopped playing volleyball about a year ago, when Kevin entered fifth grade.

"Kevin."

He turned to find Mrs. Melton towering above him. She held a heaping plate of food—three hot dogs, chips, salsa, the works.

"Oh, hi, Mrs. M."

"You're not playing with any of the boys?"

"I will," Kevin said. "I'm still deciding."

"Are you hungry?"

"A little."

"Here. Have a hot dog."

"Isn't it yours?"

"I'm not going to eat all three of these. This one's for a hungry student. Here."

Kevin looked around, unsure whether or not he should take it. Maybe he should play with the other students.

"Kevin?"

Kevin took it. He looked the hot dog over for a few moments. Mrs. Melton watched and waited, ready to pounce.

"I hope you like ketchup."

"Sure."

"And mustard and onions. And relish."

"Yeah, all that."

"I don't like relish myself," Mrs. Melton said, "but I figured a hungry student would."

"I don't mind."

Kevin looked around again to make sure no one was watching him with Melton. Then, seeing that the coast was clear, he took a bite.

"Is it good, Kevin?"

Kevin nodded, his mouth full. Melton took a bite of one of her dogs. Together, they chewed in silence.

Finally, Melton said, "Are you excited about next year?"

"Uh-huh."

"Good. You're a good student, Kevin. Don't let anyone ever tell you otherwise."

"I won't."

Kevin wasn't about to tell Mrs. Melton that he didn't want to be a good student. A good student meant a nerd, a loser. Kevin wasn't so good as to be that bad. He was cool. He might not have been as cool as Dominick or Lance or Tom, but he was cool in his own way—right? He would just have to be better at *not* being a good student when he got to the middle school. Then Dominick would be his friend all the way, and he wouldn't have to worry about just how good of friends they really were.

"Someday," Melton said. "Someday you may come visit me. You're always welcome to."

"But you'll be in Utah."

"Maybe you'll be in Utah too, someday."

"I don't think so," Kevin said. "I'm not Mormon."

Mrs. Melton laughed a little. She shook her head, looking embarrassed—but Kevin couldn't tell if she was embarrassed she was Mormon or embarrassed to be around him.

He couldn't visit Mrs. Melton in the future. That would be ridiculous! Mrs. Melton as an old lady with glasses and gray hair and wrinkly skin, warming her food in the microwave, setting out tea and cookies for him. And Kevin in a suit, not married, never married—but a professional. A professional at something.

"Give me a hug, Kevin."

Before Kevin could say a word Melton had wrapped her arms around him and drew him against her. Kevin was surprised to find how warm her body was. Even though they were in the shade, Mrs. Melton felt like she had the sun inside her. She was burning up—but in a good way, a way that Kevin liked. He felt something he hadn't expected from her: love. She loved him, or at least cared about him. It was strange, but Kevin held on, not wanting this to end. Whenever he hugged his mom and dad now he would just give a couple quick pats on their backs as they hugged him, which was not very often of course, but with Mrs. Melton now he didn't pat, he hugged her back fiercely, and he knew then that he'd been wanting to do this for the last half of the school year, since January.

Kevin shut his eyes tight, not caring that Dominick and some of the other fifth graders were watching him.

"Take care, Kevin," Mrs. Melton whispered in his ear.

If she had kept hugging him for even thirty seconds more, Kevin would have started crying, but she let go after about ten seconds and Kevin was saved the real embarrassment. Still, when he saw Dominick he knew he was in trouble.

"That was awful," Kevin said when he came up to Dominick, who was still sitting on the picnic table, his feet on the bench.

"Didn't look like you thought it was so awful."

"I did," Kevin said. "You don't believe me?"

Dominick looked him over, like Kevin was a bug under a microscope. Then he said, "I'll believe you. Are you in love with her?"

"What? No. She's my teacher."

"So, you can be in love with your teacher. Tell the truth, dude."

"This is the truth," Kevin said, and he felt his eyes getting watery. Why was Dominick like this to him? What had happened? What was going on?

"Then prove it," Dominick said. "My mom's here, so let's do this thing."

Dominick and Kevin walked across the playing field and over to the paved street where Dominick's mom waited. Dominick's mom was standing by the side of her mini-van. She was a short woman with long straight hair and a frog's voice because she smoked a lot, every day, every time Kevin went over to Dominick's house.

Dominick's mom slid open the side door to the mini-van and leaned inside. She took out a large duffel bag and handed this to her son. Dominick thanked his mother and she nodded, told him to have fun and be careful. Don't get too crazy with these. Kevin smiled too. He liked Dominick's mom, even though she smoked and Kevin's grandfather had died of smoking when Kevin was younger. Dominick's mom was kind and not too strict. She was the total opposite of The Badge, who made all these rules like you have to be in bed by this time at night, and you have to eat a certain way at the dinner table, and you have to eat the food I cook (even though it was awful), and your friends can't call before this time and after this time, and you can't talk on the phone for too long.

Dominick set the duffel bag in the grass and unzipped it. Inside were four water launchers, big cannons the kind you save up a whole year for—or just ask for at Christmas. Dominick looked at Kevin and grinned. Kevin grinned right back. Lance and Tom had brought balloons and had filled them up when the teachers weren't looking, and now they had them hidden behind some of the trees, ready for Dominick's call to action.

Still grinning, Dominick handed Kevin not one but two big guns already filled to the cap. Kevin felt extra-special now. He felt honored. He hoped Dominick saw him as his best friend, too.

Then, with a mighty cry that turned heads on the field, Dominick raised both his water cannons and ran. Kevin let loose his own war cry and followed his friend. Together they raced across the field. They looked brave, magnificent, like soldiers in the Charge of the Light Brigade, Hessian mercenaries at the Battle of Cowpens, Confederates at the Battle of Bull Run. Across the field Kevin saw his fellow students disappearing in clouds of smoke and flashes of gunfire. Now the field was littered with craters and bodies, and only he and Dominick remained to confront the enemy, and there she was, Melton, seated at a picnic table talking with Dominick's teacher, Mr. Watson. The two targets heard the battle cries but it was too late to counter the charge. Kevin and Dominick came right up to them and unleashed powerful blasts right in their faces! The blast from Kevin's cannon knocked Melton's hat right off her head. Melton took a mouthful of water, gurgled and spit it back up like she was brushing her teeth.

Her sunglasses hung on. Mr. Watson was not wearing a hat and got it even worse. Face, hair and shirt drenched, he looked like he'd just been dipped upside down in the park's swimming pool. "Dominick!" he shouted.

Melton was garbling and yelling, and for a moment Kevin stopped. But then Lance and Tom crept up behind Melton and Watson with water balloons in hand. They hurled the initial grenades at the teachers' backs and the second wave—as Melton and Watson turned—at their chests.

"Aaaaah! Kevin!" Melton cried. "How could you, Kevin? How could you?" She got up from the table and lurched forward.

"Winner of the Wet T-Shirt Contest!" Lance shouted. He pointed to Mrs. Melton as he spoke. "Winner of the Wet T-Shirt Contest!"

Kevin had seen enough to know Mrs. Melton's blouse had soaked through. He did his best to avert his eyes. No going back now. He focused on Dominick instead. Dominick was laughing, so Kevin laughed too. He backpedaled along with his friend and dodged his teacher's advances. He continued to slam Melton with gushfuls of water, so much water she began to look like a big waterlogged cat. Her usually puffy curly electrified hair now hung limp, and her blouse and shorts were dark and her eyes blurry. A couple of times she got close, but Kevin always got away from her, and every few seconds he would launch more water and laugh. He felt all eyes on him now, all the eyes of every fifth grader at Gordon Lawrence Elementary. He saw tall and lanky Mr. Watson chasing after Dominick, Dominick turning and firing like a cowboy in an old western. He heard his classmates all around him cheering and shouting and laughing, and he saw Melton get a water balloon square on top of her head. She staggered, then came at Kevin once more. "Kevin, I'm going to get you" she screamed. "Look what you've done!"

"It's fun. It's just water, Mrs. Melton! You think we'd use *bullets*?"

No bullets, Kevin thought. Not in a park. Not on a beautiful June day. Not in America, the land of the free, where students could mess with their teachers and go unpunished. His dad had taught him that, too.

Boys and even some of the girls were at the tall iron faucets over by the barbecue pits filling up water balloons. They too ran after their teachers. It was beautiful anarchy, a breakdown of everything ordered and essential, and Kevin had been the cause of it.

Melton took another balloon in the back. She turned, distracted, and Kevin raised his water cannon, came right up to her, and fired. The stream was weak this time; Kevin knew he was running low on ammo and didn't have time to refill. Melton might get him and hang him out to dry, so he turned and ran. He ran away from the oak trees and into the sun, and there was Dominick by his mom's mini-van, the getaway car, waving his arms and shouting for Kevin to get in.

Kevin glanced back and saw Mrs. Melton running for him, focused on just him. She looked like a fullback ready to make a fabulous tackle. If she tackled him he was dead. But there was no way she would tackle him now.

One of the teachers yelled out the announcement that it was close enough to one o'clock to send everyone home. Those remaining fifth graders on the field and under the oak trees and in the ravine cheered the end of the school year and the start of summer. They cheered and then ran in all directions, away from the park, down the streets and toward their homes close by.

Kevin stopped and turned just once before reaching the mini-van. In that moment of turning he saw Mrs. Melton, his teacher no more, panting and puffing, the sun and water and sweat on her face. She looked at him, her eyes narrowed, and

Kevin swore he saw her smile. That was the end. The school year was over. He was out of trouble.

WHEN HE GOT HOME his mother and father were both present, though they were getting ready to leave for their appointment. The babysitter would be by soon.

Kevin walked to his room at the back of the house, past Sandra's door through which he could hear the music blasting, and when he got to the doorway his heart just about stopped.

On his bed was the story his father had or had not written, those few pages Kevin had been reading by the light of the open microwave. They had been arranged in order, just as he'd first found them. Kevin went to the manuscript and sat on the bed. He held the pages in his hands. He heard his father's voice from the doorway.

Did you have a good school year?

Yeah, I did, Dad.

Learn a lot?

You bet.

History. Philosophy. Art. Politics. Music. Science.

All of that, Dad.

Citizenship?

Kevin nodded. He loved his dad, but it was time to let him go.

He set the pages aside. This time he wouldn't cry. He would stay strong. Someday, perhaps years from now, he would learn the truth.

10. Paul Revere:

Pray tell, Children, have Ye heard of the midnight ride of Paul Revere?

A Hollywood stuntman by trade, Paul worked for seventeen years in "the industry" before Disillusionment slammed home and he took off a ramblin' and a rollin' on a rootin' tootin' road trip cross-country to Boston, the place of this country's premature birth. Paul got a job as the town crier, and after a week he was a crying like the best of 'em, crying up and down the streets, on the T, telling folks when it was bedtime. But Paul fell victim to Temptation. A fellow crier convinced him to start moonlighting as a drag racer, and so at midnight, when the crier's shift traditionally ended, Paul and his compadre, his amigo, his head honcho of affairs and entanglements, dressed up in drag and drove off together into the Wilds of New Hampshire.

(live free or die, Cleveland Elementary is Nigh)

One night, oh starry starry night, the napalm bursting in mid-air, Paul let the speed get to him. He overcompensated on Dead Man's Curve and went over Blind Man's Bluff, but he did not die. No, Children, he did not die. For Paul was destined for Great Things in this Country, and as soon as his Lamborghini, that kind, crafty, resilient machine, hit the ground without exploding, he pointed it in the direction of the city and so sped down the streets, rapping at every window, rousing all the Bostonians with this, his famous cry: "The redcoats are coming! The Redcoats are Coming! THE REDCOATS ARE COMING..."

But by this time no one knew what he meant.

America's Finest City

I

THE TRAGEDY BEGINS as it usually does for you: in someone else's bed.

She is blonde, but not Midwestern blonde like your wife. She is San Diego blonde, her long strands streaked with darker shades threatening to overwhelm the light. Watch that hair in the late afternoon sun as she lies on her side, her back to you. She is naked, and you have to get your clothes on.

As you're pulling on your khakis she turns, breathes audibly and looks at you with half-lidded eyes. You want to say those eyes are almond-colored, but you know you'd be wrong.

"Is it time already?" she says, her voice a murmur.

"I gotta get back. Long drive, you know."

"Tell me where you live again?"

"You know where I live. It's not that easy to forget."

"It's a Latin word, isn't it?"

"Anomar," you say. "I live in Anomar. It's Latin and Spanish. 'Year of the ocean.'"

"Year of the ocean?"

Sigh. When you speak, it's as someone who's had this information fed to him from a young age. "The story goes that Anomar is where land first rose out of the ocean at the beginning of the world, billions of years ago."

"No shit."

"Bullshit is what I say. I'm pretty sure a council member came up with it decades ago to sell the town to tourists, as if there would ever be any."

"Still," she says, and she turns on her back and looks at the ceiling and closes her eyes. "Anomar.... It sounds so exotic."

"It's really not. It's a cow town. We have an ostrich for a mayor."

"You do not!"

"Yes we do. His name's Ozzy. Its."

"Ozzy the Ostrich. That's so cute!"

Cute. She also said, after swallowing your sperm, 'yummy!' Your wife would never say 'cute' or 'yummy.'

Pull your shirt on and start buttoning. You can't really look at this woman right now. You'll see enough of her tonight on the evening news.

She rolls onto her other side to observe you. Her eyes are all the way open now. "I want to go," she says.

"Where?"

"To Anomar."

"You're not going to Anomar."

"I can do a story, a profile."

"I've done enough of those. I might as well be writing a book."

"But you can't stop me," she says, and now she's on her stomach, the sheets kicked off, and your eyes move down her body, resting at last on her buttocks, the tan line in the shape of a whale's tail that reminds you of a magazine cover you saw on stands five years back.

"I can stop you," you say without averting your gaze.

"Come here," she says, and she pats a spot on the mattress next to her. Back and forth, back and forth her ankles swing, pendulum-like, upended in the air.

"I have to go." Continue buttoning your shirt.

"I have to go too," she says abruptly, and she gets up and searches the floor for her clothes. "I need to be earlier to the station anyway."

"I'm sure," you say, just to say something. "I wonder how many people they get checking in here then checking out two hours later."

"You'd be surprised," she says, and with those words you know you must end this latest affair.

IT IS WELL after four when you merge onto the 163 headed north. This summer you got your first cell phone, and you're thankful now for the ability to call from the car. The conversation goes as best it can, considering you have only one hand on the wheel and vehicles are threatening to careen into you as you maneuver between lanes for the most advantageous position. Tell your wife traffic is tight. She understands. You won't be home for a while, but definitely in time for dinner. Cut her off when she starts to ask how the press association conference went. It's too dangerous to talk now. Too much traffic all around—and the traffic's moving now. Sorry, honey.

Hit the button to hang up then throw the device onto the seat next to you. That wasn't really close. You've done this before. With a former high school classmate, with a woman interviewed on assignment, with the trips you've taken, conferences attended, all in the name of boosting the *Anomar*

Cryer's reputation, you've become something of an expert on infidelity, you think.

But not, apparently, an expert at driving. The car ahead has suddenly slammed on its brakes and you, lucky you, have just enough time in which to stop before you barrel into the back. Hear the screech of tires, your tires, swear you smell burning rubber, fear the catapulting of your car—it can all be over in this instant, you will never know how it turns out with Jess and Stephen, the woman and child you promised to love. But, lucky you, your car does stop in time, a hair's breadth from the back bumper. Exhale relief on that one. Shake it off through your fingers. Your hands ten-and-two on the wheel. You really shouldn't look at yourself so much in the rearview mirror. No wonder your sign is Leo.

Using your shirtsleeve, dab the perspiration from your forehead. Picture again how close you came to the end. It's comeuppance, you think. Bad juju, karma. A higher power is judging you from above. It'll do you in, eventually. You're sure of that now.

ON YOUR WAY through Poway think about stopping in for a haircut. At the very least it'll calm you down, take your mind off the tragedy that's unfolding in you. Finally admit there's no time for such a splurge now. It's already close to six. It's also the last day of August, and with the start of some schools the traffic throughout San Diego County has picked up. Now that you're in North County though your car has some breathing room. You should be home in about half an hour. A haircut—just a quick trim—would tack on at most, what, twenty minutes? Twenty-five tops? You've eaten after seven before. Not only that, Jess has fed Stephen long past seven, even though it's not ideal for him. And then your wife is out the door, on her way to the hospital for another night shift of nursing.

If you're not home in time to eat dinner and partake in the changing of the guard, though, Jess's guilt trip will have no end. You've cut it as close as you can this evening—best not to risk rolling your dice off the table's edge. So just out of Poway connect to the tough part of Poway Road, better known to native Anomarans like you as 'The Grade.' Shift your '88 Nissan Sentra, that little tin can, into second gear to compensate for the steepness. A few cars are behind you, but none of them honk. You are thankful for their patience.

The rattling of your Sentra annoys you, so turn the radio louder to your favorite station, 103.7 The Planet. Listen to Steely Dan's "Peg," a song you like that not everyone you know likes, including Jess. You're pretty sure your latest mistress, the newscaster with whom you spent this afternoon, would like it, if you were to play it for her. She likes a lot of kitschy things, your mistress. A lot of kinky things, too. Like her leg being stroked, gently, up and down, just one leg, like a mannequin's. Not a foot fetish—a leg fetish. Not even she can explain why it turns her on, but it does. Always has.

You'd be surprised. Inside, you shudder. How often has she been to that hotel? With how many men? How many married men? The thought of all of them in line, and you among them, angers you. In some way, you are going to end this.

As The Grade plateaus then bottoms out, you see the intersection for highway 67. Turning right will take you south to El Cajon and the San Ysidro-Tijuana border. You turn left for Anomar. The road is wide and welcoming in the decreasing daylight. Rock-strewn fields roll up to touch flawless blue sky. Iron Mountain is in the distance to your right.

You take your time, letting other cars pass by.

True, you've seen all this before, driven this road so many times, and yet you remain fascinated by your surroundings.

How strange this countryside can exist side-by-side the city of San Diego, its suburbs and exurbs, the county a double-door, one side coastal the other rural, inland, sparsely populated.

Mount Rocoso, heavily shrubbed and peppered with boulders, looms on your left, the roofs of houses nestled in amongst the green and brown hues. As you continue along the highway, now densely lined with trees, roads turn off to either side, leading to paths you've never been on and probably never will.

If you could look at your wife this way, if you look at Jess the way you look at this drive, then perhaps you wouldn't feel the need to cheat on her. You've seen her so many times; couldn't you remain fascinated by her just the same? Couldn't every man in this situation?

The road curves, but you break free from the tree-lined part soon enough and now you're in The Valley of the Cleansed, Anomar's nickname. On your left is the high cattle-less plain and the lone farm house you've suspected since you were a child is haunted. On your right are the field and corrals where the Anomar Rodeo is held every year in May, when the weather is pleasant as a silkworm's silk.

You can head straight on to Main Street Anomar, but you have to be home so turn right on Elders Road. On either side unbroken pastures reveal cattle, pigs and horses feeding fenced-in and close to their owner's dwellings.

The stench of chickens smacks you straight up your nostrils. The heat has only intensified this rankness you encounter every time you drive along Elders Road. You really are a victim of where you live, always have been. If only you could find a way out to avoid 'always will be.'

Mounting the bend in the road means you have passed the two giant chicken farms. In the hills beyond must be underground crystal meth labs. You're sure they exist, your certainty bolstered by articles in the *San Diego Union-Tribune* that claim the backcountry of San Diego County is one of the leading manufacturers of crystal meth.

At the end of Elders turn right on Vincenzo Road, which will take you to the San Diego Country Gems, the only middle-class residential sprawl in Anomar, a town with a population of just over 20,000. The San Diego Country Gems is an odd area: hilly, wild, yet entrenched throughout the land are individualized homes dating back to the early 1970s. No cookie cutters here. At night coyotes can be heard howling in the hills behind the homes. Creeks run through woods inhabited by serpents and furry critters. Seeing the San Diego Country Gems for the first time, your uncle commented that the area looked like the Holy Land.

Eyes on the road. Thoughts on your work now. Both of your women are headed to work tonight, and so are you. Think about what to pitch your editor tomorrow. You lost out to a rival reporter on that story about the AHS history teacher whose body was found in a massive nest of black widows in her cellar. A sensational story like that comes around only once in a very long while, so you need to create your own sensationalism. What will catch Piangi's ear, capture his heart? Lately, your thoughts have been turning to the high school, your alma mater. Sure, Anomar High has its own newspaper, on which you served as an editor in your junior and senior years, but recently incidences have occurred that you believe demand a professional's investigative journalistic skills.

When you attended Anomar High in the late eighties and early nineties, the years of the elder Bush's presidency, the school was tame. Tame and lame. Nothing truly newsworthy happened. Nothing sensational. AHS was just another high school in the United States of America.

But last year, in the spring of 2000 and in the wake of Columbine, the mood on campus began to change. You could see it in the articles published in the school newspaper, which as a former editor you still receive. It was an election year then, and the anxiety over which presumed poison to pick, even though the number of seniors who could vote was negligible, proved to be palpable. Not only that, but several more students than usual began acting out. Fights were frequent, tagging happened when it never had before, and a bomb threat was called in. Even though it turned out to be a nonfunctioning pipe bomb, a message of fear had been sent.

This past school year, the 2000-2001 term, was the worst yet. Far more fights, a knife drawn, expulsions, another pipe bomb, this one primed correctly, and the ultimate kicker: the threat of a school shooting. So far nobody has been killed, no property destroyed beyond repair, but you have to ask yourself and the citizens of your little town: what is going on? You're convinced there must be reasons, and you're convinced you're the reporter to uncover those reasons and publish them in a series of brilliant, blazing exposés in the *Anomar Cryer*. Writing about the high school's changing psyche—the psyche of a nation—its students and parents and teachers and administrators, will be tricky, challenging, but if you succeed, as you're convinced you will, you will have written your ticket to the big time, possibly even a position at the *Union-Trib*, or the news station where your mistress anchors. Your idea will necessitate talking to countless people, conducting hard-hitting interviews, on-the-ground detective work, going into homes and learning about inner lives. You will open up the whole heart of the town.

Watch out. Ease up on the gas. Take that curve slowly. Get too caught up in your plan and you'll end up dead. Concentration on this jagged, treacherous road in between town and the Gems is crucial. You don't want to end up like those two teenage girls who, one rainy day, hydroplaned their car off Vincenzo and into a tree since removed. At least rain was at work on their tires then. What's your excuse, besides karma?

You so desperately want to do what *she* does, the big-time. You're tired of small town stagnation, the inadequacy you feel whenever you attend these county press conferences in the city. You were born here, grew up here, graduated high school here, and you are on the path to retire and die here. There has to be more to it than that. Has to be. Even your parents managed to get out a few years back, and they're still not retired.

You are now entering the Country Gems. On your right is the Vincenzo Country Club golf course edged by condos. On your left is the corner convenience store where on weekends you have picked up sandwiches for you and Jess. Turn left off of Vincenzo onto your street promising yourself you will begin practicing your pitch as soon as you step through the front door. As much as you want out of Anomar and into the city, you are realistic enough to know the move won't happen overnight. It's going to take both work and time, and it'll take you sticking it out here in Anomar a while longer. The irony: you know you won't be able to execute your big, brazen idea with her on your mind and bugging you every day. Make a vow to cut it off with the newscaster tonight, as soon as your wife is out of the house and you can press the buttons on your cell phone.

YOU ENTER the house to find Jess stretched out across the living room sofa, reading the current issue of *The New Yorker*. An NYC travel guide lies open-faced on the coffee table close by. She's been on a real New York kick lately, your wife. She has to be. She's anticipating her trip to the Big Apple to see her best friend from college. You've agreed to go. You've also never been to New York. You'd hate to miss out.

"I was really starting to get worried," she says and sits up. "Dinner's ready. I gotta eat pretty quick."

"I know," you say, as you've been saying for so many nights since Jess's schedule shifted. She's promised you the 9 p.m.s to 7 a.m.s won't last forever. Problem is she stopped making that promise a while ago. Set your satchel on the coffee table, the same coffee table you dislike because of its surface: a mirror. You still have not gotten used to seeing yourself in a table.

"How was the conference?"

Jess stands up and comes around the coffee table, her arms open. Allow her to wrap around you, feel her softness and warmth that will be nonexistent tomorrow morning after ten hours among the recovering and the dying.

"Okay," you say. "Met some people, did some networking but, you know, it's really just a lot of self-congratulatory back-patting. Always will be."

Jess doesn't suspect, but she reaches into your pockets just the same. There her hands stay, on your wallet and keys. Could she have found an eyelash? A nail? An earring? A little red sequin? A strand of long semi-blonde hair? In all modesty there's nothing she could have found. You have been so careful these past months, this past year. You've watched a lot of movies, read a lot of books late at night, researching every possible scenario. Your affairs have been airtight. When you kiss your wife, it's as if you've never kissed anyone else. She is soft yet strong, and you feel now you could live inside her.

"Thank you for being here, Honey Pie," she says after your lips part.

Smile at the origin of 'Honey Pie,' an affectionate term that dates back to when you and Jess started seeing each other at Ball State University in little Muncie, Indiana; when you both admitted *The White Album* was your all-time favorite; when you smoked pot together for the first time, singing along breezily to "Honey Pie" while you had trouble flipping the lighter to flame. Those were the days, the days in the mid-nineties when you should've been studying journalism at

Purdue, bound for Chicago or New York to make a name for yourself, not headed back to your little California hometown to work for the *Anomar Cryer*.

"How's Stephen?"

"He managed to eat something and get to sleep, thank God. Go see him. I'll get the food on the table."

Head through the hallway and into the baby's room, where your son is at peace in his crib, his thumb in his mouth. A multi-colored plastic mobile circles above.

Stare down at your son and hope his brain is growing correctly, the synapses connecting properly; that the doctor wasn't lying when she claimed Stephen's head was not a receptacle for mush at birth. That, while you were gone today, Jess did not hit the child with a pillow to stop him from crying. Impossible, your wife doing such a thing. She takes care of people for a living. Surely she will take care of your son.

That the brain will grow strong, will grow into the best brain in the class—every class in which your son raises his hand held high. This brain will thrive, conquer.

But in order to do so it will need financial support. Some time ago you and Jess, with the support of both your parents, started putting money away for Stephen's college education, and so far you have not withdrawn from that fund. You do not plan to, although the payments are accumulating, the upkeep of this house—your childhood home built in 1974, the year you were born—is proving to be more costly than anticipated. You should move into an apartment in a true exurb of San Diego—El Cajon or La Mesa or Chula Vista or Lemon Grove—turn freelance and really make a go of it with your writing. But the thought of severing yourself from the paper you've known for so long frightens you. Piangi is your friend. You have a lot of friends there, a valuable support system that gives you the praise you crave. It's not like anyone outside Anomar is going to acknowledge your work. Why, the

Anomar Chamber of Commerce is set to give you an award for excellence soon!

Hear your wife whisper from the doorway that it's time to eat. Turn from your son, careful not to make a sound, and exit the room.

IN THE BRIEF time in which you have to eat your dinner of trout a la Navarre, brown rice and orange arugula salad, Jess anxiously inquires about your status for the New York trip. Tell her yes, as far as you know you are still fine to take off that second week in September. Unless Anomar is the epicenter of a calamitous earthquake affecting all of San Diego County, you're sure Piangi will approve your request for time off.

Jess's eyes are bright and calm. "I'm so glad you're going," she says. "It means a lot to me. I know how you are about flying."

Nod and pick at your food. "September should be fine to fly," you say. "What I'm more worried about is Thanksgiving. It's going to be really busy and, you know, it's Indiana. Not the best place to fly into."

"Honey, we've been over this...."

You have been over this, so many times. Alaska Airlines. American Eagle. Egypt Air. US Air. The flight names, numbers, dates and crash locations flash randomly in your mind, popping up like lights in a pinball machine. 990. 4184. 427. 261. 1994. 1999. 2000. This year should be safe, but still. Go to Kokomo in November and you not only must contend with Stephen's wailing on the plane, the unpleasant flight itself, and the unwelcoming weather but in-laws as well. You'll have to yet again discuss the finer points of the special coating in non-stick pans with Marion and the causes of the 1900 Boxer Rebellion with Frederick. These conversations will take up space in your mind better suited for ideas, pitches, words that could help you break free of the rut you've found yourself in for the last five years.

Twenty-seven. You're sure it has a lot to do with the fact that you turned twenty-seven in July. Twenty-seven could be the new mid-life crisis age. That would mean you'll live only until fifty-four, maybe fifty-five at most. The way Piangi works his staff at the *Anomar Cryer*, that seems about right.

Too bad Marion and Frederick didn't move out to California—to San Diego County—when their daughter asked if they'd consider doing so. They could have, they really could have. They're retired, unlike your parents, both of whom will be working until they die in their saddles. You love your parents, and you thought you would grow to love your in-laws. Turns out you've fallen victim to the cliché: you'd rather not spend any time with them. They're not your type. They continue to delude themselves into thinking Jess will move her family to her hometown after spending some time in California. They refuse to acknowledge that Jess is happier here, she doesn't get so down, she likes the southern California weather and culture. She'll never leave, but then she also won't outright tell them she's never moving back to Indiana. This will come to a head someday, you're sure. You're sure you still love your wife, sure you can afford your son and the mortgage your parents left you with. You're sure. You're sure that's not the first strand of gray hair you see, sure you have more good clippings than middling ones, sure the pages upon pages of false starts and wasted time were for something. They were for Stephen, the end game. It all goes back to him. He is the one keeping you together—and he doesn't know it. Without him, you don't know where you'd be, whom you'd be living with. This is the truth, for which you promise you will not let him go to waste. You will make ends meet. His birth will not have been in vain.

Jess drops her utensils, wipes her mouth and rises. "I gotta get out of here," she says.

"Go for it," you say. The irony of her commute down the hill to Poway four nights a week is not lost on you. Watch her come around the table and lean in. Allow her to kiss you on the mouth. Miss her terribly even before she's left.

LIKE AN ANCIENT OR A SCHOOLCHILD, you sit cross-legged with your hands folded in your lap. Soaked with rain, head tilted back, eyes open.

The rain blinds. Your mouth collects water. You cannot move, cannot close your mouth to save yourself from drowning.

All at once awake.

The nightmare sound of rain shifts into the real waking sound of Stephen's wailing. He is really going at it. Lift your head and take account of your surroundings. You're in the living room, lying on the sofa, the NYC travel guide at eye level. Beyond that is the bright flickering of your twenty-six inch TV. Through your dull groggy haze you see a commercial for a brand of jeans slip into a commercial for a kind of car. Watch until that commercial ends and a new one begins. You can't keep doing this. Something has to give. But these are empty statements, clichés. 'This' and 'Something' can't be defined. You want out—but then that too is a tired wish. Everyone wants out. Everyone comes to the realization that they didn't accomplish enough in their early years. Everyone yearns to return to youth. Everyone regrets.

Enough of this. Tend to Stephen already, why don't you.

To your son's room you bring your cell phone. You have a congealing idea of why. A memory cornering an earlier part of the day in which you promised yourself to make the call and say the words you should have said to her face. It must end tonight. Or, to be more exact, this very early morning. Your cell phone displays the time as 1:06 a.m. 1:06 a.m. on Saturday, September 1ˢᵗ, 2001. Fewer than two hours earlier you were watching your mistress on the eleven o'clock news. She looked good. Her hair was lighter, more of Jess's blonde. She must have been touched up. Her eyes certainly looked bright, her body all but spilling out of her pantsuit. You'd thought about her a lot while watching, thought about the few times you've spent together since you were introduced at a county press association function almost a year ago. It took you a while to bed this one; you had to go through a few other unrelateds first. But when you did the hunt proved worth it. You didn't even take your ring off like you did with the others. You didn't have time.

At some point, you succumbed to the flickering and the chatter. But now you're up and at 'em, in the midst of changing your son's diaper. His stench smacks you straight up the nostrils and assaults your senses more than the chicken farms you pass by on Elders Road. Work quickly to get 'er done. The faster you move your hands and fingers, the sooner it'll be over.

Stephen is still crying even when he has on a fresh diaper. He wants his father, or it could be he wants his mother, the professional caregiver he's more attuned to anyway. If your son were an article for the *Cryer* you could give him care. Lots and lots of attention to detail. You'd make sure he came out perfect. Unlike you.

Holding your son is a funny thing. You feel like laughing. He's just so small, so desperate for attention, like you. Maybe you both could go on one of these new reality TV shows —*Survivor: Anomar* with you, your son, and why not throw in Ozzy the Ostrich for good measure, the mayor skittish and flappy, eyes blinking rapidly. These thoughts at one in the morning, with that call still to be made.

Bounce your son lightly under one arm with your other hand bracing him by the back of his head. Shush sweet nothings in his ears until he settles down. Show him the love you really do have for him, despite these ridiculous thoughts and fears. These cravings. You would never let your newscaster-mistress come over to your house when Jess is at work, but you have thought of it, and you think of it again now. The call could go either way, really. A breakup or an insinuation she might just take you up on. You assume it would lead to nothing—no way a woman like that is going to drive the forty miles up to Anomar in the dead of night. You hope it would lead to nothing, if that's how it's going to play out. Jess has never come home early from her night shifts; she rarely gets sick. Still, it's dangerous. It's playing with your son's future, and you'll have none of it, anymore.

Stephen calm now and once more in his crib, you turn and start punching in her cell number even before you're out of the room. You've been careful to leave no trace of her on your phone, which you keep with you at all times, even by your head at night and beside the shower and toilet in the morning. The records of your calls to each other are always deleted immediately after completion. As your cell phone bill goes directly to you, in your name, you have complete control over what not to reveal. With the past mistresses, seen over the past year, you had to use your work phone, speaking in code they knew about from your initial advances. It was for the job, you would claim, if Piangi or anyone else questioned the phone bill or call log. Always for the job. A source needed to be verified. I wanted to make sure the quote was correct. I had to get permission, see what alias she wanted used.

The cell phone is different, though. It's all on you if you're found out. Only you won't be found out. She's not in your list of contacts, of course, and if you get voicemail this very early morning, as with every time you call, you won't leave a message. It's that simple, and you're that good.

Imagine your surprise when you get her actual voice on the second ring. "Can't sleep?" she says.

A moment as you panic, realizing you had expected and hoped to get her voicemail instead. You recover just before it gets too awkward. "Yes," you say. "Although I did...uh..."

"Were you watching me?"

"Of course."

"What were you thinking about?"

"I was thinking about...."

At this point the two of you would engage in phone sex, as you've done before on these nights when Jess is away at work. But, clamping your teeth down on your upper lip, you press forward with your plan.

"I was thinking about us."

"Us?"

"You...and me."

"You and me."

Her voice does not sound groggy at all. She must have been awake when you called. With someone else. Another. Push the murky form of the man from your mind and concentrate on her voice. Such a cheery voice, like the news, even when it's delivering tragedy. She is two years older than you, but she sounds younger than your wife.

"Yes," you say. It's the only word that comes to mind just then. You had so many more words formulated, and now you find yourself worse off than Stephen, he who has yet to speak.

"Is this it then?"

Instead of saying 'yes' again, you catch yourself. Don't say that. Say, "I just don't think I can do this anymore. I mean that. I like you. I really do. But, I was with my son tonight. My wife and my son. I know I told you I'd never bring her up, but I have to. I was with her, and I was with Stephen, and I'm in my home, and I just want to stay here. I want to stay right here. I don't want to go to the city anymore. I love the city. I do. But..."

"I understand," she says. Her voice sounds emotional.

"You do? Really?"

"I do." Now she sounds as if she's speaking to a child. Her voice is soft and guarded. She's shriveling up.

"You deserve someone else," you say. "Someone who lives in the city."

"Don't say that."

You just did. A moment of silence ensues. The moment turns into an extended period of time, then into a full-fledged lull that threatens to overwhelm. Before it can, you say, "I guess...that's it then."

"Bye," she says.

"Bye."

Press the button to hang up your cell. That was easy. Tap the phone to your lips. Too easy. Something could happen. But what? She has nothing on you. And it's not like you're going back to the city anytime soon. You may never go to her territory again. The more you avoid the city, the safer you all will be.

Yes. You are staying right here.

II

YOU CAN'T BELIEVE IT. You just can't. And you had such a nice weekend, too. One of those Labor Day weekends you really did not want to see end. Jess had Saturday, Sunday and Monday off. Not only that, but the next day back, Tuesday, she would have a normal-hour day for the first time in a while. Seven until five. Now those were the days.

Of course she would be back to the tough schedule starting Wednesday, but that weekend.... Your parents, gotta love 'em, came in from Oceanside to take care of Stephen while you and your wife had a romantic two nights in the burgeoning Temecula Wine Valley, which lived up to the hype. So did Jess, who'd promised to turn back the clock on your marriage, to the time before even the thought of your son existed. Neither of you disappointed on either Saturday or Sunday night, and for those three days away from Anomar you did not once think of your newscaster-mistress. The entire vacation your phone was silent, as if trying to tell you something.

Well, now you see what it was trying to tell you. You see it —or, more accurately, you see the big city network news van parked on Main Street Anomar as you hurry toward the Honeydrip Inn, which is exactly where the forces of evil have converged to ruin your Tuesday. Across the street from the Inn, Anomarans stand, point and gawk. You barrel on ahead, not allowing yourself to be deterred by the few shouts that rise up as you pass by the equipment set up outside, and enter the restaurant portion of the Inn.

Once inside, push past the few tech hands who try to stop you. They can't. You're big, you're strong, you played football for two years in high school before a grave injury forced you to find another calling. They wouldn't dare. They know this is your town—the problem is she does not.

And then you see her, just beyond the front entryway you've barged through. She stands, dressed in her consummate newswoman's blouse, blazer and the short skirt that shows off her legs, on a towering ladder above a table. The table is by the window that looks out on Main Street. The owners of this establishment are seated at the table across from one another, and arranged on the table is one of the Honeydrip Inn's signature uninspiring meals. You know. You've been here once before with Jess and swore never to return. The place, in your opinion, isn't much more than a gimmick, a gimmick that is again unfolding before your eyes.

From her perch at the top of the ladder your newscaster-mistress tips forward a large opaque jar with a short spout on the end. Out pours honey, long and lithe like a dancer's leg, spilling through the air and dripping onto the plates below. The gimmick continues to play out as those gathered, these city dwellers, these bona fide San Diegans, actually ooh and ah and chortle, delighted at this bit of small town charm. Your newscaster-mistress holds her arm steady as she targets certain items on each of the diner's plates. Hard bread, overcooked carrots, mashed potatoes and even the main course, roast chicken, fall victim to her delighted ire.

"Like this?" she says.

"Yeah, that's it," the male owner says.

"This is a *blast*. Are you getting all of this?"

She looks up as she says this. Catching sight of you next to the cameraman, her mouth opens into a wide O you find familiar. Watch as, startled, she loses her balance. You see it happening. See her left foot turn too far outward on the highest rung. See her platform heels slip, slide right off the edge, her entire body twisted and hurtling backward. Her arms fly up, the honey jar now detached and falling ahead of her, you see it all, and everyone else in the room cries out but you do not. You want it to happen. This is it. This is the way to make sure you're not caught.

Her landing is not fatal, though. The jar crashes and shatters, globs of honey and pieces of opaque glass fly in all directions, and milliseconds later she lands squarely on a table. A loud thwack-thud, her screams go from terrifying to piercing-horrendous, and everyone in the room has turned their attention to her without seeing the ladder that is now falling swiftly after her. It's the ladder that causes the real damage. Her leg. When the side of the ladder connects with her leg that was left to dangle off the table's edge a sharp crack is heard and you cringe, for despite your wish that she'd leave your life permanently you also don't really want to see her hurt. You care for her, even though she'll destroy you.

Along with everyone else, rush over to the table she's lying on as if she's being readied for a wake. Help pull the ladder off her leg. There's blood, and you look away and grimace further when you see a trace of bone jutting through skin. She is wailing the strength of twenty Stephens, her eyes squeezed tight, her mouth a canyon threatening to swallow you with all the 'you's she's spewing. You, you, you she says over and over, and with a sudden sharp shock you see she's pointing at *you* through her pain.

"Me?" you have enough time to say before many hands grab your arms, press into your back and drag you away from the table.

Outside, now that you've been forced there, spin around to face your handlers. Three of them, all men, all those you pushed past earlier.

"What's the deal with you and her?" one of them says. "Why'd you want to get in here anyway?"

"Uh..." Think. Think! Why had you asked Piangi for permission to check out this commotion a few blocks down from the *Anomar Cryer*'s office when you knew she was involved? Simple: you wanted to confront her, to tell her off. You couldn't believe she'd actually show up here, in your town, in Anomar. In Anomar! First a review of the Honeydrip Inn, next the history of Anomar, all the way from Ozzy the Ostrich to the world in its swaddling clothes. The omphalos. The scientists. The Year of the Ocean Parade. She had beaten you to your own story, your life! What's worse, you knew she was going to do it! She'd prepared you, dropped hints, all but announced she was going to cover Anomar. You didn't think she would actually go through with it, though. The moment you heard that a network news station van had pulled onto Main Street headed for the Honeydrip Inn, and that network was hers, the moment you knew she had gone into your town to one-up you and make you pay, you had to fight back.

Some way of fighting back, huh? All you had to do was show your face and that was enough to send her packing. No way she'll return to Anomar after this experience. But to say all that to these guys would be to acknowledge far more than you're willing. Instead, look up at the helicopter slicing the air overhead. It's as if the president's been shot. Panicked Anomarans disappear inside stores or into their cars that peel away. In the distance and growing ever louder, sirens can be heard. The scene is grander than anything Anomar has experienced in over twenty years. Not even the opening of the Big K(mart) followed by Denny's was this big.

"Wait for the cops," another of the trio commands. Now all three are advancing on you. "You're a part of this. You're gonna tell them what's going on."

Run. Turn and get the hell out of there. Back down Main Street. Only after you've passed the second block do you look back to see that you're not being followed, the ambulance zipped by minutes ago, and you're safe. Turn the corner and reach the *Cryer*'s office out of breath and drenched in sweat.

"What the hell happened?" Piangi asks.

"I don't know," you say, and, really, you don't.

YOU KNOW something's wrong when Jess isn't home by 4:45. You wait. Wait some more. Think about calling your parents, as if they could do anything for you. Maybe she's been in an accident, the second accident for your second woman of the day. She's not answering her phone, and she's usually so good about picking up. You made that promise to each other this summer.

She pulls into the driveway at just after six. From the window you can tell she has been crying, and that her crying has given way to anger. A resoluteness has invaded her purple-tinged face like the shadow of a large cloud. She is going to say some awful things to you, a whole slew of true and awful things. You want to run, but to where? It's not like you can call up your outlaws and head for the hills. Not like you can hide in the closet like you did as a child. She would find you. The law would find you. The tragedy of your past year would catch up with you. Think about all the times you cut people off while driving. All the judgments and meat-headed pronouncements you made. All the jealousy you harbored and eventually expressed. All the times Jess made mention of bad karma. It's come back to you five hundredfold. Your failure, increased in the past year, is now complete. Worse is not possible.

Don't open the door to her; she'll strike you. Wait in the dining room. No: the living room. Too many glass objects in the dining room, while in the living room there's only really the TV and the mirrored coffee table, and there's no way Jess is lifting either of those. She could hurl a lamp your way, but she'll have to unplug it first and besides, she loves those lamps.

You've figured out what happened, how your wife found out. It took you until five-thirty, but you did. Jess is here to confirm your deduction.

The front door opens and from the living room you can't quite look at her. You're sunk in the sofa, seated. Your head isn't in your hands—you're not that dramatic—but it is down and your hands are clasped between your knees as if you're awaiting an operation. Listen as your wife goes into the dining room, then the kitchen. It's over, the end of your life. She's going for an instrument of cutting with which to plunge into your shriveled besmirched little heart. You'll pull a Phil Hartman, only awake. Awake! Awake and seize the day! Seize Stephen and run out of the house, get in the car and make it to Tijuana by nightfall. Wailing all the way.

Yeah, right. As if you could actually carry out any means of escape. You can't escape. You can only wait to die—inwardly if not outwardly as well.

When you hear the fridge open you breathe a little. She's not going to throw a celery stick at you. She's going to try to settle down the best way she knows how.

She comes to the threshold of the living room and stands with her shoulder pressed against the wall's edge. Dressed in her scrubs and sipping beer from a bottle, she observes you with a newfound look of incredulity.

"I'm sorry," you say, and you don't look up.

"You know how I found out? You must because it's so impossible, the odds of it happening are…. I mean Jesus Christ."

"I know. But it happened, and I'm sorry."

You look at Jess for the first time today. Really look at her the way she's looking at you. It's not like in the movies. She's beyond hurt—if she ever got to that point. Maybe she knew. Maybe she knew from the day she met you and you told her you'd played football in high school and had your first girlfriend when you were twelve. Maybe she knew she could never keep you to herself, that you had to be shared, and that the truth of your marriage, of all marriages, is that no couple is on an equal level of desirability. One must always edge out the other in matters of the physical. Be it wife or husband, the feeling exists that *I'm* the better one here. The feeling may never be expressed, but it is thought, perhaps only once or twice early on in the marriage, or toward the end, but it is thought, and you're thinking it now, and of how it's led to your downfall.

"Just so you know," Jess says, "I would've found out. Even if she hadn't been admitted to my hospital, for a *broken leg*, which pushed aside all these people who had way more serious injuries, and diseases…. God, the fanfare. It was like we were taking care of a queen…. She's attractive, I'll give you that."

She waits, but you're not going to say anything.

Jess takes another sip and says, "She was so angry at you. She came in screaming your name. That's how I found out. That's how we connected. Your name all over the hospital. She sounded out of her mind, I don't know if you ever saw that in her. Did you?"

You both wait. After only a moment, Jess continues: "I guess you…stopped her from getting her story. Or something. You people, I swear…." And now your wife's anger is like a concentrated point of heat searing a mark on your forehead.

"You people," she repeats. "You people, you people...." You know you've lost her, you've lost them all. When next she speaks, it's in a voice removed from her heart. The hollow quality terrifies you. "She told me all about you," Jess says, "and now I know who you are. You're an awful person, and the thing is I knew that fact when I married you, but I thought, you know, I thought *Forget it*. I'm better than that. *He's* better than that. He'll grow out of it. Marriage will make him a better person. But it really hasn't, and you didn't."

You don't want to say it's the pregnancy, the baby, the future. The twilight of your twenties dwindling into your thirties into your forties and so on and so on. Don't say any of that. Don't say anything. Instead, listen as Jess tells you how it's going to be: You'll leave. You can move in with your parents. Call them up and tell them from the motel, where you'll be staying tonight (paid for with your own money, Jess makes a point of saying), or from the newspaper's office just off of Main Street. Curl up on a couch somewhere. Sleep on the Country Gems golf course for all she cares. Just, you can't be in this house tonight, or any night after.

She doesn't ask about any other women. It wouldn't matter if you were to tell her. One was enough. The one you most liked, and, of all the bad karma and awful luck, of all the statistical improbabilities and wild dice rolls and gods moving humans around on their grand chess board, of all the factors that tell you it could never happen, it did. Your newscaster-mistress was airlifted to the very same hospital in Poway where your wife was on duty at the time. And if it sounds outlandish, far-fetched and implausible, think about all that you've read in the papers. The South American fisherman who had a fish jump out of the river and into his mouth by accident. Siblings reunited after decades of not knowing the other existed. Chance encounters and ill-fated timing. These things do happen, and one of them has happened to you.

~

THE NEXT DAY IS WEDNESDAY, September 5th. Wake up in your motel bed with the sun blasting full bore in your face. You had driven out of Anomar east along highway 78. The farther away from your town the better. You didn't call your parents, not even when you stopped to fill up and grab a hot dog at a gas station outside Julian. You just kept going. It was late night when you cleared Anza-Borrego Desert State Park and pulled into the one-level motel in Borrego Springs that looked as if all sorts of sordid affairs were conducted behind thin walls and weak doors. They gave you a room without curtains, and for much of the night you awoke periodically believing you saw the faces of your wife and Stephen in the window, peering in, smiling and waving. They were going away, without you, and the thought of them doing that was what finally did you in. You cried at some point in the middle of the night. At age twenty-seven you bawled for all that you'd done to get here, from the time you were born. You cried for the fact that it will always be about you.

You'd thought of continuing east into Imperial County, perhaps lying low along the Salton Sea, or better yet pushing through to Arizona. You could make Phoenix your home. You have a couple family members there. They would understand.

But instead after checking out of that dive you headed back along 79 and settled on Julian. You've always liked Julian; it's a decent place to spend a day. Walk up and down the main drag, feeling the sun on your face. Remember a date you took here in high school. Try to smile. Stop into the general store, pick up an old paperback or two off the revolving circular rack and flip through. Stroll by the antique and crafts stores that are either closed or anxiously awaiting the kick-off to the holiday season that is October. The smell of freshly baked apple pies in your nose. Divorced dad days. The weekends when you take Stephen here, better when he's young. Maybe you'll live here. Maybe this will be your new home.

Over lunch keep your phone out and on the table to the right of your plate. Imagine what Jess must be doing now besides telling everyone she knows about your depravity. Which friend will get to watch Stephen tonight, which will get to watch him tomorrow night, which the night after. What day and time your in-laws will fly in, or she in to see them. You're going to have to talk about this eventually. You're going to have to discuss the situation. It's a question of who will call first.

The phone rings and you jump in your seat. It's Piangi. Better take it.

"I got your message," he says. "Have you seen the news?"

You haven't.

"Breaking story about breaking a leg. Anomar's on the map now. I give it, say, three days. The buzz for the Honeydrip's gonna last longer. Last night customers were lining up out the door. A couple said they came up from Rancho Bernardo. So we got a story out of that. Too bad you weren't there to cover it."

"I kinda had to leave town last night."

"So you said. Wanna tell me what this is about?"

You really don't. But you do tell Piangi you'll be at the office tomorrow, after you sort out some things. He says that's fine and thanks you for your contribution to the "accident at the Honeydrip Inn" article. "It's been getting some buzz," Piangi says. "I give that about a day and a half. Maybe if we can pry Junior Seau off the Country Gems golf course and put him up on one of those Honeydrip ladders we'll get nominated for a Pulitzer."

Laugh for the first time since the long weekend. You've always liked Piangi. He's good people, a friend till the end. An outlaw. Hang up after assuring your boss you'll be in tomorrow early. Watch your phone for a while, wondering who's going to call whom.

You can't sit much longer in this hard-backed wooden chair. Stand up, stretch, and finish digesting outside. Keep walking. Walk from what you feel is one end of Julian to the other. Walk up and down side streets, wander in and out of shops you otherwise wouldn't frequent. There's plenty of time today, your day off. It's nice. You suppose you'll stay in Anomar tonight. Another motel, but you have the money. It's not like you're in debt, not like Jess can get to your personal account in any way. Boy are you ever glad now you kept part of your finances separate. Not that you'd planned on this happening, but it was always a possibility from the day you got serious, even before marriage. Not just with Jess, but with anyone.

Finger your phone again through the outer layer of your pocket's fabric. Who will be the one to call? You figure it might as well be you.

Jess picks up on the third ring. "What," she says, not a question but a demand.

In a voice that alternates between shaky and sure you ask how Stephen is doing. He's fine. Then you ask how your wife is doing. She was doing better until she read today's *Cryer*, specifically the article on the San Diego newswoman who was injured in a freak accident while doing a story on Anomar's very own Honeydrip Inn. The article you helped pull together. She saw your name at the bottom, saw that you'd contributed to this report, as if it was an article on Bosnia and you were reporting for the *Times*. You always have to have your hands in everything, don't you. Just can't stop getting involved, even when it's business mixed with pleasure. The pen is not always mightier than the penis, you know.

You can't tolerate much more of this verbal abuse. Still, you put up with it and even laugh once or twice. The laughter infuriates Jess. She threatens to hang up. You sober up right quick and get to the point: What's going to happen next? Jess doesn't ask where you are, she doesn't care where you are. At this point she only cares about where she's going.

"What's happening next is I'm going to New York this weekend, and I'm taking Stephen with me."

"You're still going."

"You think this revelation is going to stop me from seeing Becca? Oh no, you failed there, too."

"Don't take Stephen."

There's a pause on the other end. You're also surprised you said those words, but they're true: you do not want to see Stephen go.

"We'll be gone for the week only," Jess says, and for the first time since the news of you broke you detect a hint of compassion in her voice. Emboldened, you press forward.

"Please don't take him. I'll look after him, in the house while you're gone. And when you get back, I'll leave. I promise."

Another pause, though this one is shorter. "He's coming with me," Jess says. "You can have the house to yourself while we're over there but…. Please don't do this," she finishes.

Desperate now, you relate your vision to your wife, what you saw through the window of the sordid motel room in Borrego Springs. What you felt. You stop short of relating how you cried. It's true you should only tell your dreams to your lover, but you seem to have forgotten that Jess is no longer that to you.

"I'm sorry," she tells you. "I'm sorry you experienced that but…." And now her voice has found a new resolve. "We'll be gone from the eighth until the sixteenth. You can be in the house between those times."

"We have to talk about this, Jess."

"We will. After I get back. Please don't...take anything, or do anything to any of my stuff while I'm gone."

Bristle at that last sentence. You would never—and she knows it. That your marriage has been reduced to such pettiness, as if you're roommates squabbling over food in the fridge, saddens you more than even the image in the window from the night before. Saddens and angers you. She has every right to be angry, but now you have the right, too. How dare she think you would stoop to something so low.

It's you who ends the call. You'd started out wanting to keep Jess on the phone forever, or at least until she missed her flight. Now you wash your hands clean of her from today until the end of next week. Let her go to New York. Let her take Stephen. Let her meet someone there and fall in love the way she should have. She can meet her next and last husband, Stephen's future stepfather, in a place other than a bar.

That bar. Remember that bar in South Bend the night you met. Can't remember its name but you remember the smell and thick stagnation of cigarette smoke that forced you outside to breathe. Outside you gulped fresh biting air and looked around and clapped your gloved hands and watched your breath steam in front of you like a train whistle's expulsion. It was January and thirty-five degrees, snow like coal and lumped like bodies in the gutters and along sidewalks. You were nineteen and a freshman, just returned from Christmas in California, and you were wondering now if you'd done the right thing by coming here to Indiana. You had thought the Midwest was the real America and would give birth to all sorts of stories that would launch you into a career in New York, the greatest city of them all. But you were finding it hard to deal with the weather, and maybe California was just as good as New York, San Diego just as fine as NYC. You were coming to grips with the future.

When you went back inside, your lungs open again and

tingling with anticipation of the acrid air, you saw your friend from high school standing at the bar talking with two girls. At AHS your friend had talked incessantly about going to Notre Dame on a football scholarship, and here he was just going to Notre Dame. Still, he'd maintained his impressive build, and you suspected he'd go home that night with the girl standing closest to him, the brunette, which left the blonde for you. This was what you were here for, why you'd traveled from West Lafayette to visit him and gone out on this night. Why you'd gotten fake IDs and made sure to stand near the windows so you could bolt if the cops pulled up.

Turned out the two girls were underage too. Hell, more than half the patrons were that night. Steeling yourself to say something smart, something right, you offered to buy this blonde, this Jessica, a drink, and she'd accepted. You got to talking, a lot more natural of a conversation than you'd had before with anyone of the opposite sex. You liked a lot of the same things, which meant a lot of the same movies and TV shows. You both liked sports. You were both the same age, she only two months younger than you. And the best: you both were attending colleges not far from one another, Purdue less than a two-hour drive from Ball State.

The cops did bust up the bar that night, shut the place down and cart several students off, but you and your friend and Jess and her friend were long gone by then. Back at Jess's friend's apartment, you and Jess sat on the couch in the living room and avoided looking at each other while your friend and Jess's friend closed the door to her room and started laughing and cavorting behind thin walls.

"What do you want to be?" Jess asked when she finally looked at you.

"A journalist," you'd said.

"That's noble."

It was the first time you'd heard that word used in

conjunction with you personally. *Noble.* You asked what Jess wanted to be.

"I want to help people, somehow."

"I guess we're both the same there too," you said, and you'd smiled at her and she'd smiled back, and that's when you leaned in and kissed her, and she did not draw away but instead dug her tongue in deep, and it was like the future was ready, it was like you were free.

III

WHAT'S that you hear from your seat by the window? Screams. The entire plane is full of screams—and why not? You are going down. The wing to your right sweeps over uniform houses covered in snow. This is the way it ends, here in Indiana, on the way to see Jess's parents.

Only Jess is not with you. Look to your left to find the seat empty, the seat next to that empty as well. Look beyond to the next aisle over: empty. The row in front is vacant, confirmed when you reach around the seats to grasp a hand, an arm, to hold onto another human being in your last seconds of life. The plane is empty, yet the screams are everywhere. The plane is screaming.

When you open your eyes you think you're dead. The impact was so sudden you felt nothing, and now you're more than dead: atomized. There's nothing left of you in that previous world, and in this world...

This world looks and feels strangely like the last one. For one, you are lying on your stomach in a bed. It's your bed. You recognize the sheets from the night before, the sheets you clutch now. And now you realize it was a dream from which you've awakened. The impact was never to be felt, and the screaming is the phone in the living room. Jess's mother Marion has the tendency to call at inopportune times, so the land line was moved from the bedroom to one of the end tables. That move hasn't stopped you from being woken up at another inopportune time. You answer, but instead of Marion on the phone it's Frederick.

"Has she called you?" They're the first words out of his mouth.

"What? No.... Frederick?"

"She hasn't called you this morning?"

"No, no..." Pinch the point between your eyes and shake your head. What a rude awakening.

"She's not answering her phone. Her cell phone. We don't know where she is."

"She's in New York, Frederick."

"I know that!"

Your eyes go wide. Your father-in-law has never barked at you like that before. Yet you sense the anger belies fear. Frederick is afraid. More than that: Frederick is terrified.

"Frederick, what's going on?"

"Turn on the TV."

"What's going on?"

"Did she tell you where she'd be this morning? Where she'd be Tuesday morning in New York City at this time?"

"I don't know...." Shocked, still searching for the remote...

"Of course she didn't."

The remote now in your hand, flip on the TV.

"Do you see it?"

"See what, Frederick?"

You have only two channels to go through before you're there. The previous two channels framed people talking—they sounded alarmed, and they weren't representing the news. Now you see the news, and you see why those people were alarmed.

"My God," you say. "Oh, shit, my God."

"Where is she?" Frederick implores through the receiver. "Where's our baby?"

At the bottom right of the screen, to the right of the burning, smoking World Trade Center tower, is the time, 9:01 a.m., which changes to 9:02 a.m. before switching to 8:02 a.m. Central Standard Time, and then to Mountain Standard, and finally to your time, 6:02 a.m.

"I can't believe this," you say. "What's going on?"

Stare at the screen, waiting for Frederick to say something. He says nothing. You are both waiting, watching. And then voices rise up on the screen, push through into your living room and you are falling, falling along with the plane that is just now opening up into the as yet untouched second tower. The aircraft plows into this tower, explodes—and with it the panic voiced by those in the newsroom.

"Oh shit!" you cry out. Glance back for the briefest of moments to make sure your body will actually make it to the couch. Fall back, the phone still clutched. This is happening. They've done it. They did it.

"Frederick?" you say. "Frederick?"

"We need this line open," he says and hangs up.

Listen to the empty dial tone. Watch this new tragedy that may not involve you. Hope it doesn't. But you know better. You know from now on your life is going to be different.

I want to know what you've done. I want to know why you are the way you are. Why you think the way you think, behave the way you do, pretend to love as you do. Pretend to love me. Don't worry. I'm not going to disown you. I will always own you. That's the extent of the vows we took all those years ago. It hasn't really been that long. But you really have to think so hard? Dwell on the little things? I dwell too. But I don't dwell enough in your mind to make a difference in your routine. Who said being married to a writer is a hard life? Are you a writer, will you ever be? The clink of the fork tines against your teeth when you eat, the chocolate stuck under my fingernails, your furtive glances at the wrong others, my dedication to people whose deaths are inevitably soon. What is this? What have we gotten ourselves into? This wasn't what I'd planned to be, but it is what I have become and I accept it. I wish you'd accept yourself, not keep looking for an out, not keep wishing you lived in another place. You're near a fine city, the finest of them all. But you would love New York. Take a bite of the Big Apple. You would love it here. The other day I rounded a corner on a major street and was caught up in a tidal wave of people. They wouldn't move, wouldn't budge. At the hospital, in all hospitals people move for you. They know you're coming. They see you, they know what you're doing. But here they don't know what you're doing and don't care. A hospital isn't a city, I know, but maybe in a little way it is. Both are crowded anyway, and this tidal crowd just swept me along. It surged behind me. No one said anything to me. No one said Get out of the way or Move faster. They just moved, and I would either move with them or get off the street. I got off the street eventually. A man in a t-shirt and jeans was playing a strange drum set I'm sure he'd rigged on his own. He had some CDs for sale. I didn't buy one, but I did give him a dollar. He looked like he could use more money in the guitar case. No guitar though, which I thought was strange. This was around Cooper Union, I think. Becca's teaching me the names. You'd be proud of me. I've gotten the hang of the subway—and I've only been here three days. I haven't seen any plays or musicals yet. I know some great ones must be playing in the theaters we pass and maybe later in the week we'll have the time. For now I'm getting my bearings. Being the best mother I can to Stephen. He's not holding me back. Not really. I accept I may be a kind of parasite, a mosquito that flits from one urban arm to another, sucking the experience out of a place, never adequately capturing what it's like to really be there. I want to capture what it's like to be here, but there's not enough time. Only eight days. Eight days isn't enough time for New York City, the City That Never Sleeps. I'll admit I haven't slept much. I'll admit I've met some great people, people I'd like to spend more time with, people I would see again. I think back to our summer in Europe together, the summer we graduated. You. Me. We had the world, really did have it for a brief few weeks. But you were so dissatisfied, and it showed every time we argued. You wanted the bars, I wanted the sights. Now I realize you wanted more than just the bars, the drinking. You wanted more than me, and I've never been enough. You said more than once that I think too much. Maybe you think too much. You do think too much. No, your left eye is not shrinking, it's not smaller than your right. Stop staring in the mirror. I swear you look at yourself a lot more than you look at me. I swear there have been times I wish I'd married an actual high school football player. The stereotype, the star. Someone who's a machine, who can stand on his own and doesn't need the praise of others to function. He just works. He just lives. He's just a man, a husband, a father. My former football player doesn't hold on. He doesn't hold grudges and by God he doesn't spend his life trying to be what he can never be. God, the city is beautiful in the early morning, right when the sun's coming up and people are beginning their day. God it is so gorgeous here, and you're not with me. We'll look out the window onto the world today. So high up. I'm going to do it. You know how scared I am of elevators. I'm going to do it. I'm going to swallow my fear along with that pill and have breakfast looking out on the center of the world. God what I wouldn't give to have you here with me now. To hold my hand as we go so high up. Don't look down. It's as if the building sways.

Hold my hand. Keep holding. You know you don't want to look down. We can do it together. You and me. And Stephen. Where's our son? Oh God I can't find my son.

You want to hate me? Diss me? Leave me? Walk out and never come back? Why? For what? Let's take a breath and think. What about you? What about the dishes you said you'd do. The diapers you said you'd change. The vomit you promised to clean up. Oh but that's right, you're too busy cleaning up other people's vomit to tend to his. I wish you'd never taken that career path. Too busy for me. Almost too busy for him. And you want to go gallivanting off on an expensive trip to an expensive city to do what? Explore? Explore yourself? Reevaluate your life with me? Well, I can't stop you, but think about the money and the bills and the lost time back home, think about the possibility of me not being there when you get back. We've been through so much together, and I know you want me to have more friends but I honestly don't know why she's your best. You didn't really get along with her in college. She intimidated you. Made you feel ugly. You're not ugly. You're so far from ugly you make her look like a human turnip. I'm not kidding. Stop mistaking the accepted societal norm for the physical ideal. I don't care about that, I really don't. A surprise, I know, but I don't care about what you think men care about. My actions have not always made good on that belief, I know, and I'll tell you, I'll tell you, I'll tell you, I'll tell you, someday when we're retired and on an Alaskan cruise, or sitting on a beach in the Bahamas, or fulfilling any of our travel plans we've talked about and talked about, always hoping the other will take the initiative and just book the flights, the hotel, the events, I'll tell you what made me tick at that time. If we ever get there. You always hoping I'll stop worrying I'll die in a plane crash, I always hoping you'll talk to the hospital administration about the time off you so obviously need. You think you don't need it but I know better, I know you, and I see you turning from the woman I met in college and married to more and more of a stranger each time you drive back up the hill. I don't think it's just because I'm an asshole. I am that, but you gotta give me credit for picking up on your situation. How you didn't want to get into this. You wanted to help people, yes, but was this the way? You're so good at science. You would always talk about the classes you were taking. Always talking. And I picked up on that—that and your love of children. I'm never going to forget that day we were at your parents' house for Thanksgiving, one semester away from graduation, and we were in your room, on your bed, and you were lying back bouncing your baby nephew on your breasts. And I loved you then more than I ever have. Because I saw the mother in you, I saw the glorious woman in you, I saw the future in you, my future, and it made me happier than I'd ever been up to that point in my life. I needed you, and I wasn't going to back down if you said no. You didn't say no to the next step, but you did to a lot of the steps after. I can picture that day with your nephew so clearly, the sun on your face, on his face, the both of you giggling, but no day with our son has matched that. Why? Did he not turn out the way you'd hoped? *We* didn't turn out the way I'd hoped. But did you? I fear you did. I'm afraid this is exactly what you wanted. So go. See the sights. Say hi to your best friend for me. Have a good time. Don't feel you have to call me, certainly not every day. Once or twice will be enough. And when we talk I'll tell you about the smoke I see through the buildings that never existed here, the smoke so thick it's as if the Big One was never going to be an earthquake but a fire instead. One great massive fire sweeping Anomar clean off the map. But you're safe. Safe from me, safe from the culture we were born into. At football practice one day early on, I must've been in the spring of my freshman year,

I took a hit that laid me out for what I was told was minutes. I didn't get up. I wasn't of this world for that time. Instead I was drifting through a darkness that reminded me of the smoke I first saw on the hill across from our house, Stone Mountain, the flames about to leap up and threaten the newly built Gems homes below. In this darkness I saw a light and I was sure I was dying because I was moving steadily toward it, my eyes open as if set on the future. I thought the light was the other side, but after I'd come to and recovered from the hit, and gone to the hospital then home and done all the things I normally did, I decided it wasn't the other side after all. It was me. The light was me and I know this sounds crazy but hear me out: It was a warning not to go any further. And I wish I had. I really do wish I had.

WHEN YOU WERE young and feeling lucky you would drive all by yourself down the hill into the city. It would be a school night and your parents wouldn't mind. They didn't mind a lot of things, your folks. Never raised a hand against you, rarely grounded you, always trusted you to make the right decisions. For a time, you did. Even your impromptu solo trips to downtown San Diego seemed like good ideas when you were a teenager in the early nineties.

You're no longer a teenager, and it's no longer the early nineties, but here you are again in a lounge-bar on the top floor of a downtown San Diego skyrise. This time it's Top of the Hyatt, the fortieth floor of the Manchester Grand Hyatt Hotel, and the views are exquisite. You've been here many times before, most recently a couple of weeks ago, in this exact seat at this exact table for two. Still, look through the glass to your immediate left and take in the harbor and boats lit up like stars in space. Notice something different. There's always something different to see from up here. Maybe it's a boat you hadn't noticed before that's out on the bay, or ground broken on a new building far below. You'd always wanted to live here, and now you can.

Your table is in the windowed corner so that your back is facing the skyline. You have a view of both the city and the bar that's in the center of the room. Standing by the bar now is a woman you swear you recognize. You think she might have gone to school with you at some point, but you're having trouble determining when. You went through your yearbook recently and looked at a lot of faces, read a lot of kind words. None of the faces match hers. Yet you swear you've seen her before, maybe in another life. Maybe she's single, too. You may get your chance to find out. She's looking at you now, and when your eyes meet she glances away momentarily. Smile. She smiles back without parting her lips. You don't mind. That could be a good sign for later. You've already approached her tonight, and she and her friend politely declined your offer to buy them each a drink. Undeterred, because you felt something was there with the redheaded one, the one you swear you recognize, you returned to your table for two by the window and waited. Now's your chance. The friend has disappeared and you and the redhead are locked on each other. Motion for her to join you. She looks around briefly for her friend and, not seeing her, pulls on her upper lip with her bottom front teeth then moves to join you. She's wearing a mini-skirt and matching low heels. She looks good. Her hair is long and wavy in the way you like, not curly or frizzy as you picture the typical redhead.

"Please," you say and help to pull out her chair. She thanks you before she's fully seated. She settles her drink before you. It's pink, in a thin-stemmed glass, a cosmopolitan.

You give her your name and ask for hers. "Julie," she answers.

"Julie, that's a nice name."

She blushes and looks intently at her drink. Between her index and middle finger the stem of her glass is pushed back and forth. She is around your age—or possibly a little older.

"You didn't happen to go to...Anomar High, by any chance?" you ask.

"Anomar?" Her eyes widen as she looks at you directly with the most emerald eyes you've ever seen. They are a bit unreal this close up, and you think briefly of what you mused over as a teenager headed into the city on school nights, the 67 south to the 8 west, down Wildcat Canyon Road and through Santee and El Cajon, driving fast to beat sundown: how if you didn't make it to the ocean before the sun signed off, the vampires would get you, the nightmares would come true.

"You know Anomar?"

"I'm from Julian."

"Julian! Really?"

"Yeah, really. I went to Julian High."

"Class of..."

"I'm not going to date myself *that* quickly."

"Oh come on. I'll tell you mine if you tell me yours."

She looks at her drink and smiles.

"Class of '92," you say.

"That's mine. Class of '92." She speaks as if you caught her doing something red-handed.

"Wow, so Julian High...."

"You haven't said it yet. I'm impressed."

"Say what?"

"'Julie from Julian.' Most guys say that by now. I'm serious."

"I'm not most guys," you say, and grin. "But can I call you that now?"

"I'd prefer you didn't."

"It's not like you live there now, right?"

"Well…" Julie glances over her shoulder. Her friend is still nowhere to be seen. "I do still live there," she tells you.

"No way. Really?"

"I'm a baker. I work at Mom's."

"A baker. I'll be damned. You must be really good."

"I am. And we really do bake the pies from scratch, in case you were wondering."

"I was wondering, thanks."

Julie smiles and again glances back. You wait. When you have her attention, you ask if her friend will be joining the two of you.

"Do you have a friend here for my friend?" Her eyes lock with yours. Those emerald eyes make you think of the next life.

"Unfortunately, no. I'm on my own tonight."

"Then I don't think she'll be joining us. Give me a sec."

Watch as Julie takes out her cell phone, punches a button and places the phone to her ear. She stands up. Notice her nicely toned albeit pale legs showing more skin as the skirt rides up. Don't feel dirty. She's around your age after all, and besides, you have no one to go home to, no one to answer to anymore. Sit back and listen to the piano overhead tinkle out a Christmas carol you can almost identify. A Christmas tree stands to one side of the bar, and small poinsettias have been placed on every table, including yours.

Julie stands a short distance away and talks quietly into her phone while looking out on the beauty of Coronado. The call is quick. When she reseats herself you raise your hand to signal the waiter, from whom you order a drink for you and for her. Your debonair thoughtfulness impresses her. It's like starting all over again.

"What do you mean?"

"What?"

"What do you mean by what you said? You said 'It's like starting all over again.'"

"I said that?"

You did say that. You know it as soon as you ask the question. You've been doing this lately, voicing your thoughts out loud. It's not good. Piangi has begun to worry about you.

"You did, but...whatever."

You could let your slip-up slide, but it's obvious from Julie's demeanor that she's unsettled, and so you decide to take care of the problem now.

"No, no, you're right. I did say that. I meant I'm not used to doing this. I...uh..."

She looks at you dubiously. Despite her Julian upbringing, she could be one who doesn't believe you. She wouldn't be the first, but she also would be one of the few. You press on.

"If I told you something personal, and tragic, would you promise to keep an open mind about me?"

"Um..." Wrong move, sport. Julie looks like she wants to bolt. You may have gone to Anomar High, class of 1992, but you could also be an axe murderer at this point in the conversation. Too heavy, way too soon. Watch as she shifts in her seat, preparing to propel herself up and away. Also watch as the tray of drinks descends in front of both your faces, stopping her and saving you.

"Sir...Miss...."

If you could thank the waiter now with more than just a 'thank you,' you would. Julie, with a fresh cosmo before her, hesitates long enough to stay and at least hear you out.

"The last thing I want to do is scare you off," you say, "but I have to tell you what happened to me on 9/11."

"What happened?"

"I lost my wife and son."

"Oh my God." Julie places one hand to her mouth, her

eyes widening and even tearing up a little. "Oh my God. You're not kidding."

"I'm not, no."

"I knew you weren't kidding. I mean I knew there was something sad about you when you first came up to us. You seemed sad, even though you were up front and confident and smiling. I even told her there was something more to you, I'd like to give you a shot."

"You have."

"I'm so, so sorry."

Nod. Keep your mouth tight. It's worked before, it will work again.

"Were they in one of the planes?"

"In one of the towers, actually. The North Tower, 107th floor. This restaurant called Windows on the World."

"Oh, I've heard about that. There were a lot of people in there, right?"

Again, nod. It's working. Julie takes your hand in her own, glances around Top of the Hyatt, comes back to you whole.

"She wouldn't have even been there if her friend wasn't a lawyer. She wanted to treat Jess...."

"Is that your wife's name? Jess?"

"Jessica. And my son, Stephen."

"How old were they?"

"She was, uh, almost twenty-seven, and he was...."

Here you really do get choked up, a genuine surprise. Talking about it over and over and over to different women can finally do you in, apparently. Now you're picturing things you haven't in a while: flashes of Jess in New York City, Jess and her friend riding with Stephen up the elevator of North Tower to the 107th floor, Windows on the World. The view from up there. The smiling waiter. Attractive. Your wife's age. Your age. Jess's ring is off. Her cell phone is also nowhere in sight. Stephen is gurgling and giggling in his high chair, and a shadow is gliding across the table's surface.

"He was five months," you eek out, then dab at your eyes with your sleeve. Truth be told the tears won't fall tonight either; the best you can do is a tiny wellspring. But what you've shown tonight is more impactful than what you've shown in a lot of the previous nights, and if what you showed then was enough for those women, what you're showing now will be more than enough for Julie from Julian.

"That's awful," she says, her hand still grasping yours. "You're the first person I've met who lost someone that day."

"It's okay," you say, your voice clear now. "I'll be fine. It's been three months."

"Three months isn't a long time. Not for that."

"You're right."

"Were you supposed to be with her, and him, that day?"

"I was. I missed my flight. It was a red-eye that got in early that morning. I would have been having breakfast with all of them there when the plane hit."

And you'd be a hero now, you think, instead of the husband who wasn't there. Dead, you would have been remembered for things you might never have done: shielding your infant son as debris fell. Dragging your wounded wife to what you thought was safety. He did everything he could, they would have said. And they would have been wrong.

"God the guilt you must be feeling." Julie's voice is nearly a whisper. Her head is low, her eyes maintaining your defeated level. Yet you're the one in power here. You always have been.

"We don't have to talk about this," you say.

"We do," she insists. "I mean, I don't know what to say, but if you just need someone to listen..."

"Thank you." After a few moments you release your hand from hers, sigh and look out on San Diego at night. "I can't imagine what she saw last," you say.

"I imagine she saw something like this."

Julie too is staring out the window. Together the two of you stay staring for moments on end.

Finally, you say: "I'm not a good person."

"I'm not either."

"I've never said that to anyone before."

"That's okay. It's not something we like to admit."

"I've never had to tell it to anyone before. It's crazy that I'm telling it to you. I just met you."

A corner of Julie's mouth turns up slightly. "Why did you ask if I went to Anomar High? That's the first thing you said to me. If I went to Anomar High."

"I thought you might have gone there. I thought you looked familiar."

"Do you still think I look familiar?"

"Yes."

"I used to live in Anomar. I went to Gordon Lawrence Elementary in the San Diego Country Gems, if that helps. I moved when I was in second grade."

It hits you. All of a sudden, you remember Julie through all the articles you've written for the *Anomar Cryer*, all the words exchanged with your deceased wife, all the diapers changed for Stephen's benefit, all the information you ingested in college, the roads driven, the back and forth between Middle America and the West Coast, all that is cut through, and standing before you is Julie as a second grader. You still have your second grade yearbook, but you haven't opened it in years. Julie's picture is stark in your mind now. Black-and-white, small but clear, she only half-smiles, and she doesn't show her teeth. Her hair is light enough in the photo to be mistaken for brown. At that age, her hair was curly.

"You were in Mrs. Montoya's class, weren't you?" you say. When Julie confirms this you add, "I talked with you on the playground."

"I don't remember you," she says. "I'm sorry, but I don't. I still went to Anomar sometimes, but...I just love the mountains. I love Julian."

"You love the city too, it looks like."

"I love San Diego. I'm lucky I have friends who live here."

"So you don't have to make the long drive back, right?"

"That's right."

"Me: I make the long drive back."

"What do you mean?"

"I mean I live in Anomar now."

"*You* live in Anomar *now*?"

"Does that surprise you?"

"The way you look, yes."

"Well look at the way you look!"

You both are smiling, your heads bowed. Julie from Julian. You had no idea you'd have this kind of Christmas present delivered to your table.

She's again taking in the view. When she speaks, it's to the window. "When I'm up here," she says, "I feel like I'm someone different."

"I know what you mean."

"I bet you do."

"This place wasn't here until '92, but even before that I'd pretend...in places like these.... I was in high school when I did it."

Julie nods. She's about the only person you could have met here tonight who would have done so at that statement.

"A lot of school nights," you continue, "I'd sit up here, just drinking soda, hoping I wouldn't get kicked out, dressed my absolute best. Slacks, khakis or something like that, a sport coat I picked up in Tijuana, a nice button-up shirt, and I would sit in these places looking over the city and imagine I was rich, well-off. Not really hoping to meet anybody. Just watching. Taking it all in. Convincing myself I wasn't from

Anomar. I was from Del Mar or La Jolla or North Park or even Lemon Grove. But not Anomar. Never Anomar."

"Or Julian," Julie adds.

"Do you have your own place?"

"An apartment. It's small but...it works for me. How about you?"

"A house. I'm thinking about moving here though, to the city."

"Me too. I think it's time."

Julie's words fall into silence, and you're surprised by the lull that catches both of you. Not wanting it to stretch further, you say, "So, you're staying with your friend?"

"That was the plan tonight."

Julie is leaning in now. She licks her top lip. Then, as if suddenly aware of herself, she shakes her head and says, "Sorry."

"What?"

"This isn't right."

"No, it is right. It most definitely is right."

"I just thought of your wife and...but then why are you here...because you were really forward back at the bar, in the beginning, so..."

"No," you say, and now it's you who's grasping the hand across the table. "That's why I'm here."

"It hasn't been enough time?" The way she inflects the last word makes it sound as if she's daring you to say otherwise. She doesn't know you, yet.

"It's been enough time," you say. "It's Christmas. I want to show you my home."

"I want to see it," Julie says.

It's after eleven when you leave Top of the Hyatt together. Remembering where you parked is easy. You haven't drunk that much. Before heading out of the Manchester Grand Hyatt, Julie called her city friend and told her where she'd be. She trusts you. You're safe. Her car is at her friend's place but it can stay there till the morning. Tomorrow's a Sunday, and you've promised her you'll drive back together into the city to make a day of it.

From the 5 headed north hit up the 163 going the same direction. Take the 163 all the way to the 15, and from there it's farther north to the 67 and Poway. The other route, through El Cajon and Santee and Wildcat Canyon Road, is unwise at this time of night. Your passenger knows just as well as you. Julie from Julian. Of all the luck! By this time on a Saturday night you'd be getting heavy in the apartment of a woman you'd just picked up. The apartment would be somewhere in the city, Middletown, Normal Heights, Hillcrest or Pacific Beach perhaps, the woman usually younger, sometimes in college, a student at SDSU and once, the University of California. You remember the last as being a memorable night; she didn't really know what to do, but you did. You've always known what to do. You've gotten used to this routine in the city on weekends and Thursday college nights, and there's no way you can stop.

Of course, none of this you tell Julie from Julian as you drive. You don't tell her that you started up again two weeks after the nonexistent bodies of your wife and son were laid to rest in Anomar's cemetery. You do tell her about your father placing his hand on your shoulder and squeezing as you watched the caskets being lowered. He said something like, "She loved you, son, and you loved her just as much. Look what came of it." How you weren't sure exactly what he meant but it had to be your son, you determined later. How you faced great hostility from Jess's side of the family, particularly from Marion and Frederick who, while remaining unaware of your sexual dalliances and other proclivities, believed deep down without voicing it that you should have put work aside and been in New York with your wife and son; two caskets instead of one should have gone into the ground in the cemetery in Kokomo, Indiana. You were encouraged not to come to that funeral. You understood. You braved the flight to New York, spoke to the authorities, spent time at Ground Zero, the true burial place for them all, and when you returned to San Diego and Anomar and the Country Gems the house had grown to swallow you and it was as if you were in a monster's belly, the nights the worst, and after two weeks you couldn't take being alone anymore and so went on the prowl, to the city as you had been doing all year before. The nightmares went away then. You couldn't make sense of what you dreamt, still couldn't figure out why Jess had not spilled your affair and so much more to her family and friends before the morning of the 11th, but you had your confidence back and that's what mattered most. You were safe if not entirely secure. Waking up next to someone three or four nights out of the week has been good. It's helped you to get beyond. Piangi hasn't minded. He's covered for you so many times in the past and now, in the aftermath of your loss, he's doing everything he can to ease you back to work.

Just like your battles, you have to pick and choose the information you tell others. Not all of the truth of course makes its way to Julie's ears. She listens, says little. You are off the Grade now and speeding along the 67 past Mount Rocoso, the sign for the Summarien Fellowship, Kerrier Lane, these details made out in the brief glare of your headlights and are gone.

"Do you want revenge?" she asks.

"Against who?"

"Against the people who did it. The Taliban. Al Qaeda."

"Sure." Shrug. "But what can I do?"

"You can go to war."

"You want me to go to war?" Scoff at this. "I don't think so."

"You don't *have* to go to war, but it seems someone who's been through what you've been through would be one of the first to enlist. You're only twenty-seven. You're obviously in great shape."

"They wouldn't want me because of my knee," you say. "It's no good."

You are both silent for a time. The sign for Anomar can be seen coming up in the distance on the right. You continue to drive fast.

"I'm thinking I'll do it through journalism," you say. "Fight back that way."

"That's noble," she says.

"You know she—she didn't call me...in the end."

"She had a cell phone?"

"It wasn't found in her friend's apartment, so she must have had it with her. That still bothers me."

Julie hesitates before speaking. Her mouth seems to not want to move. "Sure it does," she says. "But...if you think about it, realistically, think about what must have been going on way up there, the 107th floor you said? God, did they even get reception? And with your son, and there must have been smoke, and all these other people trying to make their calls, the circuit boards must have been jammed."

"Maybe."

"No, I'm sure that's what happened. Plenty of other people didn't get called. It's not only you."

Nod. "Let's not talk about this," you say. Feels like you've been talking about this for the entire thirty minutes of the drive so far. It's nearing midnight. You've just pulled off of Elders Road and onto Vincenzo headed toward the San Diego Country Gems. Headlights whiz by on your left. You enter the winding, wooded part of the drive and turn the radio's volume up a little.

"Do you like The Planet?"

"The Planet's great," Julie responds. "What's this song?"

"'Hey Nineteen.'"

"Steely Dan, right?"

Glance at her and smile. She's smiling back. Those eyes.

"You got it," you say. Turn the wheel and take the curve at just the right speed to keep from spinning out. Another curve is coming up.

"I can't believe how green your eyes are," you say. "They're emerald."

"I wear contacts."

Light fills up the compartment. Julie turns before you do. She screams.

Turn the wheel a little to the right, aware that if you were to turn it too sharply you would slam into a tree. A horn blares. Julie's scream continues. The headlights blind then fade from the compartment. You are straddling the side of the road, your right wheels digging into the dirt as you struggle for control. At last, you get all of the Sentra back on Vincenzo.

"Holy shit," Julie says in a grand exhale.

"What a nutjob," you say, your voice shaky. "What an unbelievable nutjob. Did you see that?"

"Yeah."

"I wasn't in his lane. I was nowhere across the line. That was all him."

"I know."

"Good thing I knew what I was doing."

"You were scared," Julie says with a smile.

"Not nearly as scared as you. Did you hear yourself shriek?"

"I heard a shriek out of you too."

"That was just the horn."

"Was not."

"Was too!"

"Was not!"

"You wanna take this out on the playground?"

Julie laughs loudly at your suggestion. You like her laugh. It sounds like San Diego.

"What kind of playground are we talking about here?" she says.

"Oh, I was thinking the kind where you show me yours, I show you mine."

Again, she laughs. That Death nearly called up two numbers in this car tonight has driven both of you into something of a manic frenzy—and emboldened you both beyond the pale. "Sicko," she says, but she has her hand on your thigh, and she's squeezing.

"Remember that song from elementary school? It was going around the playground. *There's a place in France where the ladies where no pants...There's a hole in the wall—*"

"Where you can see them all!" Julie finishes for you. Now you're holding hands, laughing, almost home.

The tragedy has passed. The comedy is just beginning.

About the Author

David Ewald is the author of the novel *He Who Shall Remain Shameless*, also published by Macromere Press. He lives in California with his family.

 facebook.com/davidewaldauthor
 instagram.com/davidewaldauthor